**Published by**
Black Candy Publishing
www.blackcandypublishing.com

4096 Piedmont Ave #722
Oakland, CA 94611

**Art and cover**
@seanfromtexas

**Printing**
Lightning Source Inc.

Library of Congress Catalog Card Number: 2017962659
ISBN: 978-0-9859572-1-6

**Distributed worldwide by**
**Black Candy Publishing**

# LOVE FAST LOS ANGELES

## BY DAVEY HAVOK

This book is dedicated to Pants.
"Write," you insisted, fashioning ladders of light, casting them down and carrying me up from my hole when I refused to climb. Without your tireless support, unique understanding, and golden friendship my life would be pale. And without you this book would not be.

# SA
# FR
# CIS

AN
AN
CO

# PREFACE

**My boss just texted.** He needs me to hit tonight's party early. I guess I've gotta cut this shoot short. Whatevs. It's cool. I've already got a memory card full of sick shit. Replying with a "thumbs-up" emoji, I pocket my iPhone, bag my camera and, from the edge of the frothy Ocean Beach tide, salute the local heroes of my sunset session photos. Still shredding the breaks, the surfers return the gesture. I turn and tread up shore to where I left my bike on Sloat Ave then cruise the few blocks back to the Victorian. Feeling pretty killer, stoked on my shoot and the ride home, I park my Boneville at the curb in front of our house between my girlfriend's lollipop-purple Fiat and an unfamiliar, white Lamborghini Diablo. Black Sabbath blasts through my ear buds and sand rains from my Vans as I dismount my café racer in the SF twilight and tromp up the blue porch to throw open the tall red door of our Painted Lady.

With my camera bag bouncing at my hip and my "FTW" helmet swinging happily at my side, I march toward the end of the tall, narrow mid-1800's hallway and announce, "Your number one has returned!" as the rich-kid junkie who has been flagrantly sending my GF pictures of his boner springs through the swaying strings of amber that separate Star's workspace from the rest of the house. The ex-boarding schoolmate who parked his car in my spot registers my unspoken reaction and begins to smugly explain, "She was just giving me a massage, man. It's her job." The top button of his jeans is undone and his familiar boner is trying to break through the breach. I think I see its tip.

Star is calling my name. I picture her frantically tugging up the elastic waist of her thin yoga pants as she imbues "Al" with tones of both pleading and warning from behind the curtain. Likely feeling the heat from my seemingly calm yet searing stare, the junkie schoolmate tells me to "chill out" and with a swift swing I introduce my helmet to his face. He collapses back into the Zen Room. The curtain of beads chatter like those weird Japanese beetles, and Ozzy sings, "Finished with my woman..." in my ears.

Wheezing, the junkie bleeds onto our mid-century hardwood floors. I step over his twitching, splayed arm and begin to collect the treasure recently dislodged from his gaping, gushing mouth. There is an almost-whole incisor beneath the massage table. I giggle and snatch it before glancing up through the shadows of the Nag Champa scented room. Star stands over me wringing her hands with candlelight glimmering in her big, teary green eyes. She shakes her head while I discourse on this fuckface's reckoning and my undying love for her.

"Al..." she says, quietly, "Get out."

At moments like these – there have been a few – Star calls my love violence. She's begged me to "channel it out" a million times. I never got around to it. Confident that I've finally exceeded her strict limitations on my love, I sigh, stand, step back over the junkie, and exit through the clinking amber.

In our former love den, not far up the hall from Star's workspace, I pack up the important shit. I'm shook. I think I really fucked up this time. I shove my ear buds into the pocket of my denim jacket and Ozzy disappears. I grab a glass perfume bottle from Star's antique dresser. From the Zen room, I can hear that funny moan of the freshly knocked-out beneath the hiss of spritzing as I mist my Disney shirts and concert tees with her Rose 31 fragrance. The words of some healing spell can be heard through the junkie schoolmate's gravely gasps. Maybe I shouldn't have hit him with my helmet. Maybe Star wouldn't have just broken up with me if I hadn't shattered his grill. But it's not like he wasn't already missing teeth. Whatevs. Fuck his mouth. I quietly shut my drawers, stuff my duffle, toss in the junkie's incisor, and then smelling like I'm in bloom, creep back down the hall toward the sound of her one-sided conversation.

I peek into the Zen Room to see if I can work this shit out with the love of my life. I've been obsessed with Star since my fifteen-year-old eyes first saw her short red dreads pop up on my Facebook's mutual friends bar. She looked like the young Catherine Zeta from my childhood obsession with Chicago. I really don't want us to end. Inhaling ceremonial incense, I grin and shrug at my ex of about twenty minutes. Pausing her conversation, Star tightly covers the phone so 911 won't hear her sternly whisper, "Don't come back." I nod, snatch my keys from the brass hooks by the door, jam down our blue porch for the last time, and hop on my Boneville.

My chestnut hair whips in the wind like a bitch'n dragon tail as I burn up Folsom St., 79 mph, helmet-free, and kinda hoping to crash. Unable to lane split the encroaching traffic, I stop short of gashing the doors of two Prii with my side mirror. A curbed taco truck's digital billboard advertises the foul odor filling the street: cabeza aka cow's head. San Francisco already feels like a bad horror movie without Star. I smack the window to my right. The rattled driver eases over to make room and, charging through the disgusting smell of deep-fried decapitation, I loudly run the red, cut over to 9th, and park in the alley behind work.

I started covering parties at Tranny Shack years ago when Star and I moved to SF. Tonight, as it is every "ShowTuesday", the floor is packed shoulder-to-broad-sequined-shoulder. I can barely see the stage over the towering wigs. Trying to focus on the vibrance of the talent, and not sob while shooting, I climb atop the far end of the bar to get a good shot of tonight's star.

A Nubian goddess enters her spotlight. Draped in the pelts of plush animals, Lucky Day caresses her luminous microphone. The audience hushes. She begins to sing "Circle of Life" and I lose it. Spotting me weeping behind my lens, the queen of the jungle steps from the stage through the crowd and in her soothing Song of The South voice, says, "This is your favorite number. Why ya cryin' sugar?" She raises the mic and with my tear dotted Canon hanging from my neck I squat down and whimper "because you're so fabulous." I keep my sadness hidden behind a snotty smile. Hundreds of queens cheer and the show goes on.

On my first night here shooting SF's most fierce, Lucky and I bonded over our love for The Lion King. We've been super tight ever since so after her set I creep into the smoky dressing room to share my sob story. As she removes her golden wig I lean in the doorway and tell her Star kicked me out. Making a tsk noise, Lucky boxes her hair then gracefully alights her enhanced buns onto a padded stool in front of an old-school vanity. One by one she carefully peels off her huge eyelashes.

"Well, sugar," sticking them to the mirror, "Looks like I just got me a handsome roommate." I'm close to tears again as I hop over scattered size 14 heels and collapse into her lap. Sniffling over her smooth thighs, feeling her sizeable bulge pressed to my ear, I agree to move in.

Lucky's loft isn't big. We're on top of each other all the time but she doesn't mind, and neither do I. Her futon is fucking comfortable. I barely leave it except when my bladder forces me to shamble to and from the bathroom, tracking stray strands of hair and groaning over the loss of my love. When I moved in I shaved my head, stopped eating, started smoking, and eventually lost my job. I suck. I know. Whenever Lucky tells me how rad I am, how any chick would die to have me, I light a Lucky Strike, tell her she's like Princess Tiana, and apologize for being a shitty frog. She opens a window, throws my cigarette to the sidewalk below, and I go back to sleep. This happens about a million times over the course of a few weeks of virtually endless slumber until after one particularly ripe sleep marathon filled with fucked-up Star dreams, I awake in a cold, powder-scented mist.

Springing up on the mattress confused, I fan the chemical moisture. Lucky blasts the chest of my dank AC/DC shirt with another Febreeze cloud. Sounding like a Louisiana drill sergeant, she barks orders over the aerosol hiss.

"Shit, okay, okay, captain!" I cough, agreeing to hygiene and retreating to the shower.

After scrubbing off weeks of grimy misery, unfiltered

smoke, and Star's perfume, I pull on a clean pair of jeans and pad out to the scent of southern cooking. I prop my refreshed and lazy ass on a chipped bar stool and Lucky, with a look that refuses to suffer resistance, turns from the stove and serves me a steaming plate of grits from an iron pan.

At the kitchen counter staring out a window toward my friend's tattoo shop Black Heart (which lately I can't help feeling was named after me), I eat the first food I've had in forever and make begrudging promises to quit smoking and start taking photos again. Lucky insists my great comeback begin immediately with her and poses with a pastel pink spatula. Holding it up like a Nitey award for most notable drag queen, she offers my lens her sizzling pan of greens. In the first shot she looks like a Back to The Future housewife with a glimmering white smile, twinkling hazel eyes, no eyebrows, and a shaved head.

Infected by her contagious exuberance, I fill a memory card with Lucky then spend the rest of the day editing a still that's worthy of developing. At dusk, feeling pretty okay, I escape the loft in search of fresh air and a print shop. After leaving a file at Samy's Camera I find myself jogging to the ocean. Passing the Painted Lady both ways, I twice restrain myself from knocking on Star's red door. To celebrate I stop in Black Heart and have my large, hairy friend tattoo a missile on my bald big toe.

The toe tattoo heals perfectly and within, like, zero time, I'm working out super hard, editing more killer photos, and feeling way better. Proud of my post-amphibian form, Lucky convinces her promoter friend to hire me to cover his parties before flying down to SOCAL to realize an online affair. Though I miss her, I'm stoked she's in love. These days she's usually in Hollywood with her mystery bae and, if not lifting, shooting the shirtless, or doing covert drive-bys of my old Painted Lady, I'm hanging in the tattoo shop and working on my revamped nightlife site. The loft is usually empty so tonight, after covering a white-trash themed Bear party, when I climb the dark stairs to find our door ajar, I'm shook – and even more shook when I hear the small sobs coming from the other side.

Carefully pushing the door wide on its creaking hinges, I see her curled up on the oversized antique couch. The little lady looks smaller than ever.

"Lucky?" I ask, easing in closer. Her right eye is swollen half-shut and her lips are puffy in all the wrong ways. Through her chipped teeth in her soft southern accent she insists "It was my fault." I look down at her crumpled, fragile frame and, trying to keep calm, ask what happened. Lucky hides her face and grips her phone, repeating, "I knew not to, it was my fault," so I freak out. I begin to threaten her unknown assailant and demand an explanation, but only after I swear on the grave of Bonn Scott that I won't tell anyone does she show me the photo. I snatch the phone from her trembling hand. On her screen stubbly, wig-less, topless, and fake-tit-less Lucky Day lays in bed with her new bae kissing his cheek as he sleeps. I'm looking at one of five secret selfies she'd taken with the pop superstar over a course of months. The fifth is gone. Just after it was snapped the phone rang in Lucky's hand and woke Jamie Shannon from his drunken blackout. He erased the last photo but never found the earlier shots because he was too busy kicking Lucky's ass to swipe deeper into her camera roll. Weeping into a silver hand mirror, my BFF tells me all of this while I secretly send myself the photos.

"He's fucking dead," I mistakenly murmur as I set her phone on the hand-painted dresser and grab my keys.

When I turn to leave Lucky is blocking the door with

her little broken frame. She's so small out of heels. I feel like I might be able to step over her outstretched arms. She makes me promise not to hurt James through sobs. I sigh and collapse onto the couch and Lucky lays her shorn head in my lap as I laid mine in hers months ago. Lightly scratching her arm, I wonder aloud how the possible fuck could she still have a thing for that fuckface. She tells me to hush.

That night Lucky and I slept together in her big baroque bed. I held her as she shook. The next morning I click through my folders to find a nude photo I took of a longtime friend before she was famous. In the shot, Stella stands onstage in the basement of an abandoned building at the edge of our tiny hometown. She may have actually still been seventeen when I covered our underground high school parties but I text her the nostalgic, flattering image and within hours we both sign the photo over to Radar Online, assuring them that she was of age. Stella takes most of the attention, and I get to keep all the money. A few days later while Lucky is at the dentist, I stuff two grand into a Princess and the Frog Card and leave it on her bed with a happy tooth drawn on the red envelope. I hang a framed 6'X8' print of the breakfast beauty queen shot above the futon, pack my shit, strap on my helmet, and roll my bike from Black Heart's garage.

Motley Crüe sears through my ear buds as I charge south with a thirst for celebrity blood. I make it to Los Angeles in three hours and thirty-seven minutes – I go fast. Unfortunately, as promised to Lucky, I'll be using my Canon instead of my hands to bring justice down upon his top-knotted head but nothing will avert me from my mission to end the universal love for that babe-bashing-poseur-fuck. Oh, and in case you somehow didn't already know, my name is Alvin. And I vow to wreck Jamie Shannon.

# HOL
# Wo

LY
OOD

# CHAPTER 1

**Holy fucking shit she's right in front of me.** I shove my hand deeper into my jacket pocket and dig through my thin wad, the remaining bills left over from selling Radar Online the nude of Stella. That was almost a year ago now. I've sold a few more shots to celebrity sites since but not many. It feels like I'm almost broke. Whatever. Posting high profile shit myself is what put me and my site on top. And I'm not about to sell ads—that corporate bullshit would rightfully ruin my cred. I find the plastic baggie hidden within my wad and pull the drugs from what feels like a few thousand—nothin' compared to what I really got. When I showed up to start ruling Hollywood I got in with some of the sidewalk scrapers that stalk the other side of the velvet ropes that enclose everything that matters. My site had already blown up with the notoriety that came with my posts of more controversial outtakes of Stella from our high school parties, so they knew that I was the shit and that I could get them closer to my best friends, the reality stars of "ALL F's: Fierce, Fearless and F*cKed UP Females!" I'd tell those fuckers when Stella was having her birthday rager, if The Barbie was secretly DJ'n some dive bar, where the other two Effs would be having brunch and if the show was filming on location. Shit like that. The Effs got more famous and the scrapers got papered up. In return those dudes brought me to gangbangs, showed me the celeb hotspots, and tipped me on superfame sightings. Everybody won. But now that I know what's up, I roll solo. Those dudes are fuckin' sketchy and, anyway, I work better alone. The promoters and young celebs let me crash their insider sanctuaries cuz they like me and B-list, A-list, superfame, whoever you are, everyone wants to be cool and like I said, my site is the fuckin' hotness. If you're not already hitting it daily, check it out: AlThisAndMore.com. I named it after myself. Bitch'n, right? I know.

Tonight I came to The Roosevelt's exclusive bar Teddy's to shoot my BF Eff, The Barbie, while she shredded her laptops for the guest-list-only clubbers. I stop in the DJ booth for a moment before jumping from its ledge down to a private table. Now, with my back to the pale, brooding, shingle-cut, brunette, reality-fame DJ, balancing over toppling bottles, force-feeding booze to my Vans, I stare down at my dream girl as one of her gooey fanboys springs up from their bench to trip on me. Her two Instafamous guardians, The Mythicals, are always at her side in photos but apparently this sucky fanboy is standing in for both. Relieved that the freaky guardians are absent, I'm freaking that my dream girl is here. This is the first time that I've seen her IRL. She's even hotter than in her old YouTube videos. I dangle an animal printed dime bag above her phone.

"It's organic!" I shout over electrocrunch-pop and the heedless demands of the whiny fanboy in the Fedora. Without looking up from her touchscreen, she waves him away and takes the coke, slipping it down her vintage dress into her bra without interrupting her scrolling. In the glow of her sacred touchscreen she looks more perfect than she does online. I'm jealous of the dime bag's hiding place and too shook to shoot the socialite superfame. My camera hangs at my hip and I twist the lucky lock braided around my wrist. It calms me. The gooey fan boy skulks off. My dream girl texts and that fucking "I'm In Love With The CoCo" song mixes in with the blaring beats. The Barbie is using the annoying track to punish me for bailing her DJ booth but I can't turn back to give her the credit she deserves for the insightful attack. I'd have to look away from my dream girl. The socialite smiles at a text from someone who's definitely way less rad than me. I wanna throw her over my shoulder and drive 100 mph toward a Vegas chapel.

"Hey! Hey! Hey!" I yell over the music, hopping down from the cocktail table and plopping myself into the booth next her. "Your hat's totally killer. It's like you lassoed a UFO with a super long scarf—totally old-skool-starlet-spaceage." She looked different in her videos–all stretch jeans, rock pins, and ripped Ramones tees. My praise of her current weird outfit doesn't even win me a glance. Raising a chrome pipe to her full lips, my dream girl points the tip downward and, thinking that she's smoking weed, still yelling over the base-boom, I ask, "How come they're not freaking about you blazing in here?" The pipe's electronic light glows blue as she looks up from her phone for the first time.

"Because, my dear," exhaling a cloud of the vape DiCaprio just made trendy, "I'm Sky Monroe." Lowering her

Chanels, Sky Monroe stares through melon scented mist at the forgotten glob of rave candy on my finger. On our way inside I commandeered the ring from a Hollywood Blvd. gypsy that howled at The Barbie.

"True!" I surrender to Sky's household name and, hoping she'll soon be screaming mine, announce, "I'm Alvin!" Hopping up and back a few inches, I plant my feet on our cushiony bench seat, drop to one wobbly knee, pull the rubber ring from my pinky, and squeeze. It blinks alive as, balancing, I extend it with my offer. "Let's get married. We can consummate our love now or after—whatever you're feeling."

Sky catches an inaudible laugh in a gloved hand, and the bottle service babe boots into our booth. She re-arranges toppled carafes and, squatting, rags up my mess. I dig through my wad and Sky takes the ring from my other hand. I watch her stretch it on, pour a stream of Tequila from a bottle into her mouth and then, saying something about a ZEDD remix, disappear into the mob of partying bodies. I frantically tip the bottle babe a couple wrinkled hundreds and follow my dream girl to the pulsing floor.

The disco ball's speckled light dances across Sky's perfect perma-pout as she gently sways to The Barbie's raucous set. Her patent flats have yet to leave the ground. Pop-locking for her, I scan the shadows of the room. Though I'm still glad they're not here to cock-block, I'm kinda dying to see her two wispy, militaristic Instafamous guardians IRL. The Mythicals both have slicked-back barber cuts and wear uniforms that look like Saint Laurent runway pieces from the wrong side of WWII. The Instafamous trio is famously inseparable so they must be close. Returning my attention to where it belongs, I drop into the splits, spring up, spin, and shoot Sky a double point.

"Alvin." She glides closer in a vape cloud. I feel her mezcal-breath-love-spell crawling up my neck as she leans in. "You didn't have to introduce yourself. I know you. You're that boy who does that delightful site that absolutely made the Effs. You kept Stella relevant even when those rehab monsters took her phone away for a week. Poor sweet girl." Her words sound sung. They didn't before, in her videos, which is weird. But whatever she says and however it sounds, I'm into it. "And didn't The Barbie get discovered on your site?" she asks, in her fancy new Mad Men voice.

"Totally!" I duck under her floppy brim to be heard over the music—and to sniff her. I do. She smells like chocolate. "We were tight before she was famous. She was just as fucked up back then." I detail my history with the somber seamstress brought in by the producers to give the show "a darker edge" and the dirty-electro house churns. "The Effs are my girls! But I'm no boy. I'm all man, baby!" Stepping back, I flex both biceps and say, "Wanna wrestle?" as the music drops. I lower my guns. Pretty positive this is that dangerous song that got us thrown out of that new 80's bar in K-Town, I look up at the Amerasian babe behind the beats and watch as Sky moves back in.

"Do you think you could do that for me?" she asks, lightly touching my solid tri. I flex again while eyeing the DJ. The Barbie, elevated in her booth, lifts her thrashed Alistair Crowley tee and reaches into the waistband of her skinny black jeans. My BF Eff and I share a smirk.

"Do what?" I ask Sky.

"Put me up on your site." Getting way up on me, she takes off her hat and breaths into my ear "...a lot. But nothing tawdry."

"Nothing what?" I yell over Knife Party, or Yellow Claw,

or whatever, turning back to Sky, ready to get my babe-to-be out of range. "Cool. Yeah…" I agree, "But we should discuss during our honeymoon…"

"No T&A. No smut. No controversy." Sky waves her pipe like she's painting virtuous landscapes. "I want you to show the world the real me." She takes a drag and French inhales. I raise my camera—*Flash Flash*—and as the babe signal is released, two blondes from the BIP (Barely Important Person) section yell my name. When I turn my lens they're already making out in their booth—*Flash*.

Sky touches my chest. I flex my pecs and lower my Canon. "I'm up for a major role in the 3D remake of a Japanese horror film" she explains, as the shorter BIP chick runs over to see how she looks in my shot. Sky removes her shades and raises her offline voice, "It's called Terror Cake. The original came out last week but the remake is going to be a real gem—a classic. The American version is set in the early sixties, instead of now. The director says I'm perfect for it but my agent told me the studio is worried. They think I'm a bit… wild."

"You wanna look all innocent? Like this?" I raise my screen so that both Sky and the BIP can see the shot of the shorty grabbing her friend's tits. Some blonde babe in a vintage Van Halen tee, and what appears to be my friend Score's studded leather jacket, sits next to them looking totally over it. I smirk at the rocker girl's sour expression as the BIP screams "FUCK YEAH! HOT." and takes an unauthorized selfie with me before wavering back to her booth.

"Seriously though. Okay, check it out…" I drop my Camera on its strap and arrange my hands in a square as if visualizing the shot. "We'll rent kittens. I'll make you look like Taylor Swift—or, fuck, y'wanna shoot with her? Wait—fuck TayTay! We'll change all my shit to 'Sky This And More' and it will be all you all day baby! Fuck everyone else—" I declare, before huffing my one caveat, "I mean, unless I finally catch James fucking up—motherfucker—" I search the room for Lucky's ex. That fuckface's Instagram put him in Vegas a few hours ago but I wouldn't put it past him to charter a PJ to catch The Barbie's secret set. I've heard he's into her. Dream on, dickbag.

"James?" Sky squints and through the speakers a robotic voice blasts "Run For Cover!"

"Yeah—" It's the song. I grin up at the DJ booth and warn Sky, "You may wannna duck... " Above the crowd The Barbie grips her pistol with both hands, aims, and opens fire. I drop, shielding my face. A pellet hits my knuckle. "Ow, Fuck! Fuck you The Barbie!" Flapping the sting from my hand, I stand, giggling, cursing over the pounding bass. "Psycho Silverlakey cunt!" I'm surprised yet honored to be her first target. My BF Eff blows imaginary smoke from her barrel and winks at me with an open mouth like a silent film star in a commercial for Japanese air pistols before proceeding to shoot up the dance floor.

When I stand, Sky has vanished. I scan for her through the pink rain of plastic projectiles. Blogger babes in Quaker hats screech "Oh my fucking god!" Fake-boobed tenders dive behind the bar. A cowering promoter rushes over to me and prods me with his cane, barking for me to get the Eff out of Teddy's. I weave my way to The Barbie and offer her a get-away piggy.

"Drive-bys on the way out!" I promise, crouching below the DJ booth. "Hop on!" But before TB can pounce from her ledge onto my back, an electric blue mullhawk trots across the dance floor and grabs me. The ring I gave Sky blinks on one of the long thin fingers wrapped around my wrist. Blue acrylics dig into my arm as I'm drug toward the exit. A pink pellet grazes my cheek. I laugh, raise a backhanded bird, and hoping my kidnapper will deposit me in a penthouse filled with only Sky, leave TB to shoot her way out of the club.

# CHAPTER 2

**The chicks' bathroom off of the hotel's lobby smells like expensive mints.** The light in here makes me feel like some witchy finger tapped the "nostalgia" filter over my life. The towering wispy babe with the blue mullhawk looms next to me making sure I don't make a dash out through the tall door of the powder room, back to somewhere that feels less like some sort of interdimensional pop-party. Perfume, candy, and Advil line the back of the counter like forgotten props arranged behind the iPad that another towering wispy babe in black just slid from a small designer backpack and laid flat on the grey stone. The Trueblood unbuttons two buttons of his dress without acknowledging my presence and slips my animal printed dime bag from his bra. He then unzips the Anger I gifted my dream girl and snows the organic coke onto the screen. Sky, in her super-slinky cocktail dress elegantly leans against the slick stone wall that separates the powder room from the stalls. She motions to my chromatic escort in the fuchsia bodysuit and The Unicorn locks us in the ladies room as The Trueblood pulls a credit card from his black pack and bends over the counter. His high collared dress rises far above the knees of his lace-thigh highs. He's wearing the same Jimmy Chu heels as The Unicorn but in black instead of white. Both Mythicals are here and, really, may have been nearby all night. I wouldn't have noticed because they've abandoned their trademark plastic-fascist look for hot mannequin manga chick—The Trueblood a lady raincloud, The Unicorn a rainbow girl.

With his golden rosary beads rattling against the slate, the raincloud works in front of the sink railing the coke. The Trueblood's metal credit card clicks as he chops Anger atop the large touchscreen. His high shadowed cheekbones angle as harshly as the A-line cut of his chin length wig. Giddy to be with Sky and her shape-shifting guardians, I open with "What's up babes? I love what you two have done with your dicks!"

In the returning silence I watch The Unicorn exchange a glance with The Trueblood before clicking across the tiles. His powdered skin shimmers like the long string of pearls hanging from his neck as he poses next to Sky and, through fanning fake eyelashes, stares super deep into my soul. Even with his lack of expression I can tell he sees rock 'n' roll. Intently, he twirls the blue tail of his hair and my ring blinks rainbows on his delicate finger.

With a heartbreaking hop Sky perches up on the counter next to The Trueblood. He cuts coke art. She palms her closed knees and smiles at me. I twist my lucky lock. She's so pretty it hurts. I want to fuck her full of babies.

"I'm sorry to so rudely drag you from your friends but we must ask if you would please not post those photos, Alvin." With a swish of her hand she absently inspects a small red blotch on her wrist. "I was smoking...filthy vice," she explains, and The Trueblood's golden fangs successfully bling for my attention. Having chopped three spooning lightning bolts on the iPad, he stares at me and licks white from the black Amex. The gold tips of his nails shine like his twenty-four karat tearing teeth as he zips the card back into the pouch of the tiny backpack. Thinking that some rainclouds have golden linings, I turn from the precious metals to scroll through my Canon.

"But its just vape...and you look hot!" I contest, holding up the controversial shot. Through her melony mist you can tell that even The Unicorn's after-market lips have nothing on Sky's super-full naturals. I wanna taste 'em. I zoom in and point at the detail, "Seriously." The Unicorn folds his arms across his diving spandex neckline like my ex used to do when I'd threaten to smash disrespectful beach rats and subtly shakes his blue mane.

"Okay, okay, I'll trash 'em..." I creep across the tiles toward Sky, "...I'll show you so you can make sure all hotness has been eradicated." The Unicorn reaches behind he Trueblood and snatches something from a candy bowl. He passes Sky a piece of gum, pops a red square past his veneers, tears the fold from the pack, and digs through his white-sequined purse.

"No need," Sky says and hops down from the sink. Her black flats slap granite, and The Unicorn pulls out a pen. He scratches onto the gum's cardboard packaging as she leans against the counter. "My confidants tell me I can trust you" she chews, "More than trust you..."

She can. I'd chuck my Canon through the windshield of my Mustang before I hurt her.

"Your confidants know what's up!" I say, deleting the last shot. No way I'd ever post unauthorized shots of Sky—or any other babe—that's not my style. The only life I want to ruin is Jamie Shannon's. "Final hotness—GONE. So..." I move closer to Sky, "What's that gum taste like?"

Sky's rainbow guardian grabs the back of my head and shoves his tongue in my mouth. I taste cinnamon, feeling blue acrylics stab into my scalp for an uncomfortable second before something falls from The Unicorn's loose hair. It bounces from my sneaker and clinks on the tiles. The rainbow releases me and looks down. He retrieves the custom coke straw without bending his knees, passes me the note, and clicks away. Like The Trueblood's, The Unicorn's newly purchased, curvy ass only enhances his latest look.

I wipe sheer blueberry lip gloss from my lips onto the back of my hand and watch as The Mythicals communicate through ESP. They stare at each other for a long moment before The Unicorn hands over the straw. Holding it up into the eerie light, twirling its blue stripes with slightly parted lips. The Trueblood inspects the thick glass for cracks. I look from the tips of his fangs down to my weird note. "Follow us and be fast" is beautifully scrawled inside an electric blue heart above Sky's digits on the Dentyne flap. This was way worth the spicy man make-out.

"You can have me" Sky promises, inspecting her reflection in the mirrored wall. "Soon. Just remember, nothing tawdry."

"Right." I slide my phone from my denim. I tap in her number quickly, glancing toward the sound of Chanel clattering against the counter. The Unicorn snorts a bolt of organics. My brain thinks it sees cleavage between the draping gob stopper-sized pearls. He unfolds, lightly brushes a nostril, and The

Trueblood takes the straw. The raincloud tucks a piece of his wig behind his ear. A skull smiles at me from his lobe, and I turn from its golden grin back to Sky. "No tits." Holding up my hand, I sigh super hard. "Swear on Lenore's life."

"Don't be glum, handsome. That's simply no tits on camera." With her beautiful bare shoulders thrown back and her hands on her hips, she does a slight dress-smoothing wiggle addressing me beyond her reflection. "You do put that thing down once in a while don't you?" I hear rosary beads clattering over cocaine, and Sky takes off her hat. With the brim crushed in her fist, she scowls at her reflection and then totally messes up her hair. Four-inch jags direct me toward the door. "You'd better go protect your shaggy friend Score. He was hiding behind that beach model in the Van Halen shirt when I got out of there. The Barbie was gunning for him too." Sky warns, turning to show me her perfect princess pout. "We can't have beautiful boys getting shot now, can we?"

\*\*\*\*

Behind The Roosevelt a self-entitled mob is ragin' around valet. Doesn't matter. I've got an invisible VIP fast-pass that keeps Lenore parked as close as the sports-fame's neon supercars. Rumbling like a kickass power-ballad, my metallic royal blue Mustang's headlights swoop over my Vans as I march out from under the umbrella over the patio lounge. The valet kid covetously eyes Lenore before opening my muscle car's buff door.

"I think some of your boys are here," he nods toward the legal side of the hotel's gates. I see the flashes of scrapers.

"Not my boys—not anymore—but thanks man." I tip the valet kid two twenties. We fist bump. He shuts me in, I buckle up, and a crying emoji buzzes my phone. Before the sad little yellow face, Marlena wrote: "He wasn't supposed to be back til tomorrow!" Whatevs. Knowing her skater-fame boyfriend will surely be gone again soon, I postpone my rendezvous with the Disney pop-superfame, wiggle my shitty charger, confirm some eatin' with my "shaggy friend" Score, and toss my dying phone into the passenger seat.

The line of expensive rides ahead of me crawls towards Orange Dr. I'm idling, yelling for a double-parked town car to bail when motherfucking Zeppelin comes on The Jack. "Been a long time, been a long time —" I sing along with Plant, crank Leonard – the chrome skull on the end of my stickshift — and edge my ride around the blockage.

"Hey dude!" interrupts my pitchy vox. The skinny scraper in the Lion King beanie breaks from my old crew. Behind him they raise their cams toward some unseen fame coming out of the hotel as he slimes toward my window. "They let you in again, huh?" Envying my ruling, the kid asks "Were you with them in there? Ya seen 'em?"

"The Effs?" I crank the song louder. "Dude, they just left with Score—pink as fuck. How could you possibly miss Stella's ride? You guys are totally lost—Lonely, lonely, lonely..."

"Sky, man." He looks over his shoulder to see what fame he's missing before turning back. "We heard Drop Dead came to meet her."

"Pshh. Jamie Shannon?" I laugh. "No way she would ever be seen with that piece of shit!" The oily-haired scraper looks at me like I'm a nut job and I rev my engine. "But dude, if you do get eyes on him once he's back from Vegas tell your boy Abbi to hit me." I motion to the massive chunk of a man at the front of his crew, chuck a deuce, and with a "Simba rules!" leave the lost motherfucker in '67-Shelby-smoke burning toward my 3am breakfast singing "Rock'N'Roll."

# CHAPTER 3

**The warm wind smacks my face to a rock'n backbeat.** I crank my windows farther down and AC/DC way up, letting all the fuckers posing outside of El Coyote know that I'm on the Highway to Hell as I blur by. I fuckin' love Hollywood. It's December but here it's Spring Break every day and Summer Vacation every night. No one has a real job and babes wear shorts year round. Breaking at 76mph, I cut into the lot across from Swingers kinda pissed-off that the post-2am swervers prevented me from really gunning it. Drunk driving seems about as illegal as smoking weed in this town. Lawlessness is cool, but I don't fuck with either—too much rad shit's going on to miss, plus hungover muscle-ups suck. I step out of Lenore, sling on my camera, march across the street and into the diner, ready for anything and everything—cuz that's what usually happens in Hollywood.

Score sits texting at our usual table in his usual seat—he literally won't sit down unless he's facing the door. The jukebox plays Bowie as I nudge through the boozy scent of the wobbly post-partiers. Singing "Ch-Ch-Changes," I drop into our booth and toss my keys with a clatter. They slide across the table directly into a small tower of phones. It topples and I vocally claim a billion points. Score catches his Blackberry before it hits the vinyl upholstery next to his tight expensive jeans and restacks it atop the two Samsungs before returning to tapping on his iPhone Plus.

"Sup?" I ask, propping my back against the wall, opening myself up to scope passing babes and fame. Score continues to type, and our waitress walks over from behind the counter.

I order a tofu scramble, a soy protein shake, and chocolate chip pancakes. Without looking up, Score compliments the buckles on the little brunette's boots, gives a history of designer knock-offs, and then fucking finally orders off-menu, "One Score Plate." She nods at his usual and closes her notepad.

"I hate that name. It sounds like poor-people food —like a Denny's special," he continues once she's walked out of earshot. Score has tons of expensive stuff but he didn't buy any of it. He never has money. People just give him shit. "It should just be called The Massi..." he insists, looking beyond his giant screen to stare at her small feet again. "Balmain. Resort collection, last year." He's mumbling so I don't know if he's talking to me or to himself as he name drops, "...Miley introduced me to the head designer at fashion week. Oliviere's cool." As he will let you know within seconds of meeting him, there isn't anyone even partially famous who Score doesn't kinda know. Pretty much everyone who meets him loves him. Though he's semi-defective, most babes think he's hot and weirdly charming. "What was up with you and Sky Monroe tonight, Al?" he asks the front door, silently rating everyone that walks through. "I saw you hanging with her right before The Barbie bullet-blocked you and almost got us banned..."

"Yeah. We got engaged. No big." The busser sets down two waters and a tea set. I fist bump him and he sidesteps an orange haired chick on his way back to the kitchen.

"You gonna sell those shots?" Score smiles and asks as the Marc Jacobs billboard-babe passes our table.

Confused, she turns. "What?" Score tells her to text him her new number as I answer the question meant for me.

"Nope! Deleted as fuck." I un-pocket my buzzing phone and explain, "I'm gonna get some better ones when we hang. She wants to be on my site super bad."

The orange-haired babe stalks away. Score taps his screen.

"Cool. That's better for the AlThis brand. You should feature her...even though you'd be giving that glorified groupie undeserved cred." He texts, yammering unsolicited advice, "You'd get a lot of new looks." He's probably sending emoji to the orange-haired babe while he discredits Sky. "You know she has more followers than me, right? It makes no sense. She doesn't even do anything..."

"I've featured you twice and you don't do anything fucker!" I plunge my free fingers in my cup and flick water at Score. He winces like a wet cat and pats his face with a paper napkin the same shade as his skin.

"You just don't understand what I do."

"Yeah, nothing is a gnarly concept to contemplate." I notice a text from my brother but I table my phone to focus on defending my dream girl. "Sky's gonna be in Terror Cake. She deserves to be on my site. She rules."

"Fabulous. At least you're over that art insanity." Whipping his packet of English Breakfast, he gazes over my shoulder toward the door.

"No, no, no. Sky's gonna be my last fame." I promise, "I still have gnarly ideas for a site revamp and a show — "

"Being poor and unknown is gnarly." Score looks at me for the first time and, emptying the little metal kettle into his mug, asks, "What if you finally catch Drop Dead in the church of man love?" He tears open his packet. "You still an artist then?" He dunks the tea bag, and steam rises to his smirk.

Okay, in case you somehow don't know, here's what's up with Drop Dead: James Shannon was the star of that totally weak, family-friendly online teen drama "Gorgeous" before he quit acting to pretend to be a Rockstar. When James was on the show he was blonde and wore stupid pop-punk shirts. Now he dresses like a vampirate, calls himself Jamie Drop Dead, and bangs everything in and out of town. He named his bogus pop-rock band "Drop Dead Gorgeous" and describes it as "a more cerebral Joy Division infused with the yearning of a fallen angel." I'd say that it sounds more like Maroon 5 playing a youth rally at The Haunted Mansion but that would be too insulting to both Adam Levine and Disney. Churchy people are way into Drop Dead Gorgeous' tameness and "positive messages", and the huge indie label that just signed James is Christian-owned. Once my site shows the moral majority who he really is, he'll be fucked.

"I shared a table with Mr. Brainwash at Greystone Manor once." Score seriously offers, "I could hook you up with him instead of trying to help you prove what half of Hollywood knows about Jamie."

"Dude, I've told you a million times, it's not street art. I'm still gonna be taking photos." I recount my well-worn plan to get out of the voyeur game and make something sick as our waitress sets down our plates. "Just not fame. But if I catch that fucker James fucking up in any way it's going up everywhere."

"He's the worst." Score smiles at our waitress like he's auditioning for a toothpaste commercial. She blushes, boots away, and he gripes on, "It's been nine days since I messaged him. He read it. No response." I try not to gag on my scramble, watching Score saw through his fried-egg-blanketed pork chop as he bitches about Drop Dead for all the wrong reasons. "But why put me in your movie when you can just pretend to be me? You noticed he stopped cutting his hair right after I did." Score stabs and waves a yolky chunk of flesh, reminding me of his father. Ironically it's because of this flesh-eater that I haven't touched dairy since I was sixteen. When we were kids I kinda looked up to Score. Back then he pretended to be vegan because it was hip. I fork spicy tofu as he goes on, "Now he's making an embarrassing attempt to dress like me and of course he's Paleo now." Score huffs and, putting down what would have been his second bite, flips out his palms. "Who did that first?" Really, the most accurate way to describe my long-time friend's trendy diet is manorexia. He'd probably be dead if he weren't too rattled to fuck with drugs. Whenever he's offered free booze or coke he declines, saying, "I'll get puffy."

As I tear through my pancakes our table begins vibrating like the Hustler Store hit by lighting. I snatch my phone, and Score scrambles to collect his toppling tower. Checking all four screens, he claims, "You know, I've heard that he and

Sky used to be a thing. You should give her my number, Al. We'd make a fabulous power couple and I'm sure she'd rather experience the real —"

"Mine, fucker! Mine." I proclaim, briefly looking up from more long distance correspondence from my brother. Zach's on the French Riviera with U2 and some Dre Beats execs who want to put our band, Band Fail!, in a commercial. "And yeah, right." I text my bro about chartering a PJ to Santa Monica for a NYE hangar party, scoffing, "Like she'd ever date a piece-of-shit-poseur like Drop Dead. She's into real rockers." I point to myself. Score doesn't notice. He sighs at his texts then, slipping his phones into his studded leather jacket, breaks the bad news.

"I'm gonna need the Twilight Sleeper, Al. I guess Stella and Franco just got back from New York on Ari Emanuel's PJ." Having picked out the rollout couch that The Barbie bought for me to live on, he claims seniority on my bed whenever his superfame girlfriend's got another guy spending the night at Eff house. "I finally convinced that Wildfox model to bring her cat over—she's got a Devon Rex—I've got to meet it."

"Wait—what's her name?"

"It's a he."

"No, the model."

"I don't know.

I take the final sip of my shake and scroll back through Zach's text stream to find a photo of a blonde sunbathing on the upper deck of a yacht. Her face is hidden by her giant shades and sun hat but her insanely toned bod is totally visible. After perving on her for a second, I hold up my phone.

"Is this her?" I ask.

"I don't know. Maybe." Score stands as our waitress sets down our check. The jukebox plays Motley Crüe.

"She's friends with the Dre Beats dude." I explain, flipping and reading the bill. "She came back from the Riv for some shoot before Zach got out there. I thought he said it was to model for Wildfox. Shit for their next winter campaign." I look back at the photo. "He thinks she's into me I guess...It would be killer if it was the same chick, huh?" I giggle. Score shrugs, says something about a threesome, and pulls up his hair. I lock my screen and pocket my phone. "Fuck..." Tightening my camera strap, I stand, and admit, "I guess I should go to the Ark anyway. Uncle Noah gets stingey and super weird if I'm gone for too long."

Okay, obviously you couldn't know this, cuz you're not Score, an Eff, or my Brother, but Noah isn't my real Uncle and his real name isn't Noah. I've always called him that because of his pets. Not long after I first rode down here, I met him outside of No Vacancy. As I was hopping on my bike to bail Score's birthday party, a tall, wispy dead-faced babe with long white hair was stepping out of a tinted SUV into the club's valet. Thinking about it now, the Rapunzel babe looked a lot like The Unicorn but then I'd only known him as a blonde plastic-fascist soldier dude. When another chick started to slide out after her, Rapunzel whipped around as if some crazy fuck were running at them with a knife, shoed the unseen babe back into the backseat, jumped in herself, and slammed the door of the Mercedes. I stomped my ratchet to follow the black G550 to whatever for-sure-crazy party Rapunzel was heading to and my Boneville pretty much exploded right there in front of the club. Cursing, I wiped singeing oil from my hands and Uncle Noah appeared through the smoke. Promising me that he'd have my bike taken care of, he unbuttoned my jackets breast pocket, slipped in a few baggies of Anger, and took me to his estate. The next morning, after picking live shrimp out of an aquarium to feed the bamboo sharks that live in his fountains, he took me to the classic car dealer on Sunset. Noah threw down his black card. I threw my camera bag in Lenore's trunk and charged my new vintage Mustang to Eff house. Since then he's used various luxurious methods to lure me back to his property, which I've named The Ark. I visit whenever I need some funding. Things have gotten a little sketchier each time.

"You ever find out what he does?" Score tugs the tight sleeves of his leather, staring at the yellow heels of a passing babe with a globe-sized afro, and mutters, "...I mean, other than get off on you watching him jerk it?"

"Who cares?" Jumping up, I sing "Shout, Shout, Shout at the Devil" at the babe and slide a hundred under my clean plate as Score props up his zillion dollar sneaker on the bench.

"Yeah. Maybe he's an agent or producer or something though..." Thumbing a spot that only he sees from his puffy leather toe, he asks, "Hey can you pay?" Drawn to my serenade, the afro babe recognizes me. She poses behind Score. I raise my Canon and, scrubbing, he says, "I'm out of cash."

*Flash Flash Flash*

# CHAPTER 4

**I lurk Instagram as I fire west toward Beverly Hills.** The loading circle on Sky's account is taking forever to whiten. I glance up from the app's annoying lagging. "Shit!" I yelp, dropping my phone to grip the wheel with both hands and screech to a stop. I almost ran over a local celebrity. Nobody walks in LA but Hollywood Jesus. The bearded savior sways across the street high off Mel's Diner grease. His two barefoot disciples frame him, carrying their high heels and wearing plush reindeer antlers.

"Sorry Jesus!" I yell, chucking a deuce out my window. "Sorry Cupid and Vixen!"

Skirting Lenore's grill, Hollywood Jesus raises his hand with godlike forgiveness then makes a gentle "bring it down a notch" motion. I take a picture. His robes flow away in the shot. "The true spirit of Christmas is a threesome!" I yell, looking up from my Canon's screen to salute the night-walking savior. He delivers his disciples safely to the Sunset Plaza sidewalk. I shift Leonard and gun it to BH. Jesus is totally gonna bang those two reindeer babes.

The Ark's security booth looks like a present wrapped in white lights. I roll up the short driveway and stop at the gate. Through his faux-snowy window, the guard nods approvingly. Martín and I were down with each other even before he replaced the last guy. After accidentally squishing some rare spider, he claimed to have been deliberately fed a bowl of poisoned açaí berries and thus bailed the high paying Ark gig, claiming that no pay was worth working for "Loco." I'm down with that ex–guard too. I used to work out with a bunch of bouncers and private security dudes before I got hooked up at Equinox. My new gym is free and filled with fame but I miss these guys—they believe in shit. You can tell by how they lift.

Martín leans out of his booth. I turn down Queen and a small chick voice singing "Riu Riu Chiu" replaces Freddie Mercury. On the counter flickering next to the thick-skinned guard's laptop, prayer candles cast shadows over the resin manger scene in the booth. As Pandora plays the Spanish villancico, I admire the image of me behind the wheel of Lenore in one of the ten monitors over his shoulder.

"Hey Chongo where you been?" he asks stoically. Martín thinks I look like a monkey.

"Me?" I fist bump the faded XIII tattooed across his gnarled fingers. "Where the fuck were you? I was worried you'd gotten poisoned too."

"Naw, my cousin got in a little trouble. I've been fillin' in for him at Soho." He reaches his bulging forearm into Lenore and furiously rubs my buzz-cut. "Got any good shit you ain't posted yet?"

He releases me, I grab my phone, scroll, and hold up a tight shot of a girl squeezing her tits together. She looks down at her pink bra and the hanging wavy hair hides her face.

"Marlena Lopez." I tell him. "She lets me touch 'm too." Martín chuckles, calling me crazy, and turns into his booth to press some hidden button.

The iron octopus tentacles of the gate silently untwine, and I roll up the smooth road. After the right at the fork, I pass the chipped giraffe statue craning up from the grass. At its concrete hooves a string of lights form a blue Star of David fading to white over the rolling lawn. I cruise down the gentle grade. Wham! comes on the radio. A cockatiel wings past my windshield and I lurch to a sudden stop. An arrogant white flock of larger birds, luminous in Lenore's headlights, occupies the small carport. I inch my bumper closer to the plumed battalion. I tap the horn, kill the engine, and step out of the Mustang. Lunging toward them, I sing "I gave you my heart. The very next day, you gave it away—" My Vans squeak to a halt on slick cobblestone inches away from their claws. The peacocks blink at me like the Red Queen's dumbass card-guards. One screeches like an evil stepmother. "Jesus, quit." I grumble with my fingers plugging my ears.

The bitchy white bird with the hearing problem fans at me from Lenore's roof. I point with purpose and threaten to feed her to the fountain sharks before grabbing my shit from the trunk and lugging my bags up the granite walkway avoiding any blind frogs or rare rodent on the way to the house. A few of The Ark critters are worth thousands but most of the pets are rescued. With the exception of sea creatures that he's deemed "untrustworthy, guilty or, whorish" Noah is a big-time animal lover. He eats those of lesser regard. I nod to a kangaroo rat reclining on the doormat and step over it to open the unlocked door.

The pool house is mine whenever I want it. I never do. I prefer staying with The Effs but sometimes a guy needs an Uncle with a pool house. I march through the pristine room straight to the nightstand. The scent of vetiver brings back sucky memories. Pressing on their tin lids, I closet the "mood" candles that I always hide—and the maids always replace— then click on the bedside lamp. My lost striped tube sock lays flat on the queen-sized mattress next to a tight stack of tees. I drop my camera bag onto the orange comforter and grab the clean Disney shirts to slide them into a dresser drawer filled only with the clothes that Noah has bought for me. As I press Goofy over multiple pairs of jeans, I pause at the sound of claws on resin. I turn toward the scratching.

One of those night-monkey things is standing on its hind legs propped next to the dresser. The slinky fella grips the edge of a wide-mouthed jar that Noah's instructed some servant to set up on a monogramed placemat. He keeps both his and his pets' favorite treats readily available in white Jonathan Adler cookie jars set all over the property.

I stand over the kinkajou watching it slurp honey from a Joy jar. It snakes its tongue into the sweet well looking up at me with its marble eyes. I don't think this kinkajou is Noah's best friend THE Kinky. I squat to face it. It watches me with smacking lips. I ask if it can hear me. It blinks with a satisfied slurp. This one might be Dom. I don't know. They all look the same. It's definitely not Sadi. I shudder thinking of her. Scooping the docile critter into my arm, I warn him to "keep your nose clean dude" before tossing the kinkajou outside and shutting the door. I hear claws scratching at the wood as I pull off my shirt and go to clean myself up.

The brick of toothbrushes Noah keeps in here never seems to get smaller. In the bathroom's walk-in pantry I snag a red Reach from a stack below the shelves of unopened soaps and creams. I step out to the sink, turn on the faucet, and brush with old-timey paste. I taste expensive, thin, licorice flavored froth, as I bite down on soft bristles and flex in the mirror. I smack my Uncle-pleasing abs, spit, kill the water, and discard the new brush. It clatters in the steel bin as I pace toward the tight sheets. They un-tuck with a clean sound. Aside from the weird jungle noises, the pool house is a lot quieter than Eff House. If this whole deal weren't so fucking creepy, the Ark would be pretty killer.

****

Gunshots and yelling wake me. A warm breeze carries the cacophony through the air and straight to my brain. Throwing my feet to the floor, I bemoan being pulled from a sex dream about Sky while giving thanks to the weather, "God damn it but fuck yeah SoCal" and salute the shining morning. I like going barefoot in the grass and Uncle Noah becomes more generous when I show off my pecs in the sun. Before pulling on my jeans, I bang out a quick fifty-set of pushups, then get half-dressed and pad over to the mini kitchen to grab some pre-breakfast.

I scarf a protein bar, swipe a juice from the assortment in the fridge, and move toward madness shirtless and swollen. But just before I reach the door, I hop back. Fuck. The kinkajou lays rigid on the ground with its snout covered in powder. Creepy little teeth point out of its gaping mouth as I follow its milky gaze to the dresser where, in front of the fucking open window, a toppled Anger jar lays puking out a pile of "organic" cocaine.

I poke Dom, or whoever, again with my toe. He doesn't move. I squat and rest my ear on his belly. He's not breathing. I curse the little fucking drug addict, clean up the spilt coke, and wrap the remains in a monogrammed hand towel before creeping over to the grove behind the pool house. I scoop a kinky-sized hole in the dry dirt with my hands and secretly bury the body in the shade below the avocado tree. This would very likely be grounds for Ark excommunication.

"Fuck you Dom." I sigh and pour some juice on the hidden grave. "Rest in peace." Kinda teary, I pat down the mound then go back inside. After scrubbing up and making sure the pool house is sealed shut, I throw the death shroud into a cabana hamper before marching toward the morning war.

Like most of the stuff living around here, the grass I'm treading is imported. Little rubbery fingers tickle my tootsies as I approach the screams. I pass a fleet of black SUVs covered in cranky white peacocks. I flip them off before cutting through the banana trees. The air thickens and moistens. The misting system hisses. Soft hyper-colored petals brush my nips as I step over two snails—each bigger than most dogs in this town—and emerge from the Beverly Hills Rain Forest. And, for the first time in weeks, I see him. Far behind the main house wearing a hooded robe, he stands on the sprawling back lawn with his phone raised to his ear and his handgun pointed at Elvis Presley.

Uncle Noah is attempting to blast holes through a Warhol. The last time I saw the print he was having it hung in his dining room, bragging that he only paid 800k for it. Noah only shoots expensive shit when he's full of rage and Anger—which is pretty much always. Once, after his ex called, he turned a Basquiat door into a 7-foot target. The sick fucker has no respect for art—or for much of anything other than his broken pets.

I pace toward him sipping from my chilled plant juice. I sniffle with ginger tingling in my sinuses and lean against a bullet-riddled elephant statue—another victim of horrible aim—watching him. Noah fires a wild shot. A cherry blossom tree far beyond his target takes a hot one. Bark explodes over the lawn. He lowers his weapon and returns to screaming in chorus with the peacocks.

"I will fucking end him! Life—over! Career? Done!" He mindlessly drops his pistol into a billowy silk pocket. "That cum-swallowing pretentious prima donna faggot might as well go back to the fucking desert right fucking now. No one will touch him. Including that ungrateful little whore who he'd suck his own dick to impress—What?" He pulls away his phone, rapidly spanks it like a insufferable child, and puts it back against his ear to demand, "Who the fuck are you to talk to me about fags and family—" When he's pissed-off his voice sounds like he's been sucking helium. The shrill tough guy threats keep coming until he whips around in a fit.

"You missed." I nod at the unscathed art.

"Honey Bear!" Flying out his Gucci draped arms like one of his necky lake-birds, Noah releases his phone. It plops onto the synthetic lawn as he scuttles towards me. "You've come home! I hope the shots didn't wake you."

"Not home—" I turn toward the small voice yammering from the Blackberry in the grass.

"Come, come, come! It's been centuries." Stopping in his tracks with a giant smile, he summons, "Hugs."

"Dude." I hold my ground and motion to the silk bag slung over his shoulder. "Is Kinky in there? How the fuck is he not freaked out by all the noise?"

"Honey Bear," Noah scolds as he pulls out the sedate nocturne, "I've told you a million times, Kinky's deaf." He speaks to it nose to nose. Noah's bugged eyes slightly cross. "That's what makes my little man so special. Isn't it?" He asks the sleepy mammal, truly believing the night-monkey can read lips. Kinky yawns. Noah kisses him and, dropping him back into his black carrier, dramatically sighs, "Alvin, Alvin, Alvin." He puts both fists on his soft hips and bitches, "Do you ever listen to anything I say? You're just like him sometimes..." He flicks his weak chin with a rodent snarl toward the discarded phone. He's referring to his ex, not the caller—I can tell. Next to the buzzing Blackberry a lizard raises onto its hind legs in the grass and challenges me with its yellow eyes. I look back to Noah and shrug.

"Well..." In a rare moment of passive aggression he shoots me an accusatory glare, "at least he's not as sensitive as Sadi. She still hasn't come home you know."

Last fall I called Sadi "Kinky". A few days later she ate some poisonous berries and Noah found her body in his bed. He was high as fuck when he exploded into the pool house screaming and waving the kinkajou corpse before collapsing to the floor. I had to bury her in the grove. When he came to, Noah killed a Koons and went on a legendary drug binge during which he decided I'd made Sadi run away by confusing her sex.

I think of the avocado tree watching him shuffle to brunch. Noah loafers onto the patio and hangs the slumbering creature's sling from the back of a lounge chair. On its pink-striped cushion a row of rifles reclines. I walk over to check out the sunning cachet while he picks over the spread on the table. Noah chooses an oniony bialy, sniffs it, then drops it back into the full basket.

"You can be very insensitive sometimes," he lilts and, pinching a fig from an overflowing bowl, drops the kinky snack into the silken carrier.

"Yep." I set my drink between a pyramid of bagels and an ominous row of parfait. I suspiciously eye the açaí and Noah opens his arms again.

"Come, come, come..." he greedily asserts. This part always sucks but after weeks of reprieve it's even worse. I go to him. I've gotta.

Noah hugs me for forever. He smells like peppercorn dipped in lemon juice. His thick cock mushes against my quad through his thin robe as he squeezes desperately, like he's cold pressing me, like my discomfort juice might turn him into a human. I barely grip his loose, stunted bod through the draping silk. Noah's much taller from the other end of a conference call. He has to look up at me when he goes, "Mmmm, you feel hungry. Let's get you fed."

"Nope." I correct. "Got a bunch of shit to do before my first client." I've told him I'm a private trainer. Noah doesn't need to know my personal shit. Luckily he's too busy with whatever he does to be interested in party sites or the talented men behind them. "But dude," breaking from his clutches, I shiver in the growing morning heat, "I'm running out of cash. Think I could borrow a few million or something?" I retrieve my green juice and take a sip.

"It's too early to be so crass my little rebel. And it's too early for a first client." He reaches into his robe and bargains, "Go get dressed. We'll talk over Bellinis at the Ivy." Noah clicks his intercom remote and summons his driver as he walks back into the grass.

"Can't we go somewhere low-pro for once?" I hold my patio position and try negotiating from a distance, nodding to the big patio spread. "Or, why don't we just eat this shit?" There's always scrapers creeping around his go-to spot and I'm constantly shook by the possibility of being recognized in front of him. Noah retrieves his ringing phone from the ground and scowls at the screen.

"How dare you fucking hang up on me?" he answers, pulling out his gun.

"Fine. Whatevs." I continue inspecting the reclining rifles—nothing killer. I prefer his pistol. "I'm driving separately though."

"What do I suggest you do?" He barks at the caller like a Pomeranian with Prada paws. "I suggest both of you find a new fucking interest."

I march over the grass and slip the HK from Noah's flailing fist. He keeps yipping. A peacock screeches and I pace over to the range. I stare at the print for a moment then, apologizing to Warhol and Elvis, blast three holes directly between the eyes of the pistol packing King of Rock'n'roll.

# CHAPTER 5

**Eating at the Ivy makes me feel like I ducked into an antique store to avoid the scrapers.** The Brazilian crew was filming Mick Jagger out front when we slipped by the brunch bustle to be seated next to a cabinet of flatware my Grandma would have sold at a garage sale. I'm editing the selfie Mick's daughter requested we take as Noah tortures our waiter over not replacing his drinks fast enough. Georgia Jagger and I both have our mouths open in a post that amasses 121 comments before Uncle finishes his second breakfast beverage. You'd think the booze would slow him down but he hasn't stopped talking since he insulted the valet. I blame the Anger.

"You are such an intriguing man, Alvin." He smacks his mouth full of a hash made of an "ambitious" lobster that Noah personally chose to be boiled alive. "You make me want to jerk off right here under the table."

"Yeah...speaking of..." I reply with a toothy emoji to a comment on the Georgia  post and look up. "I could really use some cash." I point out my eternal truth. "Clients are scarce in this economy dude."

Noah titters while chewing. His thick flapping lips glisten. I don't know what's so funny. Digging into his mouth-hole, he picks a piece of orange shell out of his chaw and wipes it from his fingernail onto the white tablecloth between us like some sick mama-bird offering. I grimace at the jagged shard, look away, and my heart begins to race like Space Mountain. My future fiancé just walked through the door following the overpriced orange sneakers of David Fass. When he's not busy being her agent or keeping Supreme in business by buying all their shoes, David teaches yoga in Brentwood. Score went to his private class once hoping to meet fame and talk Fass into representing him. I still have no fucking idea what Score would need an agent for. I watch the agent creep on the hot Persian hostess as Sky texts and Noah insists, "Don't act cold." I turn back to him. A chunk of potato clings to the corner of his mouth as he critiques my character. "You may be tough but you're not cold. You're warm, honey bear. I feel it." Loosening the suede lacing on his flayed collar, he projects, "I can see it in your big brown eyes." Noah grins and gulps his mimosa. Orange juice trickles down his chin. He's so high. "You're not like he was. You care."

"Whatever." I hide in my phone's screen. I've never asked about Noah's ex and never will. He doesn't pay me enough to pretend to care about that shit. The waiter returns to our table. I raise my glass and he fills it with Arnold Palmer.

"You're insatiable." Noah's big grin is white with crustacean carnage. "I'll have a crisp hundred—or three—waiting for you when you come home tonight." He promises the usual number of Franklins, all turned on by my violent apathy. Dipping his thumb into a ramekin of yellow Hollandaise, Noah sucks it off and points the glistening digit at me. "Don't shower." I turn back to the door. The hostess babe plays Candy Crush on her iPad. Noah loudly chugs the rest of his drink. After a toneless burp he asks, "Are you still happy with the Shelby?" Wiggling his fingers my way, "I worry about you in that old thing. Wouldn't you like something newer?" I scan the room as he baits, "I'm next on the Tesla list..."

When is my bike going to be done?" I ask Noah as I text Sky, "Where'd you go? I'm in the Ivy." The waiter sets down my plate of dry toast and I drop my phone in my lap to scoop three globs of fancy pink jelly onto a slice. "I could have fixed that shit myself by now," I carp while crunching thick, tangy bread. I cover my mouth to catch a crumb and Noah makes a shrill huffing noise.

"Well, they say the parts are backordered." Nasally, he disregards my bike's sentimental importance. "You know I really don't like you riding that thing anyway. It's unsafe." Noah mercifully wipes his mouth on a cloth napkin then digs into the Gucci man-bag hanging from his chair. "I need you safe. Boys like you don't show up too often in this town." I look into my lap. Sky hasn't replied. Demanding my attention, my drunken uncle slides a mystery prize across the table. "For my Honey Bear!" He pats the black bag. A solid box thumps beneath the canvas. "I know how much you enjoy my pets so along with the two hundred thousand acres of rainforest I saved in your name last week, I got you your own endangered species!"

"Thanks." I grab the unsettling gift by its thick chords and pull it towards me. Whatever this is has weight. My phone double buzzes. Keeping the screen below table level, I read:

"Oh, hi!!! We couldn't stay. I'm on the corner at Melrose. Get me?"

"Kick fucking ass." I mutter, pocket my phone, stand, and announce, "I'll be right back." Grabbing the canvas bag and my toast, I crunch, "I've gotta go make a call," and making for the door, mumble my crumby excuse for bailing, "client."

# CHAPTER 6

GRIM REAPER SCENT

**I dig for my creased ticket and hand it to the Valet.** I watch the kid jog away past four scrapers as the leader of my old crew creeps toward me. Two of the other three in his pack are new. They'd better be smarter or shadier than Alexei was.

"Little Bro! You're fancy now, huh?" Abbi nods toward the rich people eating on the Ivy's deck. "Whatcha have for breakfast? Lobster and Cristal?" He's always been envious of my insider juice. I was pretty rad when we rolled together but I'm way radder now.

"Nah man, just killed a bowl of diamonds. You gotta try 'em. Brutal on the teeth but tasty!" Matching his shit talk, I grip the slick cord of my heavy gift. I don't think this gorilla will get crazy in front of a hotspot but you never know with his temper. I'm ready to swing if he does. "Maybe you could trade your LED for a spoonful." I suggest, motioning to his modded-out Sony. With all that new gear, Abbi's gotta be doing okay for himself.

"Maybe so, little bro. Maybe so." He slides off his Chrome Hearts shades with furry fingers and looks to the sky, summoning a higher thread count to weave through the expanding blanket of clouds, before turning his green energy drink eyes back on me. "Who you see in there?"

"Georgia..." I pop the collar of my denim against the unexpected chill. "...Jagger. Pop's in there with—"

"No shit!" The pimply scum in the Simba beanie cuts me off. The scrapers look sweaty and hungry like the hyenas from The Lion King.

"That it?" Abbi asks. "We heard Fass was in there with Sky. You ain't seen 'em?"

"Nope." I move toward my bitchin' powerhouse as Valet rolls Lenore to the curb and holds my door. I tip the kid a fifty, toss my mystery prize to the backseat, hop in, and rev my engine. Still clustered on the sidewalk, the scrapers wait for me to throw them a bone. I roll down my window and tip, "Look... you fuckers want a sure thing? The Effs are on their way to the Chateau." With a pop of their switch, my headlights cut through the sudden gloom that came with the clouds, as I attempt to keep the peace. "Stella's been hanging with Franco pretty hard," I reveal, "he could be there."

Abbi stares at me for a beat too long before sliding on his shades and accepting the tip. "Okay. Sounds good." His nic-stained teeth look like yellow pillars holding up his death-black goatee when he bares them. "Catchya soon fancy lil bro," he threatens and follows his crew's sliming trail toward their SUV's.

"Hey!" I call toward the monster's massive lumbering back. "Any leads on Drop Dead or what?"

"It's his milkshake Tuesday bro." Without turning around Abbi booms, "Gonna be a real shit-show getting in over there."

"For you guys!" I laugh. "Next one is the Al This And Morsels. I'm already on the other side of the rope drinking chocolate almond milk. Lates!" I yell, and flipping a bitch, burn toward Melrose.

Sky, in combat boots, smokes a real cigarette on the corner in front of a coffee shop run by mustachioed men. Her open flannel looks like it would be big on me. I screech to a stop at the curb. "Missedya in there, handsome." She saunters toward my ride with a smile. "My agent had a last minute thing. I told him I'd meet him later." She leans into my passenger window hot as fuck. "You wanna hang somewhere less crazy?"

"Fuck yeah!" I exclaim, sliding across my hood, and opening her door in one totally sick, smooth motion before shooting back behind the wheel. Sky's chocolatey perfume fills my car. "You smell awesome." I tear my air freshener from my rearview and sniff its final cinnamony moment. "Love ya but fuck ya, Ol' Death" I declare as I kiss the black light grim reaper and toss him out the window. "Where to?" I turn to her and offer, "London? Paris? Turks and Caicos?"

Sky snuffs her cigarette out on the pile of change in my ashtray. "Turn right." She exhales a cloud of directions out her window before facing me with a smile. "I know a place where we won't be bothered."

"Kickass!" I snatch Sky's crushed butt from beneath a quarter and pocket it. "Buckle up, beautiful. I go fast."

# CHAPTER 7

PRINCE HONEY BEAR

**I've noticed this café.** The patio is usually full of people with scripts, high-end purses and yoga pants eating a tenth of what I would. This morning my dream girl and I are the only couple under its striped awning. The sudden low clouds are still hiding Melrose Ave. from the California sun and scaring away the locals. No one has pulled into the front lot since our busser sat down breakfast. Sky ignores hers and watches me scarf mine.

"Fuck, those cakes were killer. Place is rad." I swallow a final chewy bite of buckwheat and take a pull of pink coconut water while reaching down for my camera bag. "Wanna get some shit for my site? Beauty and the Brunch?"

Sky picks a piece of ice from her green tea, sucks it into her mouth, puckers, and shakes her head. Hiding the cube in her cheek she makes a sweeping motion toward her outfit. "Not like this. It's just for my meeting. Terror Cake may be a 90's thing now. David thinks it's cuz of the Sony leaks or something..."

"I think you look awesome... kinda like you used to in your videos." Sky crunches her ice and I empty a second ramekin of light syrup over my tempeh. "Where'd you get that shirt?"

"Oh..." Opening her unbuttoned flannel she looks down at her chest, grimacing as if she were wearing a Drop Dead Gorgeous tee. "Same place I got the rest. It's one of the bands my father used to work for."

"He worked for Sonic Youth? No way!" I pop a grainy piece of tempeh into my mouth and chew smoked soy. "Your dad must be radical." I suck my maple fingers. "I really gotta meet him before our wedding. He's gonna love me."

"I hope you never have to. He's overrated." Sky begins digging through her tie-dyed satchel. "...Just like his has-been rockers."

"Wait, what? You're not into rock? In your videos you're all CBGB tees and biker jackets with, like, Ramones buttons—"

"Rock is so done, Al. Even my idiot father moved on...to make terrible movies..." Sky pulls a fold of rolling papers from her bag and pushes aside her Benedict. The smell of rotten ocean wafts from her plate as she flattens a sheet on the table in front of her. "If it's not EDM it doesn't matter."

I grab my phone from the table. "Check this out!" I find the shot of me doing a handstand on the steps of Hyde next to Calvin Harris and show Sky. She doesn't recognize the superfame DJ. "So is your dad putting you in all of his movies?" I ask, setting my phone next to my raw juice. "He should. You'd make 'em better."

"No." Sky pinches a plug of tobacco from a sack

of American Spirit. "We don't speak." She sprinkles dark scabrous shreds across the thin paper and, after rolling, licks the fold and twists the end. The cigarette smells like a moldy, charred strawberry. She taps its tip against her buzzing phone then hangs the roll from her perfect pout. As she reaches into her bag, I draw my old lighter: matte black with "Get Rad!" in day-glow green. I snap the flint and Sky cups the thick flame to take a slow drag. The cigarette crackles and the cherry glows as she sits back in her chair, cocks back her wrist, and replies to her texts. I love her long fingers. I'm going to put a diamond on one of them—or maybe a few.

"What happened to the Vape? You should quit that real shit. I'm gonna live forever but I don't want to without you."

Her smoke snakes upward, drifting away toward an ad for a new party in Vegas. The Barbie's DJ boyfriend K3NNYDOLL has a stand at Hakkasan. The back of his dumb head covers the billboard behind Sky's stunning, downcast face. Sky says, "You really are divine, aren't you?" Glancing up from her phone she smiles like fucking Alice in Wonderland. "My friends swore you were. I suppose a Christmas baby must be divine."

"Divine as fuck!" I tug down the neck of my Donald Duck tee. "Cooler than Christ" is hand poked on my chest over my heart in celebration of the day I was born—December 25th. "I did this one myself." I tap the sacrilegious script of my first tattoo then slide my foot from my Vans and begin slipping off my sock. "My friend in SF did my missile toe." Sky laughs at the bomb on my big toe before I put my shoe back on and dig my Pluto wallet from my jeans. "Check it out, I used to kinda look like Jesus too…" I tear open the fraying Velcro flap and pass her my ID. "See?" I grin.

"Oh my god," she smiles, inspecting my old license, "you were adorable!"

"Yeah. Sexier now though, huh?"

Sky crooks her head at my ID and nods as if the official info just confirmed a hot rumor. "And your name is Dustin." I shrug and she hands back the card. "When did you cut off your gorgeous mane?" she asks, and takes another drag.

I still kinda miss Star and I don't really want to talk about my ex with Sky. "You like the long-ness better? I can grow it back!"

Sky leans across the table. "Dustin Prozen..." She whispers my real name, smelling like smoke. "I think you're hot. Just the way you are." Major goosebumps party across my bod. I move in to kiss her super fast. She backs away super-faster.

"Damn it!" I complain as she settles back into her chair. "Well, that totally sucked."

"Later, handsome," she promises, cautiously looking toward the movement in the café. Inside, two bussers ignore us and refill the cucumber-water cooler. Sky lowers her voice and places her smoke-free hand on top of my arm. "I can't risk being seen with...someone" she explains, as I flex. "My agent would kill me."

"What? What do you mean?"

"David wants me single for my fans...unless bae were A-list famous—"

"I'm Fuckin' A-list famous!"

Sky kisses my hand and takes a drag. Leaning back again, she studies me. She's either super curious or totally fucking in love. "You are adorable." Obviously, totally in love.

I prop my elbow on the table and rest my chin in my hand. Sky eyes my lucky lock as I advise, "You should probably fire David. Dude can't even recognize the divine when he sees it..." I follow her distant gaze toward a second fucking Hakkasan billboard for K3NNY DOLL. "Hey!" I ask, turning away from the lined eyebrow raised above K3NNY's oversized shades, "How'd you know my birthday? All my profiles are total lies."

"Cam and Jaq told me. They call you Dustin...they speak very highly of you."

"Who the fuck are Cam and Jaq? Wizards?"

"Well, they do keep saying you're the magic I need." Sky rests her cigarette on her untouched plate and nods toward a black SUV in the lot. "My BFFs."

The Unicorn and The Trueblood—Cam and Jaq, I presume—are here waiting inside a G550. I didn't hear them pull up. Wizards. The Trueblood emerges from shotgun, eases his black corduroy house shoes from the Benz SUV to the asphalt and turns to face me. He sucks a thick joint and parts his ruby lips. Smoke spills past his 24 karat fangs.

"Oh! The Mythicals!" I've never seen them in daylight. It feels kinda crazy, kinda impossible. I never considered them existing outside the dark—or outside the clubs for that matter. From the driver's seat Cam's unblinking blue contacts stare me down as Jaq watches me from behind golden Gucci shades. I drop my hand. I can't tell if they want to eat me or eat me. "How do they know all this shit about me?"

"They know a lot about everyone." Bagging her phone, papers, and tobacco, she explains, "They're huge on the internet." The café's window reflects her radness as she stands. Sky slides on her round rose-tinted shades. "I've gotta go. The Terror Cake producers are with David and I accidentally slept through my last meeting with them so if I don't get over there now he's gonna freak."

"Aren't you going to eat anything?" I nod to her full order. Her cigarette smolders at the edge of a yellow hollandaise pool swimming with dead salmon.

"Not today." Sky takes a final drag and crushes it in the sauce. "I'm starting a juice cleanse." She moves toward the black Benz.

"Hey, what are you doing Tuesday?" I jump up from my chair, snatching the snuffed butt before following her through The Trueblood's THC chem trail. "Pink Corvette's doing a secret thing at Sayers. Wanna come?" As Jaq spiders into the backseat, the golden FANG BANG script below his raised hood gleams.

"I was hoping you'd ask." Sky shuts her door and speaks through the open window. "I'll wear something better and maybe we can get something for your site there..." Her voice momentarily slips back to how it sounded that night at Teddy's when she says, "...perhaps get something a bit more tawdry after." She smiles like sex and, like animate plastic, The Unicorn starts the engine. Run The Jewels booms into the lot like a riot.

"For sure!" I yell over the bass. Cam leans into her covering his plump bubblegum pink lips and whispers. I watch my gummy ring change colors over Sky's ear until the disco light is muted by the deep tint of the rising window. With a calf-raise I salute and yell, "Love you hard!" as the G550 pulls away. I've got to get Sky another ring.

\*\*\*\*

Sitting in Lenore, parked in the back lot, I sing along to *You Could Be Mine* as I respond to Sky's text. Her polite request for me to bring more Anger to The Barbie's show reminds me of my mystery prize. After assuring Sky she can have anything she wants, I snatch the canvas bag from the backseat and set the box on my lap. There are no air holes in the thick mahogany containing "your own endangered species." Well, if there's some freeze-dried, super-expensive dead thing in here, I'll just give it to The Barbie to add to her collection.

I lift the lid. Axl wails toward the neighboring Spanish bungalows as a waft of peppercorn and lemon pollutes my car. On a small golden card dipped in his cologne Noah wrote: "For my Honey Bear, because I love how you shoot ~ UN"

Below the nasty note, with *Prince Honey Bear* engraved on its slide, a golden Desert Eagle nestles in the case's black velvet interior. Boxes of ammo are stacked in the compartment beneath it. I flick the scented card into the lot and, click in the loaded magazine, and raise my new toy to the windshield. "Fuck yeah, endangered danger-bird."

I crank GN'R, back out of the lot, and burn through the WEHO flats with my weapon waving out of my window, pretending to shoot every fuckface that looks remotely like Jamie Shannon. I'd probably run out of bullets if I were actually firing.

# CHAPTER 8

## Eff House is a non-stop party.

There's always some camera-worthy shit happening here in this four-bedroom West Hollywood celebration of reality radness, whether or not the show is being shot. Sleep is rare but it makes for good times, great content, and living here fits perfectly into my budget. With a unanimous vote of "fuck yeah!" from the rest of the Effs, The Barbie invited me to crash shortly after I got her on the show. One of the Producers isn't too stoked on me and, as you can imagine, I give as many fucks about him as I give dollars for rent. I pay exactly zero per night for a couch in the dead center of the action.

Score hasn't commandeered my couch since he had the Wildfox model over, so I've been able to avoid the Ark for days. Last night when I got back from shredding my quads at Equinox he was in the living room sunk into a supersized beanbag with a hot it-girl on top of him. He was petting the

Wildfox model's white bat-faced cat and snickering at *Tim & Eric* as Alexa Chung sprawled on top of him. I threw my duffle in the corner that acts as my closet and squeezed into their cuddle party. Score bailed to take a "business call." Alexa took some molly and I took pictures of them making out on the bag. The post of Score licking her face as she grimaced brought my site hundreds of new Brits and a bunch of hate comments from some kid with the handle @snowsimian. This guy claims to be Alexa's boyfriend and keeps calling me and Score "poofs". In the kitchen smiling at the stalker's lame online threats, I got a pretty rad boner. It stood strong as I downed my post-workout peanut butter protein shake and shot the Twilight Sleeper sex scene on my way to try to find a place to sleep before resorting to Uncle Noah's. I'm always far from ready to return to the Ark.

Outside of The Barbie's door, I could hear K3NNYDOLL whimpering. I'd have thought it was the sound of them banging if I could imagine him having a dick. He's so fuckin' gooey that I just can't. The Barbie's tired voice plead, "Fuck. Stop crying, Ken..." and, bummed, I gave up on my first pick for a slumber party. I still don't know how TB stomachs that guy. She doesn't need his money. The Effs' contracts are huge and The Barbie's family is loaded.

I made my way further down the hall towards the master bedroom. When I barged into the pink room, Stella was in bed with superfame. I said what's up to Jimmy Franco and complimented his ass before checking Angel and Jenny Lee's room. As expected, the other Effs locked their doors before they left to go on location in Aspen so I had to camp on the floor of the guest bathroom. It kinda sucked but at least the towels I laid over the tiles were thick and I had the Wildfox's bat-cat to keep me company.

This morning I emerge from my neck-tweaking slumber covered in sweat. It feels like I'm shuffling toward Hollywood Heaven. Bright cans flood the end of the sweltering hall with harsh white light as I follow a polystyrene trail toward it. Rubbery, white beads roll and bounce from my bare-footed steps as I enter the hot-as-fuck living room where the crew is shooting a new episode of the show. Today they're focusing, once again, on Pink Corvette—The Barbie's new electro act with her superfame DJ boyfriend.

Off camera the beanbag bleeds beads from multiple stab wounds while Score sleeps on my folded couch. An open pink switchblade wobbles on his boney chest, rising and falling with his labored breath, as the black and neon-orange plastic cat mask covering his face buzzes like a kazoo. He looks like a pale art installation for some fashion week bullshit. His striped Paul Smith boxer-briefs lay stacked below his folded Saint Laurent jeans on the mirrored coffee table. The old Ramones shirt he had on last night is nowhere to be seen.

The AD yells "Slate!" The clapperboard clacks. I high-five the groomer and, adjusting the crotch of my camo shorts, creep through the action. The Barbie and K3NNYD0LL sit next to each other in the love seat and sip off tall cans of Modelo as they go over the guest list for the event tonight. I suddenly realize it's finally Tuesday. I'm stoked to see Sky tonight.

The Key Grip squirms as I easily weave behind his rig. I avoid touching his dolly, give him a double thumbs-up, dodge a boom and, taking wobbly steps, tread thick black cables to my closet-corner. I quietly unlatch my camera bag's metal clips and grab my Canon to document the beanbag murder scene. I hop onto the arm of the Twilight Sleeper, and The Barbie glances beyond the camera crew. We say a secret hello with our eyes before she looks back at K3NNY.  He passionately tells his audience how he began fusing Big Room with Tropical House after growing up going to Gabber parties. When he says something about being raised on Kraftwerk, I pause my soft-core shoot and laugh. "Lieeeees," I sing like Geddy Lee.

Seriously. It's all fucking lies. Two years ago the world famous K3NNYDOLL was "Ken Kadaver" lead screecher of the false metal band Yesterday Starts Tomorrow. Outside the Inland Empire no one had ever heard of YST, so one afternoon Kenny woke up in his parent's mansion and decided he was a DJ/producer/songwriter/fame-fucker. He shaved lines into his eyebrows and the word "DOLL" above his new rat-tail, and changed his name. His family's alien sex cult money bought him a fully stacked recording studio/loft/art space (known to the world as *Dollhouse, DTLA*) into which—on one dark magic mushroom night—he lured The Barbie. Now he's an All Fs regular. And, holy fuck, you'd think that Pink Corvette were a year supply of Viagra for the boners it gives these producers.

K3NNYDOLL struggles to ignore my mockery while explaining his new duo to the masses. "It's like...she's the pink paint job and I'm the engine." I lower my lens and plop down from the couch. The Barbie watches me mimic her BF over his shoulder. She laughs. The director calls cut, and the male-pattern-producer springs up from his tall folding chair brandishing his Blackberry at me.

"How many times have I told you about being here when we're shooting?" he bitches. "Never. Never ever." Score's ancient Halloween mask makes a shushing sound and the producer throws back his head. "Jesus...how is this my life?" he begs the ceiling.

"He's not up there Doug." I grin at TB as she covers her burgundy lips. "I saw him the other night on Sunset rolling with some reindeer babes. We're tight. Want me to talk to him for ya?" I offer, "He might be able to get you laid – calm ya down."

"Jesus is bullshit" Score's voice buzzes beneath plastic whiskers. As if the dead just spoke, Doug drops his hands and looks back at the couch. Score goes silent. I think he's talking in his sleep.

My producer nemesis motions to me. "Someone please get this pap-rat out of my hair."

"Which hair Doug?" Squinting, I point to his five-head. "That one... or the other one?"

"Leave now." He says all serious, then looks at The Barbie like she's going to do something. TB adjusts her low bangs and stares out the window. "Your pet rodent needs exterminating." TB gives him a bratty look.

"Okay dude, settle. Settle. Don't upset the talent." Raising my hands in acquiescence I give him a wide grin. "I thought you wanted some number one ratings but whatever man..." Moonwalking through the shot, I announce, "I'm gonna go make sure Stella still likes being on top—of the charts— OHHHHH DAMMMN..."

"Does the rat pay rent yet?" Mr. Tight-assed producer addresses the crew. They all go super silent. "Find a home. And stay out of Stella's room!" He yells, having twice caught me beneath her.

"No worries Doug! We're just gonna take a quick shower." As smooth as the King of Pop, I backslide toward her door. My feline floormate springs into the hallway and paws the beads at my feet. "I'll go back to sleeping with The Barbie as soon as K3NNY leaves for Vegas." I throw up a double peace. The Barbie laughs. DOLL boy gets up, quits the show, and flails out the front door.

"Oh, great. That's great." Doug turns to The Barbie's giddy expression. "Well?" He points toward the driveway. "Get him back!"

The Barbie sighs and slumps out to the porch. Doug slams the door behind her and the switchblade clatters to the floor. The bat-cat bats its pink handle and the blade continues to spin on the hardwood.

"For fuck's sake!" Doug snaps, pinching the bridge of his nose. "Can someone please put a blanket over Score?" And the dead awakes. Score removes the mask to cover his rod and yawns. "Jesus..." the producer mutters before sternly demanding, "Score. Get up, call your whore, and tell her to come get her creepy cat..." Then yelling toward my smooth exit, adds "And ask her if she'll take a rat with it!"

# CHAPTER 9

**Listening to Sixx Sense radio stretched out on Stella's pink bed, I laugh at The Barbie's text while image-searching K3NNYDOLL on my computer.** Apparently her BF just cried during the Pink Corvette soundcheck. I quickly doctor cartoon tears onto a photo of him gritting his teeth onstage at EDC and send it to her. TB responds with a string of crying-with-laughter emoji. I close my messages and re-open my project as Score poses in front of a full-length vanity. He tells me to change Motorhead to Katy Perry. I open YouTube.

Over the sound of the Dark Horse video Score babbles about products making his hair "messy but not a mess" while Marlena Lopez sticks her tongue out at me from my monitor. Whenever her new X-games fame boyfriend is out of town the pop-superfame hits me up. This morning, after showering one pink curtain away from a pissing James Franco, I went to her video shoot and we fucked super rad on the bed at the back of her trailer. Since we're both in love with other people it's a solid sitch. No one gets hurt and whenever we hook-up, I get new shots for my site that boosts her cred and my traffic.

I suggest Score shave his whole head as I scroll through pictures of me with Disney back-up dancers to find a head to toe of Marlena in half-buttoned, candy-printed PJs. I edit my jeans out from under her feet and the pop-superfame approved post goes live. Score blurs past the edge of my monitor and I shut down, pack up my shit, and follow the frantic freak into Stella's closet.

"I thought you weren't coming with us." I lean against the molded pink frame of the apartment-sized walk-in and watch him deliberate.

"I'm not." Score grabs a scarf from what looks like a void in the corner of a pastry shop. Most of Stella's clothes are the color of frosting. His section is black.

"Then why have you changed into the same dress like three times?"

"Four." He buckles the collar of a "shirt" that goes down to his ankles. "Four outfits. Six different designers. And it's a shirt." It's like he's roped to his reflection by an eight-inch bungee cord. "I'm going to that new thing downtown—Blood Lust." Standing in the three-paneled mirror, he smiles, inspecting his teeth. "You should come."

"Grave Cutters? Post-poets?"

"Digital Ghostcore. The Meth Sentence kids are doing it." Yanking off his scarf, he throws it over his shoulder and unbuckles his neck. "...A little Power Trap..."

"Damn! That sounds awesome if you're into total bullshit!" *Flash Flash Flash*. Laughing I review the candids.

Appearing next to me, Score snatches my phone. He taps the screen then hands it back, ending my joy. "Damn it," I sigh. He erased the entire speed burst of him making the worst face.

"Tonight's thing is already the next hotness and I missed the opening," Score rationalizes, suddenly topless and back in the mirror tying up his topknot. "People are saying I was there but I can't risk actually not being there twice. They want to attach me to it—gotta make sure it's the right look first, y'know?" I can tell by his voice that he's re-checking his teeth. "It would be a good look if you covered it, Al. I really think it's the next hotness."

"Um, is it as hot as a secret Pink Corvette show?" I turn into the closet reminding my friend, "Nothing hotter than The Barbie wearing nothing but tape on her tits all up close and personal" before looking back down at The Unicorn's Instagram account. Cam tagged me in his most recent post: my gummy ring on his ring finger with the caption *our prince has come*. I guess The Mythicals like me. "I'm bringing Sky and she wants to get tawdry after."

"Fabulous. Send nudes." Score sits on the floor "shirt"-less looking like a collapsed scarecrow in drop crotch sweats and recalls something super important while switching designer boots. "Oh, BTW, I heard Jamie Shannon was at Blood Lust last month..." Lacing up, he blatantly baits me "...with Andy Kane."

"Fuck off. I'd heard they were a thing! Tell me they are!"

"I don't know. I was going to ask Andy about it but he hasn't been at Micky's in twenty seven days."

"How...why were you at Micky's?" I'm baffled by his insider knowledge of the infamous go-go dancer and the gay bar wherein he shakes it.

"Business."

Score paces by as I consider my options. "Fuck...I'd love to catch Drop Dead with Boys Town's brightest but there's no way I'm flaking on my babes...especially if it's not a sure thing," I decide, pocketing my phone. "But if you see James punching Andy with his dick, let me know. I gotta go."

As I march out of the closet toward the hall, Score turns from the mirror and yells "Tell Sky that I want to work with her!"

# CHAPTER 10

**At the top of La Cienega a billboard for a new Netflix series illuminates the block.** More LED screens flash in the distance, lining the road to the ocean with radiant fame. Siri tells me to go toward the light. I crank left and blaze onto Sunset.

Everyone bails Hollywood during the winter holidays, journeying back to wherever they came from. I weave between lanes they've left empty. On my lock-screen the time blinks on over a photo of TB pointing her air pistol toward my lens. It's 8:42 p.m. when my phone buzzes in my palm. Sky's text reads "Reggie will be down to meet you." I don't know who Reggie is.

I screech right up Queens Road past the Comedy Store. The Chili Peppers are singing something about California on KROQ. I change the station to KIIS and over Marlena's singing Siri says a bunch of stupid shit that lands me in a virtually empty lot. I reset my navigation and the voice directs me further uphill and left into a steep driveway.

I stare up at Sky's 1960's space-age dream house straight out of Tomorrow Land. I'm about to text her when a 6'5" dude walks out from a hidden breach in the concrete retaining wall. He looks like Jay Z playing James Bond. The GQ giant strides around Lenore's hood to lean into my window.

"ID?" he asks.

"What are you? A cop? I break hearts not laws man!" sliding on my shades I nod toward his sculpted mass. "Nice traps. How much are ya shruggin'?" I grin.

Reggie stares with the calm of a casual killer as some horrible garbage quietly plays on the pop station. I pull out Pluto. Velcro tears. I hand over my license and pocket my shades. I'm permanently done fucking with Sky's security. I bet he trains at my old gym.

Reggie glances at me. "Figured. There couldn't be too many of these babies around here." He pats Lenore's roof, returns my ID, and disappears into the wall.

I switch the new Drop Dead Gorgeous song over to the sounds of some dude named Francisco losing it over winning tickets to the Acoustic Xmas festival. I hear The White Stripes, Cage The Elephant, and The Arctic Monkeys. DJ Stryker announces Hozier, and Sky glides out from the secret stairwell. After looking up and down the street she lowers the hood of her red cape, takes off her shades, and smiles her Cinderella smile. The Mythicals lead her like two fallen Charlie's Angels down the path and I'm bummed. I thought we would be alone. Whatevs. They're cool—sorta. And they like me—maybe.

I jump out of Lenore, slide across the hood, and open the passenger door in one totally sick, smooth motion. Sky's guardians' skin-tight catsuits glimmer through the dark as The Unicorn and The Trueblood click toward me. "Cammmmm!" I welcome the raincloud and, ignoring the offer of my high five, he spiders into the back seat.

"That's Jaq," Sky corrects me then nods toward The Unicorn. "This is Cam." In reflective red spandex he looks like an anorexic Christmas tree ornament, strung with a forest green French braid. Cam offers his/my/Sky's blinking ring as if he wants me to kiss it.

I shake his hand. "Sup man?" Cam retracts his hoof and scoots next to Jaq. I push back the passenger seat then open my arms. Sky sits, passing up the hug. I shut her door, moonwalk through my headlights, and take the wheel as she continues to text.

"I'm a bit late. I apologize." Her voice sings, then, looking up from her phone, Sky lowers her sun visor and scowls in the dim lights of the little mirror. "Reggie saw some paps earlier. You haven't seen any, have you?" she asks, wrinkling her nose before flipping up the shade to peer into the emptiness of the road. "I mean, other than yourself my dear."

"Nah..." Behind me, squirming to keep their perfect 'dos from being fucked by the low roof of my fastback, the cramped Mythicals further investigate the streets. I look away from the rearview, "But I'm not really—"

"Good." Sky kisses me. She slowly opens her mouth and gives me a tiny bit of tongue then pulls back to return to her buzzing phone. I melt like the Toon Shoe from Roger Rabbit—minus the screaming and with a chubby. "Reggie is quite capable of keeping them away," she explains, looking and sounding way more like the sixties babe I met at Teddies than the grunge chick I picked up by The Ivy. "But a girl can never be too careful." Deep in texting, she says, "We're getting close on Terror Cake. David says they definitely want someone hip and unexpected..."

"Awesome! " I back down the grade and up her street.

"I'd never expect you! Except to kill it." I shift Leonard and head for the flats.

In my rearview The Mythicals' lips and eyes glitter red and gold in touchscreen light as I cruise past Sky's driveway. She responds to their texts aloud, "I'm sure he hasn't forgotten," before turning to ask me, "did you bring the sweet sweets, my dear?"

"Huh? Oh... shit, yeah." I pull over and reach over her to pop the glove box. "There should be one more in here!" I rummage through glossy rave flyers and gym passes. I hold up the Anger, "I guess this organic shit is pretty killer, huh? You wanna party now or at the show? Or for dessert? I got us reservations at Crossroads. They'll be stoked that you're there. You could probably have the waiter rail that shit up for you at the table with one of those crumb scraper things." The long-lost kinkajou-printed baggie dangles from my fingers. Gold nails snatch the coke.

"Oh." Nervously unsnapping and snapping the latch of her shiny black Chanel clutch, Sky says, "It's so sweet of you to think to bring us there but I'm feeling like something a bit more...low-key."

"Awesome. I hate that place." It's my favorite place. "What'd ya have in mind?"

"Burgers!" She smiles. "You choose the joint."

"Killer. I'll cancel our rez." I rev my engine kinda bummed not be heading for something un-murdered at Hollywood's best restaurant. I'd forgotten scrapers like to catch fame pretending to care about the world by eating vegan there. I guess Sky remembered. "Buckle up! That means you guys too." I yell to the back, wait, insist again, then fire downhill.

The sound of Anger being snorted from acrylics gets squashed when I turn on KIIS for Sky, and she cranks up the

Lana Del Rey remix. At the bottom of the street stopped at a red I grab my phone to text the manager of the Hollywood dining hotspot, and an incoming call from an unknown number flashes over my message. The scrapers always have new burner phones with new digits. Muttering "oh shit," I hit decline and toss my phone back into the ashtray. Just seeing the call was enough to remind me—tonight is the fucking Milkshake. I crank onto Sunset and charge east. I don't want to ruin our date but I can't risk missing defaming shit if there is defaming shit to be missed.

"Was the restaurant being difficult?" Sky casually wonders, scrolling through her Instagram.

"Nah. Everything's cool. I just have to check on something really quick." Cutting down La Cienega, I glance behind my seat. The Unicorn's red boots look super festive dusted in Anger snow and crushing my camera bag. His shimmery knees remain propped high and pressed into my back all the way to the event.

When we get to Boys Town, it sounds like Harry Styles just jumped out of a Fifty Shades of Grey cake at a twelve-year-old girl's slumber party. The squealing tweens are taking more pictures than the scrapers. At the front of the hungry pap mob, Abbi's furry fingers grip his lowered moded-out cam. He stares into Millions of Milkshakes, waiting.

"Holy fuck," I laugh, as we cruise by fans sporting Drop Dead Gorgeous tees, flags, top hats, homemade posters, old Jamie Shannon headshots, and the occasional DDG branded ninja mask. "Somewhere Justin Bieber must be plotting to kill this fucker. The Biebs and I should team up," I comment as two gasps pop from the backseat. I check my rearview shocked to have heard any sound coming from The Mythicals. Sky's guardians stare out their windows with wide eyes. Their fake lashes have lost their flutter. My dream girl glances up from a Snapchat of The Trueblood doing coke in my backseat.

"Where are we headed?" Sky asks, sounding accusatory.

"Millions." I crank the wheel to edge from the turn lane into oncoming traffic. "Fucker Drop Dead's premiering his shake tonight." Wedging Lenore in front of a family van with Riverside plate frames, I raise my voice over its horn. "I guess it's black. He said he's naming it 'Le Petite Morte' cuz 'that's what it tastes like'—fucking dork." I scan the Milkshake scene for battered Go Go Boys, and someone shrieks. "Oh my god he's coming." The hormone-riot is about to happen. Hastily double parking, I excuse myself. "I'm just gonna shoot in there for a second..." I reach for my camera bag. "Dude Cam..." I demand, smacking his candy-apple colored footwear, "Move your hooves," and Sky's voice whips me like an arctic storm.

"Fuck that dick bag piece of shit. I hope he gets his tiny wart infested cock stuck in the blender when he whips it out for all these little brain-dead cunts. Get us the fuck out of here. Now."

"Woah! Um—" laughing, stoked, I look up at her.

Sounding more like Uncle Noah than a fancy sixties babe, Sky hunches down in her seat as if we're about to do a drive-by and dumps her clutch. She stares at the loose cash, pink slips, parking tickets, credit cards, and make-up in her lap. "Oh my god, they're not—" she begins, horrified, before The Unicorn's green acrylics shove something into her mouth. A shiny black arm follows with a squirt from a golden baby bottle. My dream girl swallows, wipes her lips, and throws her seat back into Jaq's lap as cheers and shouts burst through her open window like a Tower of Terror drop.

I scan the mob for Andy Kane and Drop Dead but see only promo posters of Jamie drinking a black shake and mall people having heart attacks. "Jamie, Jamie!" His dumb followers chant. I'm dying to go in there.

"Shit. Sorry, I—" I stammer. Sky's drained face matches her cashmere sweater. I squeeze her hand then release it to grip Leonard. "Hold on kids!" Downshifting before throwing up a preemptive flip-off finger toward the inevitable honks, I crank around a Forester and leave Drop Dead's lame fans in clouds of smoke.

# CHAPTER 11

**"I'm sorry. I must control my outbursts."** In the patio, Sky sits across from me in the glow of the neon, Astro Burger sign and vapes, apologizing. I sip blended strawberry iced coconut-cream and tell her the Milkshakes meltdown was totally awesome. "No," she insists, in her sixties song, pushing aside an orange tray to prop her elbow in its place. "It was terribly un-lady like." The Unicorn reaches over the golden baby bottle to retrieve the crinkle fry he's been sharing with The Trueblood as, with two tiny red blotches spotting her wrist, Sky flits her e-pipe and says, "That boy just pushes my buttons."

"Fuck yeah. I'd like to push his off button." Sky's open-faced burger cools next to a full paper boat of onion rings. She peels a thin bacon strip from the glistening cheddar and I pull up Instagram. "I'm hoping get a photo of this kid's tongue in Drop Dead's butt to show his Jesus-freak fans." I scroll to Andy

Kane's account. In his last post the cropped platinum-blonde stands on the back patio of The Tenants of the Trees cocktail compound, punching toward the camera. D R O P D E A D is written on his knuckles in the same lipstick framing his glossy snarl. "You know him? I think he'd be stoked on me featuring that kinda thing."

"We do." Sky affirms with a nod, "We used to see him all the time." She passes the fatty slice of pig flesh to Jaq and asks, "Didn't we?"

The Trueblood glances at my phone then looks to The Unicorn. Cam squeezes my thigh. I turn my screen and, like slow parrot wings, The Unicorn's green lashes bat once at the photo before he stands and clicks into the burger joint with The Trueblood.

"The sweet boy was smitten with Jaq." On her own phone Sky shows me a selfie of Andy Kane snuggling The Trueblood in a dark booth at A Club Called Rhonda. "This was a long time ago. We were celebrating. Andy had just done his first webcam." In the go-go-porn-star's post, The Trueblood looks like his old slick fascist-soldier self. Andy looks like a kid hugging a militaristic wax pop star that walked out of Madame Tussaud's. "I hope for his sake that he's not involved with that cad James." Sky says, pursing her phone, "Though I wouldn't be surprised if he were. Andy's just his type—broke and fame-hungry."

"So..." I palm-press a stack of grilled soy cheeses, take a greasy bite, and, covering my mouth, ask, "You actually know Drop Dead or you just hate him for the obvs?"

"No, I know him. Unfortunately..." Sky exhales. Melony mist mingles with the scent of the patio's natural Christmas tree. "Daddy created Gorgeous. He made James. And I, being an impressionable girl of fifteen, was smitten with him.

I begged daddy to introduce us but he refused. He was so protective of James, more than protective really. It was like..." She shakes her head as if dismissing her first thought. "...It was like he was jealous of anyone who got near him." I blindly reach for my missing shake and Sky passes her cherry coke. "He'd even have James stay on our property but only when I was away at mother's. It drove me mad. Then one night I was at an after party at The Ace Rooftop—the year James hosted the MTV Movie Awards..."

"Yeah. The suck year," I nod, sipping diet soda.

"I didn't think he'd actually show up but there he was at a table full of reality girls. James left them to come talk to me then took me to his suite." Sky's Bambi eyes go all dreamy as my brain starts to scream with the growing nightmare. "We drank most of the mini bar while watching new episodes of his show and then he took my cherry..."

"Ugh! What? Fuck! Gross!" My fingers fall with my heart, and I drop my sandwich. Sky keeps super cool so I get it together. "You know what? Doesn't count." I calmly wave away the disgusting truth. "Since I'm gonna be the first real man to do it to you we'll say I'm taking your V card." I take a saccharine gulp, hand back her artificially sweetened fountain drink, and ask, "I'll be your second right?"

"Sixty-second."

"That'll work."

I frown at my suddenly unappetizing dinner and cover the tray with its waxy paper placemat. My pocket buzzes. I reach in and kill the call. No one is gonna compromise the deep connecting happening between my babe and me right now. "I can't believe it. I can't believe you fucked Drop Dead. Must've sucked."

"It wasn't dreamy. He usually fucked me like he treated me—horribly." She peels the last strip of bacon from her burger and offers it to me. "We secretly dated for over a year."

Unable to keep my cool, I bail to the ground. Splayed out over the concrete I stare at Sky's beautiful ankles from up close. I wanna kiss 'em. Wondering if Jamie has, I interrogate, "How the fuck did you even date him for a day?"

"James always said I'd never do better and I believed him. I loved him," she easily admits. "We'd fight a lot..." Sky lightly scratches her wrist and gazes wistfully at the electric icicles strung from the awning. "I broke it off at a house party in Malibu. I caught him getting blown in a hot tub by one of the waitresses. When I said his name, James looked right at me and laughed."

"Holy shit." I pop up to my feet, revitalized by the spark of rage charging through my disbelief. "What did you do?"

"I went back into the house and had about twelve drinks."

"Wait..." I take The Trueblood's vacant seat to be closer. "Seriously?" I ask, "You didn't say anything? I'd have thrown them both off Point Dume."

"He was never the most faithful. I thought I'd gotten used to it but on the way home I broke. I started screaming at him and he grabbed my face and pushed my head against the window...hard. Like he was trying to squish a bug. I had to claw him off." Sky absently checks her ruby manicure before looking back to me. "I drew a little blood. It dripped onto his scarf. He saw it and started giggling like an idiot, calling me a stupid worthless cunt, so I told him to fuck off and James had the driver pull over and he kicked me out of the car—literally. While I was banging on the window begging him to let me back in, he opened the door into my face."

"No fucking way." I hide my hands below the table, trying to chill and dying to tell her about Lucky. I tug my lucky lock.

She shrugs, "Then he drove away."

"He bailed?" I'm losing it.

Sky sucks her pipe and puffs, "I was crying on the side of PCH, bleeding all over a dress he'd bought me that day." She squints at her reflection in the burger joint's window. An airbrushed elf smiles at her as Sky touches her nose. "I've had it fixed four times but those BH quacks can never get it right." She pulls her perfect pout into a frown. "That's why my face looks so funny."

"What? You're fucking beautiful! I've been jerking off to you since before we even met." I didn't think I could want to murder Drop Dead more but I was wrong. I can't comprehend how great babes like Sky and Lucky could be into this motherfucker. "You can have anyone you want!" I insist, grabbing her cold thigh as I rant. "I'm 100% killer and I'm barely good enough for you! Fuck that—" She silences me with a kiss.

As we make out I taste booze, but I'm only wasted on her radness. I press my hand beneath her soft sweater and up her warm ribs. She hums like a love song. Sleigh bells ring, and Sky pulls back. Standing a foot taller than the jingling wreath on the dining room's door, The Mythicals stare down at me before strutting over.

"So did you tell your Dad?" I turn from them and ask.

"I told him." Sky pulls herself deeper into the billows of her hood. She's a true Christmas miracle framed in green satin lining. "Daddy was only upset that I'd been seeing James. He forbade me to speak to him and told me never to tell anyone." The Unicorn places a comforting green claw on her shoulder before Sky reveals, "Cam and Jaq said I should tell you. But you can't—" and The Trueblood swoops in fangs first.

"Dude, wh—" He kisses me. Golden acrylic digs into my scalp before I can escape. I taste licorice lipstick, strawberry-coconut-cream, and cocaine as Jaq molests my mouth. Just before releasing me, he bites my cheek. I yelp and, taking my old seat, The Trueblood pulls a golden compact from his golden clutch. "Seriously, man?" I ask, rubbing sandy golden glitter from my face. Jaq, places one finger on his smeared lips, gesturing for me to hush, then reapplies his makeup. I turn to Sky. "What the fuck?"

"We adore you," she says and I notice my shake is back.

"Okay." Snatching my cup, I suck down the organic-cokey taste of Trueblood. "So, yeah, believe me, I can totally keep a Drop Dead secret." I assure her, and give a thumbs-up to the mute Mythicals wondering if the wizards know about Lucky Day. "I'll only talk about it with you guys." Sky's guardians ignore me.

"Daddy overheard me talking about it to these dears and he poisoned my breakfast. I threw up for days." I look up from my chewed straw in total fucking horror. "Blood at first…" She casually details, "I handled it better when I was a little girl. Or maybe he was actually trying to kill me that time…" Sky scratches behind her ear, "Anyway, it can't get out or—"

"Fuck this." I lob my cup into the nearby trash and make moves toward my ride. My spark of anger has turned to an electric storm. I feel her hurting and I can't fucking take it. I'll beg Star's and Lucky's forgiveness after my killing spree. "Let's go." I grab Sky's hand. "We're going back to Millions. I'm going to choke Drop Dead with his stupid fucking scarf and then you can show me where your dad lives."

"No—" Sky rises with The Trueblood. The freshly preened raincloud circles the table and takes his place by her side.

The Instafame trio stands united as Sky reaches for my arm. "No, no. Though that candy ass surely deserves nothing less, it would be bad. For both of us." She insists, squeezing my tri. I flex, as she advises, "I think your plan to reveal his secrets to the public will serve that child molester a bit better. The scandal would utterly destroy him."

Everyone would be over Drop Dead if they knew his thing for gay and straight babe-bashing. "Okay—yeah," I agree, "except it's like impossible to catch him with these dudes. I've hit up Andy Kane a million times but he's dropped off the face of the internet. His last post was weeks ago."

"I know where James takes them for his 'bromance,' as he calls it." Sky slyly smiles, mocking his bogus term for boy-on-boy touchin's. "It's always the same—same place, same price, same witness. He insists on paying them and having a girl there. That was me."

"Holy fuck." I'm stoked on our conspiratorial love and mutual Drop Dead hatred, "That's so much rad fucked-up shit." My phone bursts with another series of buzzes. I pull it from my pocket and glance at my rapidly incoming texts. Most of the messages are from scrapers: Joaquin Phoenix (who is into my site) is at Jumbo's Clown room. I've wanted to feature him forever. Fuck. Shooting him in front of the bikini bar would be insanely killer. Ignoring their tempting lead and all their questions about Sky, I only respond to my defected defective friend.

"Who's going on early?" I ask Score. "Where are you?"

# CHAPTER 12

**Wilcox smells like weed.** An outrageously hip line snakes down the avenue as I cut Sky and The Mythicals past it straight to the door, and yell the hostess's name. She's ignoring the Israeli kid waving a stack of hundreds at her as she glances up from her clipboard and consults the slick dude in the grey three-piece suit with a look. The promoter tells her the AlthisBANmore has been lifted for the evening. Last time I was in his club I posted a candid shot of a Karadashian that apparently made her look "gigantic". Whatever. I hold up my ID and grin. The head of Security, who always treats me like a scraper, casually threatens, "Don't fuck around." I throw up an "OK!" He stamps us and opens the door to the Papaya King.

A waft of sausage and onions hits us as we march through the fast-food limbo between the outsiders and the in-crowd. The back wall thuds at the end of the yellow counter. I open the frameless hidden, door, holding its painted yellow handle that most would never notice. Sky slides her red nails along the dark quilted interior of the tunnel, leading the way into Sayers, and I follow behind The Mythicals. Beneath the chandelier shadows we brush by trashed chicks, loaded dudes, and young fame, as The Barbie's cold flow grows louder: *If you wanna be my sugar you're looking for sweet heartbreak. I'll lick up all your frosting then eat you like a cupcake...*

Pink Corvette is onstage in the main room. Crouched on all fours atop a four-foot speaker stack, The Barbie's lips graze her discarded mic. I was like that mic on a few nights, back before K3NNY was a DOLL. Every morning after, I'd tell The Barbie all the rad shit she'd said and done in the sack the night before, and she'd say she'd been too wasted to remember—even when I showed her pictures. The Unicorn grabs my hand to lure me away from my lurid memories through the packed lounge and into the long, elevated, VIP area that fills the entire wall to the left of the stage.

Security gives me a salty look before unhooking the rope. We step up, and I squeeze next to Sky, behind the railing that separates us from the BIP below. They span towards Pink Corvette. I look over them. Onstage, slouching, K3NNY DJ's with his back to The Barbie and her fans. He's probably crying. Laughing at the gooey superfame, I lean over the rail and scan for Score as The Mythicals heel onto our bench to see and be seen. They gaze over the audience in sultry surveillance, their glitter eyes sparkling in the sheen of their cat suits.

TB pounces from the stacks and strikes a feline pose with jutted hip while singing with confidence. The strip of skin below her bellybutton shows above her low riding jeans and the black sad-faced pasties frown through her mesh top toward the lucky hundreds in the audience. I smile back at her little boobs and raise my camera. My flash only goes off once before someone yells my name from the gen-pop below. A rich babe with a shoestring tied over her hair starts making out with a chick in a "SLUT" beanie. *Flash. Flash.* More horns are thrown. The bass drops. The crowd cheers and drinks rise into the fruity vape fog.

Sky is pressed next to me, watching my BF Eff while yelling, "The Barbie is choice. Singers are dreamy." I drop my camera and face my dream date, singing "I wanna know what love is…" hoping Sky will show me as I slow dance all up on her. She purrs in my ear. As I inhale chocolate, she tells me she wants to do a shoot backstage with Pink Corvette for my site.

"Fuck yeah! I'll get TB to put her tawdry tits away." Pink Corvette hits the final chorus of their first YouTube hit *RCHBCH.* "Fuck yeah, TB!" I scream. "Fuck you K3NNYDOLL!" I put up both middle fingers for the pouty DJ. Sky bails to "powder her nose", and my party crawling friend creeps over from the neighboring booth of imported strippers and DJ fame.

"Supporting your friends now, huh?" I ask Score. "What happened to Fame Lust party? Wrong look?"

Score stands at our rail with perfect posture and flips open a Japanese compact. "I had to meet with an agent. See who's here?" Keeping his eyes on his reflection as I shoot his LED-illuminated primping, he asks, "See those two runway girls at the end of the bar?"

I drop my camera on its strap and watch a Belarusian brunette trade a full black milkshake for a massive bouquet of white roses with a translucent redhead. "They're agents?" I ask. "Of what? Anorexia?"

"Look down." My adrenaline hits. I feel like I just downed a tub of T-Total. A few feet from the far backstage door, Drop Dead lurks between his young accessories.

"What the fuck is that candyass doing here?" I yell over a pulsating synth line.

Score unleashes his topknot. "I think he wants to fuck The Barbie...though he hasn't taken his eyes off our table since you showed up. And yes, he's wearing my boots and my jacket." He details, mussing his hair in the tiny mirror. "What'd you call him?"

I immediately scan Sayers for abused go-go boys and make eye contact with Jamie. My blood sizzles. "Dude," I turn back to Score. "Please tell me those training bra whores are hiding cocks in their tights."

"I'll be able to check on that for you in a second." He quickly smiles at himself then shuts the compact. "They're definitely coming over."

I turn toward The Mythicals. The square dimples their designer holiday heels left on our bench expand in their sudden absence. "Fuck," I utter. "I've got to get Sky out of here. She's gonna freak."

Gripping my camera, I spot-jump the rail and almost land on two hot BIPs with half-shaved heads and sour expressions. I ask if they want me to finish their haircuts. Their faces turn even bitchier. Then they recognize me. "This next one is called Cunt Magic," The Barbie, sounding bored, covers her crotch, and I blaze past the kissing BIPs.

As I push back into the tall shadowy hall, Sky glides out from the ladies room. "Hey, Belle buns..." jamming toward her, I grab her hand and start making shit up. "I guess Joaquin Phoenix and this stripper..." I begin and, with her raised red riding hood swathing her innocence, Sky's beautiful brown eyes go wide. She drops my hand, and I turn to face him.

"I hurt." Drop Dead gazes at her like he's gonna cry. Oozing between us, he says, "The days of silence are suffocating. Why do you abuse me?" Fucking shocked, I reflexively step back and, having possibly felt me trying to stop his heart with my mind, James pauses and stares at me for three wordless seconds, then takes both of Sky's hands. I want to skin him. "I told them I wouldn't sign on unless they went back to this period." he brags about some unknown bullshit, looking her up and down before saying, "We always loved you like Hepburn." I think he's talking about her outfit. I edge to his side and face his shaggy profile. With a self-loving smirk he adjusts a perfect piece of Sky's hair, tainting it "... but I still miss our playful grunge-moments. We did flannel a favor... You know, they've been asking me whom I'd most like to work with—"

"Okay." I step between them into an invisible cloud of rose-scented mothballs and smile. "I'm playful." Mentally apologizing to Lucky and Star for the impending violence, I suggest, "Lets have a moment." Jamie's surprisingly astute accessories step further back while a confused Drop Dead pulls his flowers to his chest like I'm gonna steal them. This guy may have beaten up a few waifs but he's has never fought anyone who could possibly fight back—not a fucking chance. I'm going beat him to death with his bouquet.

"Alvin..." Sky grabs my delts. Lightly pulling me back, she motions towards the fucking fuckface as I flex. "This is James," she says with a nod. The rash that had calmed after dinner is back on her wrist. "James, this is Alvin."

Drop Dead tells me he's "a fan of my work" and pulls his flowery fist behind his back and bows. I restrain myself from kneeing him in the face. Then, as if Jamie had just rubbed a knockoff magic lamp, Score materializes.

"Hey Al, Ari Emanuel just texted me and—" He glances at me for a zillionth of a second before turning to Drop Dead and feigning surprise. "Oh! Hey Jamie! Comme de Garcon?" Score asks, nodding in approval at the studs in Jamie's designer jacket (which, yes, is identical to one of his own) before introducing himself and extending his hand.

Drop Dead bows. Score repeats the bullshit greeting then recalls something he's certainly never mentioned to me. "You know, we've actually met before at Beacher's Mad House with Miley..." He flips James a business card: black on black, name, Facebook, Twitter, Snapchat, Vine, Viber, Raya, and Instagram. "I heard you're looking for guys for your video. LOVE the new track." Score degrades himself as Jamie passes the card to the Belarusian model. The redhead trades the brunette her black shake for the black card. Score hands out two more cards—one for each of them—then pulls out his most expensive phone. "When are you shooting?" He taps his iCal, promising, "I'll block out..."

James slips stem after long stem from his bunch. "Drop Dead Gorgeous is hosting a private event. I'm directing a three part film created around *Meet Me at My Funeral.*" He pauses as if expecting applause from the reveal of the wildly weak name of his new album. I guffaw. "The event shall celebrate the first movement." He hands Score the roses. "These are your invitations. Please share them with The Barbie and the rest of your housemates."

"Fabulous," Score says, accepting the bunch. "She'll be ecstatic." The Barbie will not be ecstatic. Sniffing a bloom, he lies further. "These smell fabulous."

"They're keepsakes—woven with the silk of Orb spiders from Madagascar and anointed with my new fragrance."

"No!" Score gasps and touches his chest. "I love the spiders there." Man, I truly love my defective friend but sometimes I wish that pink switchblade would open in his pocket and stab him in his dumb dick. Score buries his face in the bouquet once more, deeply inhales, then, with an outrageous look of satisfaction, turns. "I'm gonna go bring these backstage." He takes off then suddenly halts. "You can come if you want but, spoiler alert, K3NNY's back there being dramatic." I look to the stage and wonder how long the laptops have been on autopilot before Drop Dead draws me back into hell's mouth.

Jamie faces Sky and sighs, "I cannot leave." She turns to me. I tug my lucky lock. Score says "fabulous" and bails. Enthralled by his exit, as if watching the midnight fireworks over Sleeping Beauty's castle, James calls out, "Score! Do you dance?"

"I do it all." Creeping around the unwavering Mythicals, he literally sings "Whatever you need. BRB!" and pushes into the lounge. Cam stands rigidly in the doorway with Jaq, a tiny red taser at his side.

Drop Dead pulls out another rose and holds it up to Sky. "I can barely look at you," whipping his hair over one eye, he gazes down at his boots—yes, the fucking same as Score's—and bemoans, "you're too beautiful."

I take the flower. Sky scratches behind her ear and, before I can clean house, The Mythicals strut in to tidy up. Jaq covers his metallic fangs as he hisses into Drop Dead's ear. His golden acrylics glimmer. Jamie's tinted lashes flutter. "...organic?" he asks, then nods and wryly smiles. "Rock 'N' Roll."

I don't understand what the fuck is going on. With all the weird notes, Instagram tags, and make-outs, I felt like The Mythicals were on my side. I had expected to see Cam send 5000 volts of justice into Jamie's exposed neck. I turn to The Unicorn like, what the fuck? He bows his plump red Christmas lips and turns his braided head. Electric contact lenses shoot an emerald laser-beam-arrow toward the exit. I get the point—I guess that The Mythicals like fucking Jamie too. Or maybe they've got something else up their shiny sleeves. I don't know. Whatevs. They can stay. I'm taking Sky.

"Let's bail." I grab her hand. From the stage TB spits, *Colder than ice, blacker than pitch, tonight you're gonna be my—*

"Yeah." In her cold milkshake voice, my warm babe quietly agrees. "Let's get the fuck out of here before I punch this asshole in his diseased balls and make him watch you fuck my mouth."

I pull her from danger and Drop Dead breaks his concentration on TB's frowning tits, shoots out his hand. "I miss you Sky," he blurts. "You are my heaven."

That fragile face was used at least three times in every old episode of Gorgeous. I'm dying to break his extended fingers but I force myself to focus on bromance and keep my hands on Sky. Pulling her close, I guide us through the crowd as whispers of "Jamie, Jamie—" spreads beneath the chaotic, grinding, autonomous beats.

The backstage security dude is basically licking The Barbie's pasties with his eyes when we storm by and into the dressing room. There, sitting next to K3NNY on the velvet couch, Score makes modeling faces into a dirty wall mirror while Stella sucks him off on sticky knees. I salute them as we fire past and, as if we're about to trample a rescued Kinkajou, Sky hits the breaks. She wants a picture with K3NNY. Throwing herself on his lap, she removes his DOLL flat-brim, tosses off her hood, and puts on his cap. The sullen glassy-eyed DJ, suddenly super stoked, throws up the horns. Sky pretends to smell his Drop Dead flower as I capture his shit-eating-grin on my phone before dragging her out of the club.

The alarm doesn't sound when we charge through the fire exit but the scrapers wouldn't notice us if we were aflame. Abbi and my old crew are clustered around a town car in front of Papaya King with the rest of the paps ravenously waiting for Drop Dead to come out and pose. I cut away in the opposite direction down Wilcox, burned that they didn't hit me with the tip that James was here. Motherfuckers.

# CHAPTER 13

**"God, fuck him.** Of course he'd show up. L'fucking Morte couldn't possibly be enough attention for one night." Sky is quietly freaking in the passenger seat, digging blotchy hands through her purse. I throw open my driver door. She's hyperventilating and speaking in her cold compressed milkshake-voice. "Fuck—Cam has them all."

When we fired away I offered to circle back to Sayers to save Cam and Jaq from Jamie. Sky said they'd be fine. I'm still picturing a bloody AlThisAndMore Mythicals bromance feature when I step out into the semi-sketchy Rite Aid lot hoping those two are only getting laid and not lacerated. Sky pulls down the sun visor to see what the close encounter with James has done to her skin. "Jesus fucking Christ, I look like a monster." Scowling in the mirror, she touches a tiny hive on her neck. "Oh my god I'm disgusting—did I look like this in the club?" Clouds crawl above us to help her hide as she grabs her phone and dials.

"I can barely see it. You're seriously the hottest girl ever. I'll fucking dip my tongue in Calamine right now." Smelling the coming rain, I lean into Lenore for directions. "What do I get? Benadryl? Claritin? I'll steal some Oxy's from behind the counter if you want—"

Sky speaks into her phone. "Hi. Hi, it's me—a guy is coming in for me right now." She releases me with a look, and I lock her into Lenore.

I shoot up the steep concrete stairway and push through the annoyingly slow automatic doors into the fluorescent glare. The one cashier behind the row of registers texts as I pass him on the way to the unattended ice cream cooler. Sky's voice calling me "A guy" echoes from my brain and bounces off the glass as I moisten the dipper and pull out two plugs of mint chip, towering them onto a plain cone. I leave a ten in the napkin dispenser then make my way up the toothpaste aisle feeling guilty about holding the torturous factory farmed treat—but Sky's worth it.

At the back of the store the pharmacist waits gripping a white paper bag as I dig for a handful of crumpled papers in my denim. I drop them onto the counter. One flutters to the floor. Retrieving it, I ask "This one?" I hold out the pink slip and smile.

"She doesn't need instructions." Without unfolding any of the prescriptions, the lady gives me the meds for Emily Golden eyeing the ice cream in my grip.

Confused by the sticker on the bag, correct address, wrong name, I ask the pharmacist if I've got the right shit. She nods. I pay in cash and she refuses to keep the change. I shove a couple of twenties back into my dangerously thinning wad with relief and leave the Rite Aid knowing I'm gonna have to do some shit I don't wanna do soon.

The first drops of rain have sent the natives screaming into their bungalows. The streets look beyond December empty. The passenger door is open, and Sky is nowhere to be seen. Green cream drips from my fist as I run through the rare downpour with dread alligator-crawling up my throat until I'm close enough to see through my open window.

Sky reclines in shotgun holding a small golden flask in her lap. On the floor next to her shiny black flats, her bare feet bunch her red cape. I throw open my door, drop behind the wheel, and hand her the bag. "The pharmacist sends her love to Emily. Aren't you cold?" I ask, and shut myself in. I adjust my jeans as rain spits through the open window into my face.

Sky inspects the two translucent orange bottles. "Can you? Please?" She asks, her hands trembling as she passes the pills. "I can't right now. One of each."

I balance the cone on my damp dash, twist the caps, and pinch out a Zoloft along with something I've never heard of. Sky props herself up and pops the meds, and I reach behind her to rifle through my gym bag. When I offer the electrolyte water, she already has her flask pressed to her lips. Gulping, she tilts her head back. The clear liquid briefly flows until the last drops drip into her open mouth. "It's cool to mix those with whatever that is?" I ask concerned, and Sky reaches for my Trader Joe's bottle. I pass it. She pops another pill, sips, and hands back my water. I taste booze lingering on the plastic rim as I chug. Lying back down, Sky snaps her golden flask into her black clutch.

Rain pummels Lenore's roof. Minty trails stream toward my steering column. "You want this?" I offer the treat. "I got it for you." Two red dots like tiny high eyes watch me from her wrist as Sky wipes her mouth on the back of her hand and shakes her head. I toss the rejected confection out my window.

The ice cream explodes into a sad green burst on the wet asphalt. I watch my dream babe melt.

Sky rolls over and faces me. "You are divine," she purrs in conclusive agreement with her Mtyhicals' review of my character, curling up in her seat and closing her eyes. The song in her voice has come back with a slur. "An angel...magic...just like Cam and...Jaq said." Her breathing slows. I reach behind her and whip a stolen Ark towel from my duffle. The cashed Anger baggie flutters to the floor. The Mythicals sucked up a lot of coke before the show. I'm still shook over leaving those boys with Drop Dead. I wipe my sticky hands on the couture rag, flip up the golden "JG" initials, and, briefly wondering what they stand for, scrub the dash with Noah's scratchy monogram.

"I've never really met anyone like you, Alvin," Sky mumbles in an entirely new voice that immediately becomes my favorite. "Pure. Too pure." Barely opening her eyes, she reaches over. "Thank you for putting up with me." Sky's hand crashes onto my thigh, and my rod instinctively inches toward her fingers.

"Fuck, c'mon. I love you hard."

"Do you?" she asks with genuine and insane disbelief.

"Fuck yes I do! I'd ghost ride Lenore off a cliff for you..." Her hand cruises up my jeans to my button fly, and all thoughts of Canon-crashing a Unicorn, Trueblood, and Jamie threesome disappear. I crawl out of my seat and straddle her. Sky rolls under me onto her back and I further profess, "I'd burn my Disneyland pass. I'd—" Undoing my jeans and considering some really crazy shit, I look down at the lock tied to my wrist.

So, yeah. The real story here is that when I shaved my head, I sent my hair to Star along with her boyfriend's tooth. In return she mailed me a letter forgiving my having permanently disfigured her new dude and enclosed a magic-potion bathed braid woven with my locks and her old red dreads, saying it would, "center you, bring good fortune, and peaceful love." I do kinda still miss my ex but Sky is my calming spell, my lucky charm, and my peaceful love. She's brought me closer to Drop Dead—who I will totally resist murdering—even without the help of this magic bracelet. Star would approve of its new owner.

"Here..." I slip off my lucky lock. "Until we get married." I gently tie the coarse weave around her speckled wet wrist and ask, "You wanna be my best chick?"

In her damp matted cashmere Sky inspects the scraggly love lace. "Um...?"

"Promise hair. It's mine, mostly." I smile down at her. "So whataya say? Just you and me? Status updates? I'd never cheat on a princess with a crappy waitress—or anyone else."

Sky turns away. She stares through her open door. My heart pounds in my chest like a 22" kick drum as rain thumps on Lenore's rumbling hood. Drops burst onto our faces and I watch her waiting for an answer—any answer.

"I—I'm sorry." Her speech momentarily loses its slur as she turns from the empty lot. "I adore you but... my agent—"

"Oh right. Totally. A-list." I feel like I just fell from the rooftop of a Movie Award's after party at The ACE Hotel. "Yeah, we can just be secret until you're mega-superfame." I reach down to her wrist and twist my lucky lock. "I'm totally gonna help you get there and then you can fire David. He's fucking lost. Stella can date anyone she wants, you know? I mean, fuck, Score is her boyfriend and he's E-list. I'll have her hook you up with her people—"

"Al." Widening her welling Bambi eyes, Sky shakes her head. "I don't want to hurt you—I'm terrible—you're too perfect and deserve so much—"

"What the fuck? You're perfect! Don't cry! " I'm trying to keep it together. "Forget I said anything. I was being dumb." I insist, pulling out my phone. "How about we just fuck non-publicly?" Sky smiles from my touchscreen when I open my camera. "I won't send the video to David. Just for me. Swear on my broken Boneville."

"How could you even want me right now?" She covers her face with her arm. "I'm more hideous than ever. And my lips sting—" She is fucking beautiful in and out of frame.

I'm not gonna fuck her without kissing. "What if I just jerked off?" I suggest.

My nine-second video shows Sky squint at me like I'm from planet radness right before she knocks my phone to the floor, pulls off her sweater, and asks, "To these small things?" She's not wearing a bra and I'm not not getting a boner. "I don't know how I could possibly turn you on." Her nipples stand hard through the invited storm.

I reach into my jeans and release the raging Kaa to hypnotize her. "Does it look like I'm not turned on?" I hold out my hand. "Help me out?" Sky spits into my palm, and I start pounding my python.

Reaching upward, she pets my head and my whole body gets a hard-on. I tell her that I want to fuck her. "Don't stop." she begs quietly. "I want it all over."

As I jerk it, Sky listlessly plays with her tits and mumbles about how bad she wants me to blow. I kinda don't believe it. Her lids blink like they're wearing weight belts. Occasionally her eyes swim up in my direction but Sky is somewhere else—Planet Pills, Terror Cake County, Drop Dead Dreamland—and wherever she's gone, my boner followed. Fuck. I can't do this. Releasing my worm, I climb back into my seat.

"Rain's a real rod killer." I apologize, reaching over her

to grab the door. I tug the handle, and the slam bangs through the lot. Sky mumbles that she adores me then rolls over and throws the fight with her weighted lids.

I pull off my shirt and jacket and blanket my sleeping beauty. She doesn't move as I kiss her cheek or when I bump her knees while scrounging for my buzzing phone from her wet clothes on the floor. The Unicorn just tagged me. In his post my blinking ring is edited onto a guitarist's finger. The rocker with the bowl cut shreds in his biker jacket on some old stage. I crank the engine and the heat, reading the bizarre hashtags: #TooSlowFor32 #FastFastFasterNow. My blasting vents melt the steam from my windows as Lenore crawls out of the lot. I can't shake the feeling that I recognized the rocker wearing my ring, and at the red light I unlock my screen to check the weird post again. The tagged photo is gone. Cam must be high as fuck. I toss my phone in the ashtray. My wipers tick and, cranking west with the green arrow, I focus on the slick road. I've got precious cargo.

When I park beneath her dark house, Sky is still passed out. Lenore's engine churns as I step out of my ride, open the passenger door and unbuckle my dreaming dream girl. Snagging her clothes from the floor, I wrap Sky in her damp riding hood and lift her. Even wet, she only weighs about a buck twenty.

Sky breathes sweet medicine onto my neck, and I cautiously carry her up the streaming driveway toward the large dark man holding a big bright red umbrella. Reggie silently strides towards us from the concrete retaining wall and stops in my headlights. We face each other and looking down at Sky, he sighs through the storm's whisper, "Damn it, Em." Emily. I guess Sky has two names just like me. We'll call that destiny.

Reggie takes my dream girl into his giant arms. He cradles her as I slip her clutch, flats, and wet sweater-ball into his fist. Sky groans and hides her face in his chest like a poisoned princess. "Girl." He shakes his head. "You need to slow down." Sky mumbles something that sounds like "I hate James" and Reggie carries her through the secret doorway.

I stand in the driveway half-naked staring up toward her spacey house. Rain rages down my back as, twenty feet above me, a blue light flashes in the towering southern windows. Striding through the ghostly blush, Reggie squats, with perfect form, to deliver Sky onto an unseen bed. Water drips from my eyebrows. He rises back into view, turns and nods through the arching panes. I salute, drop back into Lenore and bail.

****

hoping she'll regain consciousness and ask me to come back, to stay with her. A Smashing Pumpkins song plays on The Jack as the looming, rustling hedge drips in triplets on my roof. I slow the wipers. The Hollywood glow reflects from the clouds illuminating the flats. On Melrose Ave the Blue Whale changes colors. To the east, an urban Christmas tree made entirely of red lights peaks from the top of Capital Records. Planes blink over the DTLA skyline on their way to and from LAX. Billy Corgan sings about 1979, and I check my rearview. Sky's intergalactic bedroom is dark. I'll be up there soon. We're gonna be together for real—profile relationship status changes. She adores me, and deep down I really do think The Mythicals have my back. I just have to hang in here, take it slow, and help her get where she needs to be to feel comfortable. "Fuck David Fass." I grab my phone and open VSCO Cam. I'm about to import the backstage shot of her and K3NNY to edit it to AllThisAndMore radness levels for immediate posting, when my phone buzzes. The text isn't from Sky but it doesn't suck.

Here's what's written below some unknown 323 number:

*Yo Crazy! @Hollywood Forever.. Sunday@3ammm@ JohnnyRamone Bring what I neeeed n I'll bring the$$$ PLAYER!!!!!!!!!!!!*

"What the fuck?" I laugh and rev my engine, release my e-break, and fishtail down toward wherever, loving this town.

# CHAPTER 14

## Last night I covered an event that I was going to bail on. I haven't seen Sky in days.

I've tried to hang with her, but she's been super busy prepping for some Terror Cake thing. So I went to Beverly Hills.

ZEDD was spinning on the third story of this industry dude's house party. When he started to tell me about his new collab with K3NNYDOLL, I fired down to the backyard where snowmen were getting their noses eaten by reindeer. Marlena sat on a bail of hay with Taylor Swift feeding a buck a brownie and sipping her fifth eggnog. I tromped through the manmade snow to show the pop-superfame the candids I'd taken of them sledding. I held out my screen. They opened their plaid blanket, and I slid under. As I dug my hand into a drift, Marlena started telling Taylor why we should have a threesome. Fully agreeing with her points, I packed a snowball and pegged Terry Richardson in the center of his chest. He retaliated. Taylor pulled Selena from the war and after getting tagged twice in the head, I called a truce. I was super tempted to follow the chicks back into the house but figured I should maybe wait to bang anyone 'til Sky is ready for me to be her first real man. I bailed the party and returned to Eff house to work.

At around 3 a.m. I sloshed my Vans up our porch and into the living room. ELF was playing on the flat screen, and the three babes in my low laying twilight sleeper had kicked off my Alice In Wonderland sheets to partially cover a thin body on the floor. Stella and Alexa's slow dream breaths emanated distilled ripeness. Between them wavy blonde hair peaked out from under my Chesire Cat pillow. It looked like someone had tried to suffocate the mystery chick in the orange-sherbety underwear. As I circled my mattress, this third of the half-naked threesome particularly inspired the horniness that'd been brutalizing me since I'd failed to jerk off on Sky. Staring at the blonde's shredded abs, I was wondering if she had a hater agent and a princess perma-pout—if she was still breathing—when a hand reached out from the sheets on the floor and landed on Alexa's boob. I laughed, got a shot of Score's sleep-molestation, then bailed to Stella's bathroom. After jerking-off into the deep pink tub, I draped my wet clothes over a pink spot heater then sat my ass and my Mac down at the pink desk. I'm still here now. The sun is just coming up. I should be posting a snowy superfame set of party photos for my site but I couldn't help moving on to more important, yet super disheartening, window-shopping.

With my clothes cooking behind me, I scroll through jewelry for rich people. "Fuck." I close the Tiffany window, say "fuck it" once more, and call Noah. I let his phone ring once, hang up, hit speaker, and finally tap my packed voicemail. Marlena slurs rad filth about what I should come do to her right now in a succession of drunk-dials. Even while inhaling the scent of baked foot, her voice almost gives me a boner. I glance back at my smoking socks and reopen the uploaded image of Sky sitting on K3NNY's lap. She keeps asking me to post this shot but I'd rather wait and get more, then do the full-on feature she deserves—one that won't include this gooey grinning DJ-superfame. Marlena's solicitations end and my salacious boner begins to chill in the quiet as I attempt to edit the backstage photo into something that doesn't bum me out.

Dawn flows through Stella's pink curtains as I move the red spots from Sky's wrist to the DJ's face. I grab my sunglasses from the desk and slide them on, hoping to get this shit finished before production shows up. According to The Barbie, K3NNY hasn't stopped crying to Doug about me. If I want any sort of diamond, I'm already gonna have to deal with one nasty old dude this morning. I sure as fuck don't need two.

A string of random emoji buzzes my phone off the desk. I cease adding girth to K3NNY's chin to grab it from the pink carpet. Marlena is still awake, texting and nog-wasted. I reply to her NSFW nonsense with a smiley face in shades, and Noah finally calls back. I can't believe it took him over twenty seconds. "Yep." I answer.

"Are you awake Honey Bear?"

"Obviously."

"Are you hungry?"

"Duh."

"Come outside. Bring your present."

CHAPTER 15

## Standing in the Eff driveway, Sal holds the door of the Maybach. I fist bump

the slim suited driver, adjust my belt, toss my bags into the sedan, and step into the massive backseat. Though Noah is next to me, he's still pretty far away–which rules. I motor out my footrest, kick back, and Sal lurches into our 'hood.

Peppercorn permeates the leathery air and Noah bitches into its cloud. "Art film?" Menacing a silenced, disembodied voice, he leans toward the back of his driver's seat. "I don't give a fuck if Buñuel comes back from the dead and personally sucks my cock. The only film that shit-dick should be making is a snuff film staring himself. Listen you fucking retard, he'd better be paying you a lot because if you continue on this job it will be your last—" The guy on speakerphone starts talking about his family: two children, another on the way, all going to private schools. Clearly not into hearing it, Noah taps his gritted teeth with a tiny silver spoon pendant. A disco beat clacks over the voice's every excuse for doing some shit Noah doesn't like. My uncle flops back into his seat and sighs. "Fuck your fag sons and fuck you." Then, raising his Mimosa to himself, commands, "Sal, shut off the fucking phone."

"Sal, shut on the fucking KROQ!" I request, adjusting the Deagle in my denim. "Por favor!"

Noah's driver glances at me in the rearview. The Chili Peppers sing California. Sitting up, I poke a monitor and kill the radio before kicking back again. Silver clinks against white veneers. My phone buzzes. I can feel Noah watching and attacking his teeth, as I read through stream of texts from unknown numbers. Since Sayers the scrapers won't stop asking me about Sky. They think that we're a couple. One of them must have seen us running out of the alley. I wish they were right about our status. Ignoring their prying texts, I copy, paste, and send the same reply I keep shooting to the unknown dude freaking about tonight's cemetery thing. Hoping he'll make a deal for something other than a shot of Sky–or a shot of us together, which doesn't exist—I ask the freak for the fifth time what he wants to buy and how much cash he wants to drop. As I watch his deliberating thought bubble, Marlena sends a photo. She's topless but covering her tits. I'm fucking horny and I want to enlarge it, but Noah gets super jealous of all babes.

"You know how fucking annoying that is, right?" Locking my screen, I slide on my shades to face him. "Where are we going?"

Noah relieves his enamel and like a fucked-up faery-godfather, waves his spoon. "Someone is hangry!" he happily proclaims, before dropping the charm on its long chain. It thuds on his bloated belly. "Home." I stare. "You're excited.

Carmen is making peanut butter pancakes." Quickly sniffing three times, he pinches his pointy nose job and pulls down slowly. Plastic or not, I'm surprised it doesn't come off. "Peanut butter pancakes with almond flour...not that you deserve such treatment after leaving me stranded." I recall my bail from the Ivy as he insists, "I felt like a sixteen year old with bad skin." His eyes go all spicy. They're beadier than usual. Or maybe his face is just puffier. I peer at the moist clump of cocaine clinging to the divot above his dry lip. He's so high. I wonder how he's still alive. I hope I don't have to bury him beneath the avocado tree. "It's like you don't even care," Noah pouts, and the shrillness of his claim breaks my Anger fixation. I turn away.

"I don't really."

Noah giggles, "You're so bad." He loves it.

Sal crawls into the turn lane, and I stare out the window. Neil Patrick Harris is lingering in the back lot of Fred Segal. With the cash I'd get for the right head-to-toe of him I might not have to go back to the Ark. I'm way over stalking and selling fame but I shouldn't be doing this shit with Noah anymore—Sky would be bummed if she found out. As I think of art shows, a site revamp, and what A-List men might be staring in Terror Cake, NPH disappears into the boutique. I turn back to Noah.

"I know you love me," he insists, and downs the last of his drink. Setting his Mimosa flute in its holder, Noah drags his sleeve across his mouth. A yellow streak stains the raw linen. He snatches a bear-shaped bottle from the refrigerator compartment. Frigid air seeps into the heat, giving me a moment of relief before Noah shuts the hatch. The cool dissipates with his words. "You're not like the rest of these selfish shits—nothing like him." Noah flicks his hand toward the ghost in the speakerphone then traces his lips with chilled honey. He puckers, and I retreat into my phone. Sleep deprived and empty, my stomach croaks. "Did you remember your gift? Is it in your duffle?" The Deagle is stuffed in my waistband, framed by my plunging obliques. I lift my tee, and my uncle makes a nasty hungry noise. "Such a beautiful gun." Honey threads his lips. "I look forward to seeing you shoot after breakfast" he oozes. "You're such the marksman." I turn away, pull down my shirt, and unlock my phone.

Below my post of Score molesting Alexa, the Brit It-Girl's stalker has left a zillion threatening comments. @Snowsimian says he's coming to fight me and "...the uphill gardener with the friendly fingers." I open his Instagram. Scrolling past photos of the soccer-playing, barbering, coffee-making blonde poseur, I like all his shirtless selfies. Sal turns into Melrose traffic, and I open Sky's account. Her last post is a throwback selfie with The Mythicals standing against a graffiti covered wall in a trashy hotel room. Below the photo, Drop Dead commented #sweetestsweets #32forever. I reach for my lucky promise hair that isn't there, and Noah politely instructs Sal to honk at the line of cars stopped for the red.

"Hey...can I borrow 30K?" He puckers and pats his chest making a kissy noise. My stomach twists before Kinky peaks out of the deep pocket of his draping coat and yawns. The night monkey, sniffing and scratching up unbleached linen, props it's paws on Noah's face, and licks his coated lips. "How bout a hundred?" I bargain.

"There's already money waiting in your room." Little claws dig into the tiny blue veins in his red cheeks. I may actually puke.

"That's not my room." I roll down the window and gasp. Semi-fresh West Hollywood air blows in as we cruise toward The Ark. "And it won't be enough."

"Cash cash cash! Money is cold, Alvin." A beam of sunlight briefly catches a gold thread hanging from Noah's chin. The honey line is so thin, I'm not sure it's there. I wish I weren't here. "You know you can have anything you'd like..." he lures, "Just tell me what you want."

No way. He'd cut me off for sure if I told him that I want to buy a ring. My phone buzzes and a new nude fills the screen: Marlena is covering her face but not her tits. I quickly screen-lock and shove my phone into my jacket. Sal breaks. Noah mists his face as Kinky continues to lap pucker-honey in the herbal scented shower. The monitor on the passenger seat says its 69 degrees and I'm fucking melting. Noah's rose-scented toner deepens my nausea. This fucking gun digging into my belly isn't helping either, but he'll say some gross thing if I adjust it.

I sit like a statue wondering if Noah saw the nude. He fidgets in my periphery, squirming like he did the last time I disappeared for weeks. He furiously mists himself again. Sal stops at a crosswalk. Noah politely commands him to honk at the bearded pedestrian in white robes. The sound is awful. The oppressive sweet floral scent is killing me.

"I've gotta bail." Throwing open the door, I grab my bags and step out into traffic. "This client just hit me up about maybe training him on location in New Zealand. He needs to meet now," I explain, leaning back in with more lies, "I'll come over after."

Noah bitterly questions Kinky, "He should do that, shouldn't he?" The kinkajou dangles from his fist and with thick sticky lips, Noah whispers, "Famous little rich girls don't like unappreciative broke boys." Kissing his deaf pet, he gently sets him onto my seat, reaches over, and slams my door. Cars honk. I dodge a Prius and flip them off as Sal cruises away.

Noah totally saw the nude.

A wannabe model posing poorly against the pink wall of the Paul Smith boutique doesn't break pose as I fire by her and her wannabe photographer. I crouch behind the windowless building and count what's left of my wad. "FUCK!" I scream into the empty alley. The curse resounds from the stucco Stella-colored walls. I can barely afford a protein shake. There's no way I can afford diamonds. Regretting having let Neil Patrick slip away, I grab my phone and, swearing that it will be the last time, dial.

"Meeting's cancelled." I mutter, swooning in a pothole and feeling totally fucking sick. "Tell Sal to pull back around."

# CHAPTER 16

**Back when I "made Sadi run away," Score's LAPD friend swiped a bunch of police targets for me to give to Noah as an offering for the hallucinated kinkajou shaming.** At breakfast this morning, unnervingly happy-as-fuck, my uncle missed every one. I blasted a hundred holes through the hearts of pink paper assailants, ate an eight-stack of peanut butter pancakes, and grabbed the cash. Tonight the money is dirtying the pockets of my clean jeans as I scale this rock wall groaning. Noah only gave me the usual three hundred bucks, but whatever I'm about to get into will hopefully keep me from having to go back to the Ark...for a while.

Still beat from weight training after pulling an all-nighter, I push myself up onto the ledge and wearily look over Hollywood Forever. Silhouettes of skyscraping, threadlike palms frame the island mausoleum. Violet LEDs light its roman pillars and the cropped lawn stretches toward me under a blanket of moonlight. I stand atop the Paramount Studios corner of the cemetery feeling like the prince of the dead and famous, thinking of good times gone.

The last time I snuck in here, I came to meet The Barbie. The XX was playing while we laid down amidst the tombstones on a blanket. She drank a bottle of red wine, and we made out. TB says she doesn't remember that second part, though. I think that was the night before she went to Dollhouse DTLA and hooked up with K3NNY. Right now he's in Vegas and she's raging. Earlier she called me from the Cloak & Dagger party, about ten times, to tell me he's away. I was worried she was too fucked-up to be out alone so I shot to the hidden basement in the center of Hollywood, scooped her out from under the DJ desk and carried her to Lenore. On our drive back to Eff house she dropped a bag of mushrooms. While scrounging beneath her seat for the fumbled drugs, she found my Deagle, grabbed it, and flew out of my ride before I could even finish parking in our driveway. I chased her, begging, but TB wouldn't give my pistol back. At gunpoint she locked us into her black-hole room, undid my jeans, and blew me. I definitely almost came after she switched to two hands but when she dropped my weapon, I snagged it and escaped from her den of darkness. The Barbie was high enough that we could've banged without any weirdness, but I had to get here. And yeah, the waiting for Sky thing or whatever. Doing it with TB wouldn't really count cuz we're so close—but anyway, now I'm a lot horny and a little late.

Gripping my camera, I salute the stars and spring super high into the air. A floral wind whooshes through my ears like a Malibu wave. When I thud down into a three-point squat, my Deagle pops out of my pants. The scraper scene has been kinda crazy since our Russian guy screwed my old crew on some weird stalker side deal. Abbi found out he'd gotten ripped off by Alexei and beat him with a mini Dodgers bat. Abbi hates liars as much as he loves money. Now Alexei rolls solo. I guess he still does shit for the guy that hired him for the stalker side job, and from what I hear, the unknown dude paid to fix Alexei's broken hands. I wipe my grassy palms on the arms of my denim and shove my gun back into my waistband. There will be none of that bone-breaking shit tonight.

Adjusting the barrel away from my rod, I march the path that leads to the water. In the distance a shadowy shape sits on top of Johhny Ramone's grave bouncing its puffy black sneakers against the stone. Dried petals scuttle around my worn Vans. That's definitely not Abbi over there–doesn't seem like scraper at all. This dude looks more like Score. Pacing closer, I pull out my phone and unlock my secret app, confirming Marlena's nudes are inside. I really don't want to fuck with her life, but Sky's engagement ring is going to cost way more than I've got. If this guy wants superpopfame nipples, he's gotta be ready to drop some real cash. Not that he's ever told me what the fuck he wants. I breast pocket the dirt and, with betrayal pressing against my heart, step off the paved road.

The fragrance of rotting flowers grows as I approach The Ramone's grave. When I get close enough to realize how much money my rendezvous really has, my heart kick-starts. "Are you fucking serious?" I want to break into a running tackle but, halted with disbelief, automatically raising my Canon, I ask, "What the fuck are you doing here?"

Jamie Shannon poses for my lens. The tail of his hooded tank top hangs past the cuffs of his black sweat pants which,

I fucking swear to all Ramones, I've seen Score wear. James reverently reaches up to the cement guitar stalk and makes an even douchier face before suddenly getting shook. "Wait! Shit!" He jumps down from the ledge and hides behind the statue. "No pictures!" He stage whispers "Are you fucking crazy?"

"Y'just look like another witch in the cemetery, dude," Reviewing his unidentifiably blurred photos, I walk toward him taunting, "Or Score...you know Score, right? The guy who owns the ass you're way up?" Cautiously, Jamie peeks out from behind the grave. I drop my camera. "Relax. I'm done shooting." He steps out into the moonlight. Tightening my strap, I slide my Canon behind my back just in case. I don't want it to get hurt in the event of a beating. Floral decay mingles with the scent of mothballs as I stalk towards him recalling his first cryptic text. "I've got what you want? What's that fucker? Say Sky." I'm grinning. "Please fucking say Sky–"

"What? No! Dude, dude." With his hands up, he jogs backward towards the water's edge sensing the likelihood of his hospitalization. His intuitive, brunette and redheaded accessories must have given him a lesson in reality after I left him with them at Sayers. "It's not like that. You don't have to get crazy. Didn't they tell you?" He fearfully begs, "I brought the cash!"

"What the fuck are you talking about?" I pause my imposing march. "Didn't who tell me what?"

"Cam and Jaq said to hit you up. Isn't this your spot? They said that this was your spot. I guess we were pretty fucked up," he nervously chuckles. "Shit bro, I swear to god that organic shit was the sickest shit I ever had." I glance at the statue of the Ramone. Johnny was the old rocker wearing my ring in The Unicorn's disappearing post. I realize those

Machiavellian mannequins set him up when Jamie pulls a thin stack from his vest. "Here!" With fingers trembling in a fingerless glove, he pushes the cash through the night and into my face. "We're cool, right?"

Cam and Jaq probably expect me to bring them Jamie's teeth–a great fucking idea–but they don't know about my promises to Sky and Lucky. Thinking of them and my lucky lock, I breathe deeply, and stare at the fold of new bills. Drop Dead looks like he's going to piss his drop crotch. "If it's not enough I can—"

"Shut the fuck up." I begrudgingly decide The Mythicals will have to settle for a public shaming, and snatch the cash. "My shit is one hundred percent organic. Three hundred dollars-a-gram-fucking-organic." I have no idea how much coke costs. Everyone I know gets it for free from some nast like Drop Dead or Noah. I lick my fingers and start counting the bills while freestyling rad bullshit. "Erewhon would shelve this shit if they could get their rich hippy hands on it. But last I checked they don't got this shit at the market. Lucky me...and lucky you, dude!" I hold up the six hundred. "You're covered for two grams." Folding the crisp bills, I slip them next to the dirty money in my jeans. "I don't sell to just any fucker...but Sky tells me you're rad." My insides twist with the lie. "So you're good."

"We've shared raptures." He switches effortlessly back to the role of the dramatic dick worshipped by the world, tossing his stupid hair like he used to on his show. "She said you two are official now?"

"Fuck yes." This lie twists harder. "Shared raptures-as-fuck." Now a little shook myself, but not showing it, I wonder if he's lying about having spoken to her, if he's just prying. He must be.

"So...may I have those sweet sweets?" He asks, and

turns toward the fading sounds of sirens on Santa Monica. "We should probably be leaving..."

"Hey!" I bring his attention back to business. "Since you're a friend of hers, I'm gonna make you a deal."

"You are a prince."

"Fuck yeah I am. Check it out—" pulling out my phone, I unlock my secret files. "I'll throw in three free grams. You give me 20k."

"20 thousand for an eight ball?" Slipping a black band from his wrist, he ties his shaggy locks into a topknot and scoffs, "That's mad."

"True. True." I agree, "But you can't get it anywhere else..." I swipe past Marlena's awesome tits, the nudes TB used to send, and a shot of Score in a pink tracksuit and tie, then motion James toward me. I throw my arm over his shoulder, "And that price includes my word that no one will ever see or hear about this." I show him the shot of him in bed with Lucky Day.

Drop Dead drops. He begins to hyperventilate with his head between his knees.

"Great. No hard feelings dude." I stare down at the tittering panic party, wanting to kick him in the mouth. "It's still a fucking bargain. Trust me on that shit. Just let me know where to make the drop." James freakishly giggles. The wind kicks, rippling the water beyond his man-bun. A dizzying stench spirals up my nostrils. "Fuck man. I figured there was an open grave somewhere." Fanning the pungent air, I ask. "What the fuck did you swim in?"

"Paralysis," he gasps without looking up. "It's my new fragrance."

"Cool. Cool name. Text me when you have the cash." I turn from the mess and bail through the fetid breeze, weaving between tombstones. I can hear Drop Dead giggling before he pukes into the pond. I can't believe Sky used to love that candyass.

* * * *

With my gun in the glove box and my camera-bag sitting shotgun, I fire up Lenore and flip through the radio. I stomp the gas when Alice Cooper comes on. "No more Mr. Nice guy!" I screech along, picturing Mickey Mouse as he bears witness to my (Jamie Shannon funded) marriage proposal, and roll down the window to battle the scent of Paralysis that's lodged in my nose. I don't believe Sky actually talks to Drop Dead but if she does, at least she's telling him I'm her man. Cool 4am air blasts in from Melrose Ave. as I wiggle my phone charger and begin to text her questions about her current status with the superfame before erasing the whole interrogation. I can't tell her about any of this. The ring has to be a surprise, and she might break out in hives if she finds out I'm dealing with that poser.

I downshift and scroll through his Instagram profile before jumping to Sky's. No communication anywhere except Drop Dead's comments on her posts. I check The Mythicals' accounts. Both have tagged me in a diptych they've made of Score and Jamie. I notice diamond emoji and the same hashtag Drop Dead keeps referencing, before Cam and Jaq delete their identical posts. Wondering what #32 means and why The Mythicals said I was "#tooslow" for it, I glance up from my phone.

Just east of Highland, a blonde babe is standing on the curb wearing a brown and red beanie with ears. She kisses a little dark haired dude before they get into his Aston Martin. I screech to a stop next to his open window. Inside the silver sports car the couple is full-on making out. I lunge for my camera. Taylor says, "Shit!" and I look up to catch hate from the dude's pretty blue eyes just before they take off. I peel the fuck out as my brain catches up to what I just saw. That "dude" was a young chick with short hair—this chase was just elevated to diamond status.

Four phantom cars ahead of me, the pop-superfame and her bae speed east. I trail them. An exclusive of Taylor Swift with a fucking girlfriend would buy me out of the fame game, make The Ark history and, most importantly, bling out Sky like Beyonce. I crank the radio and catch up to the Aston Martin at 71mph. "Tay Tay! Don't be a fucking bitch!" Steering with one hand, I shove my cam into the wind, screaming over Alice Cooper, "It's me, Al! Roll down the fucking window! Tay!"

The shorthaired chick swerves across the double yellow, barely avoiding the Lexus stopped at the intersection. I pass the IS on the right as we both run a stale red at La Brea. I pace the couple—past the car wash, past the pink, Paul Smith building, past Crossroads, and through a gracious green light at La Cienega. Fucking finally, with The Beverly Center mall as her blurry backdrop and her reindeer beanie pulled over her face, Taylor rolls down her window. She looks like Rudolph, flipping me off. I laugh at the lewd reindeer, call her a bitch then, facing the road, scream like Slayer.

My breaks screech. A flutter of white cloth drops below my headlights as the heavy latches on my camera bag smack my windshield. Thin cracks form a web in the glass. Through it, the silver Aston Martin disappears past the Blue Whale. I frantically unbuckle my belt, throw open my door and jump out of the car. "Oh fuck. Oh fuck. Oh fuck..." I just killed Hollywood Jesus.

Splayed across the asphalt, the local savior reminds me of 80's Ozzy. His robes are still white—fully bloodless. He looks like he's sleeping. "Holy fuck dude, are you dead? Can you hear me?" Standing over him breathing in burnt rubber, I beg, "Jesus. Fuck, Jesus, don't be dead... Jesus. Your birthday is coming, man."

With his hands folded across his chest like an old-timey vampire, he opens his steely eyes. "You should slow down my son. You might get hurt." Suddenly standing, he offers me a high five. I smack his wide palm with a limp shell-shocked hand, and he strides away flowing into the night.

"Holy fucking shit." My arm is still raised to the heavens. I slowly lower it before shuffling back to Lenore.

For a minute I sit breathing, pulsing, holding my head. I check my camera–nothing. I never hit record. Video was never my thing. Fuck. I rub my belt-battled shoulder, shift Leonard to neutral and start my dead engine. "Send me an Angel" plays on the JAK as, at about 1mph, I creep over to the curb, throw back my seat, and try to settle. "Yeah." I reconfirm with myself, "that was really totally fucked up."

# CHAPTER 17

**I headed straight to Equinox and went big on a full body workout despite being twisted and tweaked from passing out in Lenore and being rudely awakened by LA DOT banging on my windshield at dawn.** I'm digging my Iron Maiden tee from my locker when my phone rattles out. I snatch it from the air before it smashes on the tile. It's Sky. She wants me to meet her. Killer. Without showering, I secretly borrow cologne from some unaware dude in the sauna, spray it on, drop the skull bottle back in his bathroom bag, dress-super fast and, majorly bummed on how I smell, bail.

Stella and Franco are talking to some dude with neck tattoos about Sundance outside of the gym. The Lullulemoned Eff invites me to yoga. I say, "Can't—in love" and kiss her on the mouth just to fuck with Jimmy. When I pull into the basement lot of the 9200 Sunset tower just east of Beverly Hills, valet parks my ride next to a Ferrari. Puffy is on his way out of SOHO House. We fist bump as I barge past him through the heavy glass doors. The reception chick asks my name from behind a high wooden desk. I tell her she's totally my type but I'm already spoken for. She smiles politely and asks me whom I'm here to see. "Sky Monroe" I proudly proclaim and, telling me that I smell good, she directs me to the elevators.

This place is pretty exclusive but even if I were to forge a perfect recommendation letter, I couldn't afford the dues. I watch the floor numbers blink and wonder if Score is here. He somehow hustled a free membership. I take a selfie next to the events calendar and send it to him. "What up, uphill G?" I type, clowning Alexa's stalker, before asking what a Paralysis bottle looks like. Google struggles to load an image of Jamie's unreleased cologne. Before Score can reply, the doors open at the penthouse and I fire out past a short dude waiting to go down. Recognizing his orange sneakers and agent expression, I point to a Ruscha painting that hangs above the pool table. "I wrote that." I hook my thumb toward my Number of the Beast tee and declare, "Fuckin'-A list!" I throw up a double-deuce as I back-step up the wide staircase, and the elevator doors close on David Fass' baffled face.

Far above Hollywood, Sky sits alone at a cocktail table in front of an empty bloody mary with her legs crossed. The speckled dress she's wearing would only look half as hot on January Jones. The babe of Mad Men casting agents' dreams touches her perfect nose then taps her phone. She's taking selfies. No one sees this but me. Except for the occasional clink and a low tense murmur, the whole rooftop is pretty quiet. The only other people inside are the staff and two chicks talking at the end of the huge rectangular center bar. A brunette babe in a white dress and white hat drinks something blue as a heavily tattooed Asian girl chatters at her while crunching colorful Taro chips. The runway babe looks like one of Drop Dead's accessories but she could easily be any other model. The bleached-blonde Asian girl with the bad boob job looks familiar too–maybe I've seen her working a pole at Jumbo's Clown room. Wondering if Joaquin Phoenix throws dollar bills at this chattering tattooed chick, I turn from her bad tits toward the men on the balcony. Standing poised in shrunken tuxedo jackets—one black, one white—The Mythicals silently sip wine facing west. The Pacific appears more distant than it is beyond their pointy padded shoulders. They must sense my rockin' vibes because they turn from the view and stare at me like Si and Ami from 101 Dalmatians. I wanna thank those cats for setting up Drop Dead but I've got to be sly. I tap my nostrils and rub my fingers together, giving the universal hand sign for being papered-up, before turning up two thumbs. With zero reaction, The Mythicals turn back toward the ocean and text, keeping our little-big secret, and I move in to interrupt Sky's private photo shoot.

"Hey beautiful." I drag out a chair and plop down. "How hard did you miss me?" My seat is still warm from David Fass' stupid ass.

"Shit! Hey…" Startled, she tables her phone next to a cocktail napkin dampened by her discarded celery. "I didn't see you come in. How long have you been here?"

"One second. I skipped my recovery shake and came straight over. I like your dress. You look like a hot Dalmatian." The waiter sets a fresh Bloody Mary in front of Sky. I'm starving but she looks too upset for me to fuck with ordering. "Are you okay?"

"Yeah..." Her stormy eyes are cloudy with unspilled tears. Tracing the condensation on her second round of breakfast with her chipped robin-shell nails she admits, "Well, no, not really..."

"What's going on?" I ask, feeling watched. If the chicks at the end of the bar aren't talking about me, they're definitely staring like they are. "Did David yell when you fired him?"

"Did you see him?" Sky asks, concerned. "Did he see you?"

"Yeah. He just bailed. I said what's up. I think he sucks too much to recognize me though..."

"Oh, well, that's good at least..." She sighs like she did when I told her I'd edit the hive from her wrist in the backstage K3NNY shot, and chugs down half of her drink. I ask for the celery on her napkin and press her to tell me what's up. "I didn't get Terror Cake. They gave it to Alice Always."

With my wilted vegetable waving toward the curious chicks at the end of the bar, I ask, "Who?"

"That 'My Undies' model that's all over your site!" Sky scolds, as if I should already know.

"Fuck. Which one?" I drop the stalk immediately and go for my phone. "I'll take down all her photos right now." My accounts are open before my celery hits the floor.

"Stop, no. It's fine." Sky reaches across the table to still my deleting hand. "They said they wanted a more 'all American girl.' She's the pretty blonde. The Australian with the perfect nose."

"But you're perfect."

"Stop fucking saying that." Sky pulls back. Looking at me like I was the one who cast the chick, she seethes, "Clearly I'm not." I touch my wrist then notice hers is bare. "But C'est la vie... James has the male lead...better to not be attached to that kind of thing." She stares wistfully toward the DTLA Skyline. "David says I might have a shot at Pac Man, though. Bruckheimer. With Disney. Live action. I'd be Pac Man's virginal girlfriend who gets possessed by Ghost Monsters." She smiles sadly and shrugs.

"You'd be perfect for that!" I pretty much scream, and a tall glass of pink appears in front of me.

"Plant protein smoothie with almond milk and raspberries." Our waiter swishes away.

I look up from the shake to Sky. "No way! Thank you!"

"I figured you might be hungry." Pinching an ice-cube, she sucks it and smiles. Like, for real smiles.

"You're gonna be the killer-est Pac Babe." The tattooed chick heels by with her eyes cast down toward her big bad tits.

"I don't know, Al." She picks polish from her nails. "David says they're worried."

I slam my shake down mid gulp and wipe my sleeve across my mouth. "Fuck they! Worried about what? Having a fucking blockbuster? Who's they?" I notice the brunette model has disappeared from the bar.

"One of the producers who worked on my reality show is involved in the film."

"Oh yeah! Whatever happened with that show?" I howl with a brain freeze then, wincing, whisper, "I couldn't wait for that shit."

"I ruined it," Her phone buzzes on the table between us. We both glance at the text preview until her lock-screen eats David Fass' unanswered text. "Daddy put the show together for me." She pulls out her pipe. "I was so worried about making him proud back then that I started breaking out on camera. It was a disaster. Sometimes I'd pass out on set. Reggie would say it was because I'd drink with my pills but I think it was from the stress..." Sky vapes. Behind her The Unicorn paces the balcony arm and arm with the brunette in the white hat heading for the southern railing. I inhale melony mist as Sky divulges. "When I told the director that I wanted to fuck him, the show was over. They claim I said it in front of his wife but I don't remember saying it at all..." She flicks her wrist. "They like that kind of stuff on camera but not in real life."

"Fucking hypocrites! They can't take the real thing." I scan the windows for the white-clad couple again but they've disappeared. When I look back at Sky, Jaq is standing behind her. A dark stripe runs down the side of his sheeny tights as he smokes something scentless, and surely hallucinogenic, from a long thin vaporizer. I raise my glass to him before promising Sky, "I'll start making movies and you'll be the star. They'll rule...Maybe you shouldn't drink when we're shooting, though."

"Maybe not..." Sky finishes her Bloody Mary before suggesting, "How about we start with my AI This And More feature—but ditch the shot with K3NNY? I don't think he's the right look." Though her reasoning kinda reminds me of Score right now, I'm super stoked. "Maybe a set at The Happiest Place on Earth?"

I picture myself down on one knee surrounded by mice and princess superfame. "You want to go Disneyland?"

"Have you done Club 33? I think I can get us a reservation for next week...if you wanna go." She smiles. No one but major Disney royalty can get into this fucking club.

"Fuck yes I wanna go!" The Trueblood folds over to whisper into her ear like a black Slinky with gold fangs.

"Already?" She seems unpleasantly surprised. The gold lining of Jaq's tuxedo tails disappears as he unfolds to stare at me through wintery blue contacts. Sky pulls her phone from her purse and mutters, "How'd he get back here so fast?" She stands. "Al, I have to go. I have a meeting in the Garden Room that I forgot about." The Trueblood boots away and, popping something small into her mouth, Sky dry swallows and follows him toward the dining garden at the east end of the tower.

"It's cool..." I trail them up the long shadowy Polaroid-adorned hallway. "I've gotta go finish some shit I've been working on so I'll be done before Disney."

When we reach the photo booth, Sky pulls me through the velvet curtains and kisses me super good. She tastes like spiked Campbell's soup. I secretly press the sunken red button in the carpeted wall.

"I'm sorry I snapped at you. I was just upset. I adore you." She whispers, pecking my neck, "You smell delicious." The camera beeps, flashing as we make-out. I reach up her speckled dress and hook her lace panties with my thumb. As I begin to pull them down she breaths, "I'll text after we're done."

Sky slips out of the heavy black drapes leaving me with my boner. I peak out through curtain and watch Jaq lead her to the rooftop garden. The Unicorn and the brunette model are posed in the restaurant's entrance waiting with a tall redhead babe dressed in black. I salute Cam. With zero reaction, he turns into the dining room. The warm photo strip is four dark blurry frames.

At the bottom of the stairway, Steven Tyler and Adam Levine come steppin' out of the elevator, and I pocket my beloved prints. "Adam and Steve not Adam and Eve!" I cheer, barging between them and offering a double hi-five. "Mickey Mouse is gonna help me propose, dudes!" Only Tyler is prepared for the celebration. In a flurry of long colorful scarves, he smacks my left palm.

"Right on, brother!" he congratulates before recommending, "Might wanna lay off the Paralysis a bit on the big day though."

I double spin and push the lobby button. As the doors close, I think I catch a glimpse of Score booting for the stairway in his overpriced studded leather jacket, and I stop wiping my Paralyzed neck on the padded wall to pull out my phone. The text I sent him never went through. He doesn't know I'm here. I figured this place would have fancy elevator reception but when I tap his number the call is dropped immediately. Whatevs. I'd rather tell him the rad news in person so I can watch him freak. He's gonna be stoked to dress up for our wedding.

# CHAPTER 18

## "Your brain is drowning in semen.

You're gonna be over it once you fuck her...or anyone." The Barbie grips her pistol and points it into the closest of the boutique's million mirror columns with a sneer. Below the barrel, a diamond glimmers on her left ring finger. The Tiffany's chick, acting as if the glass counter will serve as a billion dollar force field to protect her from chaos kids, watches us. She's shook but there's no way she's kicking us out of the Rodeo Drive jewelry shop. She's already got the The Barbie's Amex which TB asked her Dad to get her, mostly because it's black metal. The Barbie doesn't normally buy expensive shit but we're not here for her. "And what if she's no good?" Her words are infused with the smirk she's too cool to actually make. "Bet she doesn't swallow."

"Pshh. She's for sure good. I'm going to be her sixty-secondth." I defend the cred of my wife-to-be as the Barbie turns her barrel on me. I put my hands into the air. "And, yeah. I'm crazy fucking horny right now. But it's not about that."

"That's what I'm worried about, babe. Rich girls have no hearts."

"You're a rich girl." I smile fearlessly in her line of fire.

"Yeah—" The soft-spoken Eff sets her plastic pistol on the glass case and slips off the ring. "That's how I know." Lowering my hands, I eye the fifth rejected diamond as she passes it back to the blushing shop chick. "Champagne would speed this process way up" TB advises, and the chick heels to the back of the shop.

I hated asking The Barbie to front me the money for Sky's ring but as soon as I deliver the 5 golden grams of organics to Drop Dead, my BF Eff is getting a pile of cash and a new dead thing to hang in her black hole. Not that TB would really care if I never paid her back. She's in this for the cause. A few years back Jamie roofied her ex-girlfriend so, even beyond her innate love of bedlam, The Barbie fully backs my blackmail plan. My imminent engagement, however, isn't really stoking her out.

"Don't be jeal, evil stepsister." I throw my arm around TB's shoulders and squeeze. "I'd marry you but you only like horny Martian-worshipping poseurs with in-patient haircuts."

"Kenny only worships me. BUT..." The Barbie squeezes her little boobs together and raises her voice a hundred octaves. "He stops makin' hits, he stops hitting this." Her bare ribs show through the sides of her slashed Skinny Puppy tee as she holds an emotionless pucker. The shop chick clicks out of the back room and sets down our champagne. Dropping her tits and voice back to their former position, The Barbie insists, "I just don't want her using you to be cool or make James jealous or whatever." She passes me a long stemmed glass of booze. "Unlike me, you've got feelings babe."

I raise my glass. "More than a feeling!" The Barbie shakes her head at my bitch'n Journey reference. We clink glasses, and I toss my champagne over my shoulder. As it fizzes on the floor behind me, The Barbie downs her drink.

"You know Sky talks to him right?" she says while passing the chick her empty glass. "Seems like they're fucking."

"Uh, he's talking to her. Sky doesn't respond and she definitely isn't fucking him." I set my glass upside down on the case. "She's allergic to him." The shop chick pulls another ring from the case saying something about "pave" and a VVS canary. TB slips it on, and I challenge, "Why are you lurking Sky's shit anyway?"

"Just lookin' out, babe." Fanning her fingers in front of her porcelain face, The Barbie vogues. "Already looks better on me." Her sharp brows disappear beneathe her low Louise Brooks bangs.

"It's perf, huh TB? It's gotta be perf...fuck, it's hot in here." I grab the bottom of my tee and knot it into a bikini top. "Can I get a free Slurpee with my million dollar diamond or what?"

The Barbie's half-Asian hazels look up from the ring. "This is the one." The shop chick vehemently agrees with the decision as she clicks away to run the Amex. I yell at her tense back, "That one comes with a 'yes' guarantee, right?" A bead of sweat forms on the rim of my belly button. I tap it away.

"Fuck, Baby." TB finally gets it. "You actually think you love her, don't you?"

"Hard." The shook shop babe jams back with the loot, and TB scribbles on a payment screen. "Thanks!" Snatching the blue bag, I smooch her high cheekbone. "You're really the best."

"I know. Anything for you, babe." The Barbie's soft subtle smile looks uncommonly fragile until she grabs her gun from the counter and jabs the barrel to my belly. "You smell awful." She pulls the trigger, and I scream in point blank pain.

# CHAPTER 19

**I crank off the third showerhead and the water rush dies.** Over the few plunking drips, strange imported night birds cry on loop like a car alarm. I stop myself from yelling at them to shut the fuck up, palm the hot water from my head, and reach toward the sink. The white towels on the marble counter glow in the dark. I grab one and wipe down the shower tiles before pulling another from the stack. Drying myself, I step out of the vast walk-in and march through a beam of moonlight past the bed. My clothes lay in a pile on the floor by the dresser. Noah doesn't know I'm here and never will. Even if he woke up now he wouldn't suspect it. I parked Lenore on Sunset, hiked all the way to the gate, showed Martín Marlena's nudes, crept into the pool house, and pocketed a baggie of coke. I'd take more but I'm not really into stealing from anyone, especially someone who's admittedly been super good to me (even if he is a nast). And

I'm not trying to sling Anger; this mission isn't about making money. It's about love and justice.

After my first shower in days, I slide open the windows inviting in the night air to further cleanse me of my thieving sins. Steam rises from my body and floats around the pilfered Anger Jar and out toward the pool. A three-legged dog-like creature drinks from the shallow end. The coyote, or dingo, or more likely some thing that I've never heard of, pauses and looks up at me. I throw it a double-peace. It dips its muzzle back into the salt water. It laps. I pick up my denim jacket with an enormous yawn, and extract my phone. "4 a.m…"

I'm demoed from car camping followed by 3 a.m. drug deals and surprise SOHO brunches with my babe. I stretch my lats and carefully, so as not to muss the comforter, lay my naked ass down on the bed for a nap. Little claws scratch against the front door and I pass out hard for I don't know how long.

"Mmhh," I groan, barely conscious, thinking I'm at gunpoint with The Barbie, "you know I love you but…"

"Oh Honey Bear," Uncle Noah slurps. "I know… I know. I love you too."

I reach out, grip my hand around his throat, and push him off my cock. He gags and gasps with his floppy bare ass in the air as he claws at his bow tie. I jump out of bed and stand.

"What the fuck are you doing?" I yell, deeply inhaling Vetiver. In the nasty "mood" candlelight, my erect rebel rod glistens with Noah's thick spit. I'm so relieved I didn't fucking blow. I grab the damp bath towel from the floor and wipe down. My rogue boner retreats as, trying to keep cool while furiously scrubbing, I calmly remind my benefactor of the rules. "You can't just fucking do that. That's not how this works. I watch for two hundred. You watch me for three. That's it. No touching."

He's so fucked-up that his ashy dong is as hard as a salted slug. It pokes through the unbuttoned hem of his tux shirt. "You'll get your money you ungrateful little shit!" He yells in a flabby rage and grabs a thin stack from the nightstand. "Does your wet-back whore do this?" Screeching like a pissed-off peacock, Noah flips hundred dollar bills at me after each question. "Does she? What does she give you? Bad Disney head!" Having cashed his cash, he points at me trembling with rage. "You're in my town. Don't think I can't find out what you do when you're not here, you fuck shit! I am God and you are shit! Shit!"

I count three bills on the floor and leave them where they landed. "Fuck off." I pull on my jeans and button my fly feeling queasy from the violent ball-scrub—or disgust—or maybe even fucking blue balls. The thought deepens the sick feeling in my stomach. I pull on my shirt and grab my jacket. "I'm not doing this anymore." As I snatch my phone from the bed, Noah rushes me like he's a scraper and I'm Taylor Swift holding hands with a buzz-cut chick in front of Mickey's on ladies night.

"Yes. You. ARE!" Gripping my triceps surprisingly hard, he shakes me. His eyes look like they're about to explode into cocaine clouds. "You will fuck me and you will love me."

I throw off his hands and strongly caution, "Don't ever fucking touch me." Noah smacks me. As I contemplate murder, he stares, scared and frozen, except for his jaw. He chews his thick dry bottom lip, and I twist my phantom lock. Grabbing my shoes I bail toward the pool. "Later freak."

"Oh, no! No later!" Flailing in the doorway with his pants partially held up by one thick resilient suspender, he yells. "Never! Never, you fucking whore shit liar! You're through here—this whole town—over—go! Never come back!"

With a backhanded double flip-off raised into the night, I march across the damp grass directly into a slumber party. The attack-peacocks awake on the wrong edge of the rainforest. White wings beat in a cacophonous whooping flurry. Menacing tails mad-bird me as I sprint through the flock waving fistfuls of keys and cocaine. In my slow-mo nightmarishly surreal escape, the live-action angry birds peck at my legs, screaming along with my ex-uncle as he brings up his ex.

"You're just like him! A loser faggot! You hear me you whore loser faggot?" Noah threatens, sounding completely unhinged. "Your slut spic girlfriend is through too! You hear me?"

# CHAPTER 20

**The Barbie is blacked out in her hole.** Her head rests on my chiseled chest as we recline comfily on her frameless mattress. Through the dark I can smell her amber oil floating around me like an unseen familiar, mingling with the vanilla body wash I used to scour off Noah's molestation and unreleased Paralysis. I stare at a baboon's humanoid tongue. A bottle just escaped from our tangle of sheets and clunked onto the floor, colliding with the animal's glazed wooden base. The ghostly clink rouses TB into migrating across two feet of courtesy friendship space to curl onto me. I was already awake before the sound stirred her, watching the taxidermy in the corner bare its massive yellow fangs. I turn from its teeth and look up toward the bone-yard suspended from wires and nails in the wall above us. TB's drool pools in the soft spot below my sternum as I gaze at a small deer skull. I wonder if someone murdered that baby deer. My phone is double buzzing. It's been constant since I plugged into my fucked car charger and called TB. She told me she was still up celebrating K3NNY's extended absence, and that since All F's has a super early living room shoot on my sleeper, we should have a slumber party. I came straight over but she was passed out when I crept in.

I'm relieved to be in an actual bed that doesn't belong to Noah, though I'm stressing about tomorrow: David Fass' A-list. Drop Dead hashtags. My site. My art intentions. My phone double buzzes again. Normally I sleep super hard with TB but the texts are creating a Hollywood hale storm in my brain. I lift my hand from the back of her thin Coil tee, reach down to the floor, grab The Barbie's charger cord and, carefully so as not to wake her, reel in my phone. Sliding the brightness all the way down, I scroll through a scraper inquisition hoping Score has finally hit me back.

The Barbie rubs her ankle across the beak bite on my calf. I clench my teeth silently through the pain. The fresh wound throbs as I squint at the poorly encoded texts from what is obviously Drop Dead's newest number. He keeps changing burner phones like a scraper to avoid getting caught in the drug deal–which, I've recently learned, needs to happen tonight. He's got some super early flight tomorrow to go do some self-promoting. Fucking worst timing. At least I've finally just learned what #32 means. After what Sky told me about his bromance ritual, I should have already known.

I doubt the shaggy haired ghost will answer my call for assistance but I dial Score anyway, and The Barbie makes a cat noise. Her warm skin feels killer against mine as she slides up to kiss my collarbone. Immediately I have a shredding boner. Immediately her hand finds it. I toss my phone and, from our black-sheeted feet, it glows through the black-hole-room. Score might have some rad shit to listen to if he ever checks his voicemail.

**\*\*\*\***

"What the fuck—" A stream of hot fluid drizzles on my eyebrow, and I pull the sheets over my face.

"Get up, babe." The Barbie pokes my head with her toes. "Today's the big dumb day! Love in the shittiest place on earth!" Though she complains the rides are too fast, TB says she hates the humans at Disneyland more. She's the only babe I'd forgive such sacrilege–cuz she's the best. Another scalding stream patters over my cover. "Drats. Empty."

I peek out. The blackout curtains are open. A misty morning light washes over the black walls and the antique fit mannequins, creeping up the corners of the room. The Barbie stands over me holding a burning man-shaped candle with her ankles locking my ribs. Zebra striped panties peak out from beneath her thin vintage shirt. They aren't the pair I licked off before we went to sleep. Those were green.

TB cocks her head. "Did you fuck me, Al?"

"No way man." I insist, picking hot red scales from my neck. Last night when she grabbed my rod, I'd figured she was drunk on wine. I don't know if TB secretly took some black-coffee pill, or what, but when I slid inside her and she started talking about what we meant to each other, she seemed way sober—so I put on the breaks and pulled out. Even though we'd only fucked for mere seconds, I immediately released my baby brigade onto the sheets between her thighs. I've been deprived, and TB is fucking hot.

"Your loss." She smiles, blows out the flame, and bounces from the bed.

My BF Eff skips across the room. I flick a red ball of wax toward her black bob and she deftly dodges. She's for sure sober now. The crimson wad sticks to a bolt of black lace leaning against the wall. Setting the smoking headless wax figure on her bookshelf, The Barbie slides out a large fabric-bound bible and flips it open. Quietly singing "She doesn't deserve you" in a recess melody, she pulls a small blue box from amidst the drugs and ammo in the hollow. "Congratulations" she says, and arcs it over.

"You rule." I catch Sky's engagement ring with both hands. "Thanks again for sponsoring me on this and letting me stay and everything. You f'real rule."

She pulls an ancient medicine bottle from the book and skips back to bed. "Anything for you, babe." The Barbie presses her bare thigh to mine as she props herself against the wall. I roll off the mattress. At its foot, next to the migrating Badoit bottle and under last night's panties, I find my dying phone. I'm shocked the empty bottle had been drained of water and not Syrah. I hit dial—straight to voicemail. "Seriously? Is Score dead?" I drag my denim out from below an antique sewing desk. "He hasn't responded in days and he's offline as fuck. Did the show take back his phone? Where the fuck is he?"

"Probably somewhere pretending to be someone with someone pretending to be someone else." TB squeezes an eyedropper into a half-full Fiji. The clear drops could be minerals, Chinese herbs, DMT, or some shit I've never heard of. "That beach chick has been posting pictures with him" she shrugs, twisting the rubber plunger back into the caramel colored glass.

"Shit, okay, well... I was gonna ask him cuz they've obviously got some weird thing for each other, but fuck..." I stash the ring in my jacket and pullout the Anger. "Drop Dead's leaving tomorrow. Obviously I can't go so...would you maybe be into getting him this tonight?" I wave the animal printed baggie. "I'll love you even more forever...and it might be fun...?"

"Because I'd be the first girl to ever receive twenty thousand dollars directly from a bag of limp dicks? Bitch'n..." She places her thumb over the mouth of the bottle and begins to shake her solution. "Don't you think you should postpone your terrible idea and be there yourself? Way better terrible idea if you ask me."

"Dude, TB, the place he wants to meet is where Sky told me he takes his dudes! The Mythicals keep tagging me in weird disappearing shit, and I'm pretty sure they're telling me Drop Dead wants to get fucked-up and fuck Andy Cane, or them, or whoever, and he totally wants to fuck you too. You'll get the cash handed to you and if you semi-play along, you'll get the scandal shot that fucking destroys him! Glory! I bet ya Cam and Jaq will be there too... I'd go but..." The Barbie raises an eyebrow, sips her drink, and I drop to my knees. "Please! Please! Please!" I clasp my hands together and shake them at her. "I'll buy you an aborted fetus. I'll order you a lifetime supply of pink pellets. I'll get Mickey's skull and frame it for you. I'll—"

"Okay, babe." TB chugs the rest of her drink and tosses the bottle. The creepy primate silently screams as the cashed Fiji bounces from its freeze-dried paws. "If you don't wanna return the ring after fucking me, I'll fuck up Jamie for you."

"Whoa. You're already that fucked up?" I ask, eyeing the discarded bottle for visible traces of some potent mystery drug. "You eat mollymeal for breakfast while I was still asleep?" She gives a guilty open-palmed shrug and smiles. I toss her the Anger. "We've gotta be super fast." The Barbie catches the coke as I jam toward her. "I don't want to be late to pick up Sky."

# CHAPTER 21

## The alarm screams, ricocheting off the windows like a Noah misfire.

Security is staring up at us from the ground floor. I don't give a fuck. I'm in a French lift with my mouse ears on and Sky's tongue in my mouth. I told her my post from brunch caused a site-traffic Carmageddon and she called me "radical" in the weird valley girl voice that she's been using all day. I hit the emergency button and pressed her against the glass wall. I taste champagne and strawberries as she breathes, "It should totally be like this, like, always."

"Fuck yes!" I agree, shoving my fingers through the shreds in the ass of her jeans.

I don't ever want this to end. We've been at Disneyland all morning and I have a million great shots of her: dancing with a gingerbread man at Sleeping Beauty's Castle, laying by a tombstone outside The Haunted Mansion, wearing deely bobbers in an arcade while playing a rebooted Ms. Pac Man machine. Sky said she's going to forward those photos to her people but had me immediately edit and post the shot of her and Marlena in Club 33. When we showed up to the exclusive restaurant for brunch, Miss Lopez was there with her ex Justin Bieber. A reunion shot of that superpopfame power couple would be worth a zillion but I fucked it off like an untimely drug deal cuz this trip is pure pleasure. And I think Marlena hates me right now. She hasn't responded to my texts since I tried to shoot Tay Tay. And yet, when Sky asked her to join us, she was into it. Marlena totally iced me at brunch but whatevs. The post of her and Sky sharing macarons is red hot. It went live right before I left a hundred dollar tip and by the time Sky and I stepped into this elevator, everyone started blowing me the fuck up.

Having lurked the post of my two babes, Jamie was freaking about me flaking on tonight. When I told him that The Barbie is bringing the Anger he was so stoked that, after sending a string of heart-eyed emoji faces, he stopped texting me entirely. The scrapers, however, wouldn't shut up about my Disney date. I denied rumors of the return of the supercouple "Mustin" and my soon-to-be-eternal romance with Sky, typing "I wish. Just right place and time as usual dude. I'm out to Marmont to meet Stella, Franco, and DiCap—" then happily pocketed my dead phone. I don't really know where any of them are, but no scraper is gonna ignore that lead to come down to see if I'm full of shit.

Sky stops kissing me to pick up her fallen bowler hat and read a text. I pop off the alarm. Well-oiled cogs whirr. I lean against the glass and grin toward the sour looks on the faces below. "What is this, Tower of Terror?" I ask Club 33 Security, stepping out from the sliding doors and sliding on our shades.

"You've really gotta get that fixed. Shit's dangerous." Sky and I jam back to the park holding hands.

Near the edge of the Rivers of America, a Dixieland band plays. Approaching the bandstand, watching the drummer, I snap along to hot jazz wondering if my brother will want to work on some new Band Fail! tracks when he comes back for New Year's Eve. I can't wait to make Zach my Best Man. I shove my hand in my pocket and the Tiffany diamond stabs at the calluses in my grip. Anxious to propose beneath the fireworks, I check the time. An actor, resembling my friend, boots past the town clock. His long ratty coat dances in a cool gust. "Hey, that explains it!" I point to the pirate deckhand treading the dock below the rolling clouds. "Score got a real job! No wonder he's been ghosting." Sky tightens one of her five day-glo Swatches, glances up from her texting, and laughs at my mockery of the missing man.

"Oh my god, fer sure. James must be like, totally playing Captain Hook somewhere right now." My guts squirm at hearing Drop Dead's name, but I laugh anyway. "Let's jam." Sky snaps the elastic at my chin, says, "These clouds are a bummout. I wanna do Splash Mountain before it's arctic," then dives back into the text deluge that has begun pouring into her phone.

We escape the briars of the flume ride barely moist. Taking Sky's free hand, I march us out of Bear County towards Fantasyland. As we pass a babe dressed as Alice, Sky, speaking to me for the first time since she mentioned Jamie, glances up at the character actress in the blue dress and asks if I think Ms. Pac man would be blonde if she were a real woman. I put my arm around her, telling her that if Ms. Pac Man were Sky Monroe, she'd already be totally fucking perfect.

"As if." Sky scoffs, tapping her screen.

I release her unresponsive bod and pull up my hood. With the snowy peak of the Matterhorn behind us, I shove my fists in my pockets and, silently pacing by her side, grip her ring as she texts.

**** 

I've led us out of the main park and into California Adventure. I'm not sure Sky has noticed the change of scenery. She doesn't seem to care where we are or what we do. We haven't ridden a ride in hours. Every time I suggest one she mutters "hm?" so I've just been wandering around gripping the ring.

From our wander past California Screaming, we shuffle into the food court inhaling the scent of fried dough and cinnamon (though I don't know if she smells it.) I scan the fast-food options trying to decide which empty calories I'm going to scarf and how I'm going to propose tonight—if I'm going to propose. Sky's being so weird—super detached. She usually spends half of our time together on the phone but today it's nonstop and her uncharacteristic silence has an anxious energy to it. That shit The Barbie told me about her talking to Jamie echoes in my head. Wondering if Drop Dead is the one responsible for distracting my girl on our big day, I ask if she wants a churro. Sky lightly giggles at her phone for the millionth time. I buy a fried treat from a passing cart and try to hand it to her. Without looking up, she shakes her head.

Still holding the warm donuty tube of rejection, I lean against the glazed wooden walls of a little bakery eating the tortillas we were given after the factory tour. A round girl sitting at a table in front of the Lucky Fortune Cookery grips a drippy vanilla ice cream cone. Its citrus swirl glows like orange neon in the dusk as she licks, watching me. At first I figure she's into my unwanted donut wand but no, she recognizes me—or us. I'm not sure she knows why. But then I see her father standing next to her and realize he would. He would for sure.

I turn to Sky. Beyond her a vendor parks his cart at the edge of the court and bang, a suicidal balloon rains glitter onto his shoulders. The noise doesn't divert her eyes from her phone or help my tweaking nerves, but it does draw the young girl. Dashing toward the flashing inflatables, she leaves a trail of soft serve speckles and her father behind. Her dad paces between the picnic tables shoving down a flakey egg roll and speaking into a blue tooth earpiece, waving a broken hand. I'm pretty sure he just asked, "Monroe or Lopez?" between a million other secret Russian things. Alexei often breaks into his native tongue, regardless of whom he's speaking to.

I stand in front of Sky to block her from the shady scraper. "Hey. It's almost dark." I swallow the last of my tortilla as I attempt to interrupt her typing. "The grommits should be leaving Fantasyland. Let's go back." Barely glancing up she says "...K" and, tossing her eggy churro into a trashcan, I drag Sky away.

I can't let Alexei see us. He would have us online before Tinker Bell lights the first firework. David would drop Sky, her Pac Man role might get fucked, and that hothead monster Abbi would be far from stoked. If his betraying Russian piñata sold a rumor-affirming exclusive of Sky Monroe coupled-up with me—his lying, evasive, totally killer crew defector—I'd be dodging more than broken contracts. I lead the iBlind like a rattled guide dog through ambling tourists while keeping close eyes on our backs. The top-secret marriage proposal will have to wait. This fucking sucks.

I jet us toward the exit maneuvering like a Radiator Springs Racer. We cut in and out of a gift shop then, just before the gates, I notice two security guards at the 50's gas station facade. They question a little Russian girl who's sitting on the curb crouching by a pump. All three of them are smiling. I pull off my ears and tug on my hood. Walkie-talkies crackle cryptic alerts of a lost child in happy Disney code. Sky texts through the turnstiles then, in the middle of the courtyard, she stops.

"Al." Sliding off her Vuarnets, she drops them in her day-glo rubber bag along with her phone. It seems like forever since she's looked at me. Her eyes are more magical than this Kingdom. "My socks are still wet from Splash and I'm, like, freezing," she says, lightly scratching her neck. "And these Capezios are a major bum out. My feet are totally dying." Sky wiggles a pink-striped dance sneaker. "Could we maybe motor?"

"Now?" I squeeze the ring as my heart collapses. We definitely need to bail, but Sky doesn't know this. She doesn't know anything other than what's been going on in her phone. She shouldn't want to go.

"I guess David wants to meet early tomorrow too." I take off my shades. Though I'm relieved to think she might have been texting her orange-shoed agent all day rather than James, I also want to cut off David's feet. "I know it's totally lame," Sky admits, "But he's going out of town early tomorrow, so..."

"Oh. Okay, cool—"

Breaking my stammer, Sky smiles, tells me I'm radical, and kisses me. Her lips are more electric than The Light Parade. I edge her back and lift her onto a circular planter. She wraps her acid washed thighs around me, digging her fluorescent fingernails into my traps, and we make out super hard below a bush shaped like Olaf the snowman. When I crawl my hand into her short hair, her bowler flips off. Children cheer. Flashes explode through my relaxed eyelids like fireworks, and I feel better.

"We'll come back again," she promises, ending our extensive DDA (Disney Display of Affection) and the cheering morphs into a high-pitched squeal. Not even Axl could hit this shit. Wincing at the high note, I watch Anna and Elsa posing by the ticket booths. The Frozen princesses are surrounded. Their handlers can barely keep back the rabid little girls in tiaras. I think I see Alexei's daughter bouncing in the throng.

"You're totally rad for understanding." Sky smooches me again, and I hoist her to the ground. She dusts a clingy leaf off her hat and asks, "Race ya to the tram?" I turn back from a frantic, inconclusive double-check of the round-girl's proximity. Sky jogs in place, puffing her cheeks and exhaling in cute little bursts. "Come on!" she challenges, and I squat.

"Here, don't run." Opening my arms, I offer a piggyback ride. "Hop on, I'm not letting your feet get more fucked."

# CHAPTER 22

**Traffic was kinda crazy on the way out of the park but when we parted the Orange Curtain the road to Los Angeles opened with it.** I've got Lenore cruising at around 90 mph, and Commerce Casino's arching hotel shrinking in my rearview mirror. But that's not all I've got. Laid back and buckled-up next to me, Sky luxuriously sips her golden flask looking way pretty. She's a ton more relaxed and a little less sober than when we left Disneyland. Even though shit got weird, I'm still stoked. This is the longest I've ever hung with her.

Sky pumps her drink to DOLL beats and raps along to Pink Corvette, her voice blending with The Barbie's dark detached words. I wiggle my charger and checking the clock on my dash, realize I'll be back to WEHO in time to meet Drop Dead. I should probably relieve TB and go to the hotel myself, but she did write, "Tonight should be amusing," and I don't want to leave Sky. I pinch and twist bare wires then, slightly electrocuted, unplug at one percent battery life and, telling it to say "Sup to Ol' Death for me," fling my annoying charger cord out my window. Sky smiles and chants, "If I weren't rich, I'd still be a bitch." I drop my drained phone in my ashtray, and the DTLA skyline welcomes us home.

"Check it out." Kinda creeped out by the Barbie/Monroe duet, I kill "RCHBTCH" and point toward the flashing sky. "There's a Crüe Concert in Heaven! Pretty cool, huh?"

Sky sits up to watch the rare lightning over Hollywood before curling back onto her reclined seat. "You're Heaven," she corrects. With my eyes on the road, I smile imagining her enraptured stare and turn on KROQ. The Chili Peppers sing something about California. Sky cranks the volume and springs up. "Where are we? I totally want fries! You want fries?" Pointing to the quickly approaching exit, she directs, "Get off here!"

Fucking stoked and fucking starving, I cut across three lanes and burn west on the edge of the new storm.

****

French fries are everywhere. "Holy fuck, is he fuckin' dead?" Glancing into my rearview, I wrench Leonard and swear to fucking Bonham, "I seriously didn't mean to kill him."

Sky's laughing, and I'm gunning it out of the drive-thru. When I turned into Astro Burger my old crew must have been inside stuffing their faces at a window booth cuz seconds after we pulled toward the take-out window to grab our order, Abbi appeared.

"Goose chase? That's how you repay your old friends?" With one hand on his cam and another in his track pants pocket, he barked from the end of the tight alley. "Maybe you want your goose cooked, huh Lil Bro? Franco's in New York. Stella's in Miami." My windshield wipers sliced his blinding spotlight as he slithered toward Lenore, and I wondered if his hidden hand was holding a little bat...or a gun. "So what I wanna know is where's your girlfriend, lil full of shit fancy Bro?"

Sky started to sit up to check out the drama. "Shit. Stay down." I tossed our to-go bag and threw my arm across her while stomping the gas. Abbi hit the stucco Astro Burger wall. I think my side mirror clipped him. Like I said, I f'real wasn't trying to run him over. I just wanted Sky out of there.

We flee the scene, and I cut right into a rainy warzone. Dry Hollywood drivers are dangerous, but just add water to'm and the roads are Grand Theft Auto. Sky's salty middle finger rises at the sounds of honking. I think she's flipping off the horns, but it could be the wounded raging scraper behind us. I don't know. Looking over my shoulder, I see Abbi standing in a puddle on the sidewalk. He points at me before gripping his arm in pain and involuntarily dropping it.

"Okay, totally not dead." Pretty much talking to myself, I watch the road. "But I think I got him pretty good."

Sky gleefully chomps fallen fries and starts to sit up again. "Fer real?"

"Whoa, no no!" I push her back to her seat.

"I wanna see!" She pleads.

"I'm pretty sure David will not be stoked on seeing you and—"

"As if." Sky retrieves her toppled flask from the cup holder. "David is boring and his usefulness is, like, totally evading me right now." She raises her drink and, toasting herself like Uncle Noah, says, "Fuck'm." Thankfully she stays down.

A black SUV idling at a meter wildly cuts away from the curb as we pass. I check the rearview. Illegally tinted windows are charging on an indirect path up my ass. The Cayenne tailing us goes for like 150k. These scrapers obviously know how to get paid if they're rolling a Porsche. I crank right at Fairfax and catch my buzzing phone mid-bounce. These scums still don't know that Sky is in here. I put a finger up to my lips and answer the call.

"Fuck you! Bail!" I demand and run a red at Fountain. A filthy voice bitches through my speakerphone. I figured I'd be talking to the creep that's chasing us but it really sounds like Abbi—although most of those fuckers sound the same. It could be the scum that just barely got his Porsche through the cross traffic behind me. I can't see anyone else tailing as the voice continues:

"You fucking owe us big time—"

"I don't owe you fuckers shit! You can—" and my battery dies. "Fuck."

I toss my phone toward the backseat, downshift Leonard, and flip a bitch. Lenore fishtails on the slick road. A silver Maserati coming toward us swerves. My Cayenne tail could have easily maneuvered to keep up with me but it's stopped at the intersection. Whoever's behind that wheel is a super sucky driver. No chance he's catching me.

"Ditch'm Alvin!" Squealing like she did on Space Mountain this morning, Sky grabs my leg and I fuckin' ditch'm. I cut west, and we disappear into the secret alleys below Santa Monica. "Faster!" she yells. "Faster!"

I dodge dumpsters, pass empty loading docks, and burn through side streets. My shocks slam into a huge pothole and speeding across Orlando, I turn up Doheny. I slow it way down all the way to Sunset then crawl east. As we approach her street, Sky pops her seat. "Here! Here! Pull over!" I stop at the curb in front of my friend's tattoo shop. Lenore's engine rumbles. The rain paradiddles on my hood.

"Shit..." Gripping my wheel, I take a deep breath and turn to her. "You okay? I think we're okay."

Sky traces her finger through the steam on my windshield. At the center of a bubbly heart, she writes A&S and turns to give me a liquored kiss laced with salt and grease. "That was, like, totally hot," she slurs while digging through her bag. The relatively new cracks in the glass reach into her heart and jag through our initials.

"Yeah?" I ask, straightening my mouse ears over the sound of rattling. "Killer. I'm just glad you didn't get caught on camera with me...fuckers." I glance in the rearview mirror. The steam on my back window is too thick to see through. "You're okay, right?"

"Paps don't drive Porsches handsome..." Sky shakes two white tablets from a little gold box, "...and maybe I wanna get caught with you." Sky feigns shock at her own words and opens her mouth wide to toss back the pills. The Shamrock Social Club's neon clover glows green beyond her. Rain spatters into Lenore. This rules.

"Where's your phone? I'll tip those fuckers that we'll be finishing the fries at your house!" I exclaim, wondering if popping the question over fast food would be too fucked.

The heart on my windshield begins to drip as Sky stares toward the shop. "I wanna get tattooed" she informs the rain then fixes me with party eyes. "Let's get each others' names."

I fire out of Lenore, slide across the hood, and open her door in one totally sick smooth motion. Sky steps onto the curb. The rain stripes her Spandau Ballet tee as I take her in my arms, step through the Shamrock threshold, and walk her toward permanence.

# CHAPTER 23

**Sky's space age bedroom hovers like a UFO over Hollywood.** I watch the city lights through the arching glass as I plod up the hallway toward the open door carrying her like a bride. Far below us The Blue Whale design building blushes to crimson and, recalling the dying words of Jesus, I slow down with my beak-wound burning from the pressure of each deliberate step. The needled skin above my eyes stings. I tried super hard to convince my friend to tattoo Sky, but he insisted she was too wasted. After her early meetings tomorrow I'm going to hold her hand while she gets my name tattooed on her ass.

"Whoa. That—" A giant framed Friedman photo of Tony Alva skating a pool in the 70's hangs at the end of the hall. I point, and Sky begins to slip from my arms. Catching her, I finish, "—is fucking shredding! I really wanna do that kinda stuff again. But sicker. I'm thinking of—"

"Take it!" She flicks her wrist back toward the print as I carry her across the threshold over her shaggy carpet. A four foot lava lamp veils Sky's white room in a minty blue. "Take anything—except them." My dream girl motions to two stuffed animals chilling on her round bed.

"Awesome!" I lay her on the plush unicorn and bat. "I'll take the wasted princess!" Sky smiles, pulls off my mouse ears and throws them. They hook over a glass column of jellyfish gurgling next to her cluttered desk. She kisses me as I tear off her torn jeans.

Sky naked is seriously unreal. Even before I got undressed my boner was out of control. A wayward wind rushes in through an open window to watch her grip it. Sky sloppily rubs the tip of my rod against her ass like Pollock painting with pre-cum. I bite below her ear and squirm behind her trying to slide my rod up between her legs. She wriggles. I can't get it in. I think she wants me to put it in her butt.

"I want you in me," she slurs. Beyond her powder blue shoulders, the lava orbs ooze like un-oxygenated blood cells floating in plasma. "Fuck me, Al."

I begin to flip her over. Sky resists.

"Okay, um…" I pant, my bod throbbing like an 18" kick, "I just…I don't wanna hurt you."

"You can't—" She turns her head back and kisses me with a dry mouth. "You can't. You won't. There—" She nods to a low dresser. "In the bottom drawer." It's so far away—from her.

"Can we start normal?" With the exception of those few killer seconds in The Barbie—which totally don't count—I can't even remember the last time I've had actual sex. It's been at least a week.

"Okay," Sky accedes, "Get the lube first."

Prying myself from her heat, I jam across the room and

throw open the drawer. It bangs on its track, rattling the slimy, artificially scented sex toys inside. I dig through black ankle cuffs, red vibrators, a gnarly whip covered in wilted pleather feathers, flavored lubes of every color. "Do you care what flavor?" I ask, holding a small bottle beneath my nose and squeezing to inhale puffs of a tropical surf-waxy scent.

"Huuurrrrrrrryyyyyy..." Sky opens her arms and arches her back like a cat. My boner kicks at the view. Her boobs stand up like little blue snowballs. I flashback to sledding with Marlena and Taylor as I shoot back to bed. Kneeled over Sky squirting a handful of goo, I slime up our rad-parts then slide inside her.

Everything below my abs is slippery and smells like coconut. I thought I was really going to have to work so to not immediately explode, but after a few wet, smacky thrusts, I feel—fuck—I feel weird. Sky was grinding back at first, for like a minute or two, but a second ago she stopped moving. She's probably just taking a break, I think, then pump a few more times and slowly pull out. Propping myself up on my palms, I stare down bummed. There's no fucking way I'm finishing inside her while she's a million miles away from me in drunken dreamland. Leaving Sky blacked-out, I kiss her dry, slightly parted perma-pout, and bail to the bathroom.

In the shower I think of The Barbie and giggle to myself as I blast a gallon of sperm against raspberry tiles. I wish she'd been here to witness the bogusness of our first bang sesh. She'd have loved it. I hope everything went cool with her and that dick-bag James. I crank the water to the handheld nozzle and hose jizz-cicles from the soap dish fixture, using my missile toe to wrangle the streaming troops around a bottle of peppermint-stick body wash and down the drain. Sky will be rad at fucking when she's not wasted. I know it.

I stare at the empty towel racks through the open shower door then take one long step to the thick bath mat edging against the open wicker hamper. I pull a towel from the top of the pile and pinch its corners. When I spread it to read the huge, swirly "SM" monogram, a ratty Drop Dead Gorgeous shirt falls to the floor. I unlatch the little bathroom window, toss the worn tee over a cliff, dry off, and creep back into the bedroom.

Sky's white desk is covered with Lucite ashtrays, pink note pads, and super old Tiger Beat magazines. Snatching my jacket from beneath it, I dig through the pockets then gently lay my denim on the curvy couch. My dream girl sleeps through a gust that rattles the shades, blowing blank prescription slips and ash across the icy carpet. I scavenge a handful of her butts from the floor, stash them in my denim, plug my phone into her wall charger, and drop to one knee. Her diamond sparkles like winter in the cool lava light as I raise it, blow off some ash, and whisper unrehearsed words of undying love to the darkness. Sky can't hear me now but she will tomorrow. Proposing at the tattoo shop after my name is permanently in her skin will be perf.

**** 

Sky's voice is muffled but the intensity of her murmur pulls me from a peacock nightmare. She's on the phone... somewhere. In the bathroom. From deep within her fluffy comforter, I squint at the hands of her antique bedside clock. Between the brass bells, I watch a luminous jellyfish descend in its tank and disappear below the desk. The shower turns on, and I fall back asleep until keys rattle me awake. "Sky?" I creak, "It's too early. Fuck David. Stay here." Through the dark, my dreamlike dream girl paces back from the hall. She crouches and kisses my cheekbone smelling like Christmas candy. Her lips are warm. I smile. In a slow blink I see checkered Vans bathed in a blue haze.

"I'm so sorry." she whispers. A massive Louis Vuitton overnighter is slung over the shoulder of what looks like Gumby PJs. "I adore you."

# S K Y

# CHAPTER 24

**Low clouds block the sun as high-end rides make their early rush hour crawl to and from Beverly Hills.** I'm perched and shivering on the LAXPRESS box outside of Shamrock Social Club watching for a black Mercedes SUV to appear from the east. My phone rattles on red metal next to me. I glance down at a preview string that reads *Fuckyoufuckyoufuckyou*. This kinda shit started coming in overnight. Except for Marlena's, the hate texts are anonymous. I'm over checking them. I pick up my phone and reopen Sky's accounts. I'm only worried about her.

Across the street Jamie Shannon's giant stupid face pouts at me from the Drop Dead Gorgeous billboard filling the whole west wall of The Roxy Theatre. A half block west, The back of K3NNY's head blinks onto the LED screen above the One Oak nightclub. I flip them both off and hang up on

Sky's voicemail for the zillionth time. It's time to call my BF Eff.

"Where the fuck are you?" The Barbie asks, speaking even more softly than usual. "Did you get my messages?"

"Not til a second ago, sorry. My phone was dead then I was at Sky's..." I look through tattoo shop's window and point at Mark Mahoney. He's on the phone too. "That her?" I mouth to the shop owner. He shakes his head as he continues to speak into the landline. I sigh and return to TB. "So what the fuck was up with last night?" I ask, recalling her cryptic but intense texts. "Did he stiff us or somethin'?"

"It got weird—shit—" I can hear Doug yelling for her to hang up. "I gotta go. Get over here. We need to talk."

Mahoney leans his old-timey pinstriped suit against the door jam and watches me hop down. The neon shamrock in the window glows green over his slicked, silvering hair.

"Fuck, sorry man." I pull out my thinning wad to try to make up for his super valuable time. "I don't know..." I break off four hundreds, and he waves away the cash. "Fuck. Thanks Mark." I pocket the bills and gaze east toward an untinted G550 headed our way. "She must be with Bruckheimer or somethin'—"

"Or somethin'..." Mark grabs my chin and turns my cheek to squint at his work. "We could add the word 'blue' above it," he suggests, breaking my balls. "Glad I talked you out of 'Monroe' now?"

"Aw, c'mon man." I smile, shaking my head as I shuffle to Lenore. "That's messed up. I'll text ya later to rebook."

# CHAPTER 25

**Kenny DOLL stands in front of Eff House behind an idling Bentley as it's being lit.** I park at the end of the driveway, blocking in the production trucks, and ask Doug if The Barbie is coming to set. The cranky producer mutters something unintelligible, and his PA tells me my BF Eff is waiting for me inside. When I march into her black hole room, TB springs from the edge of her bed, squints at my face in disbelief for like one second, then licks her thumb and starts rubbing at Sky's name.

"Fuck! OW!" I bat her hand. "Seriously!" My back slams against the black wall in retreat and a shelf of formaldehyde filled bottles rattles above my head. Ivory bones clack a witchy percussion—like a voodoo ceremony to rid me of my passions. The Barbie stays on me. I shield my face and reach up to unhook a bouncing antler. "Back off Cunt Dracula!" I raise the dead deer's defense like a stake. "Shit's fresh! I don't want whatever secret sex sores Kenny gave you—"

TB drops her hands and huffs. Walking across the dark wooden floor, she shuts her black door then sits back down. My BF Eff stares at me with disapproval beneath her octopus chandelier. I lower my brittle weapon and grin.

TB shakes her head and sighs, "I love you, babe, but you're an idiot."

"Love needs no IQ, TB." Rehanging her bones by their wires, I slip off my Vans, sock-slide across the room, and collapse down next to her. Her bible bounces near my face as I curl around her waist. "Ugh" nuzzling her tight black jeans, "I'm fucking demoed." The Barbie absently pets my head before flipping open the hollow scripture and pulling out an ivory pipe. The stinky buds are the strongest shit from the weed store down the street. They hook up all the Effs. "So what the fuck happened last night?" I ask, looking up from her thigh. "You catch James grippin' the Kane or what?"

"I think we might be in trouble, babe." TB slides open a matchbox. The devil on its cover sticks out its tongue at us as she strikes a black match against his sandy horns. She takes a dank hit before exhaling the whole story:

Last night, when she knocked on door #32 of the Alta Cienega Motel, Jamie undid the chains. Inside the lights were off. So was Drop Dead's shirt. "Wow," he said, "I can hardly look at you. You're too beautiful." He whipped his hair over his eyes and bowed. "Please enter."

The scuzzy room was just as Sky had described it. Sticks of burning incense poked from white crystals arranged across the nasty inset air-conditioner. Drop Dead's favorite Black WICKed candles lit Jim Morrison poetry scrawled all over the walls. I guess The Lizard King actually lived there for a minute.

As she stepped through the doorway, James told her he and Jim had a lot in common, asked for the Anger, and she tossed him the coke. Catching the baggy, and doing what she described as an "elf dance," James clapped, tied his hair on top of his head, and sat down at a small table by the window. The thick smoky drapes were closed. Railing up on a beat-up bible, James snorted over the croak of draining water as light and steam seeped from under the closed bathroom door. Red clippers sat unplugged on the counter next to the sink amidst skull shaped bottles of cologne. Long black locks wormed over the chipped floor tiles toward the thin stained carpet. With her Balenciaga boots crunching torn psalms and clumps of hair, The Barbie demanded her money. James wiggled his fingers toward the nightstand without looking up from the silver straw. She marched over and grabbed the thin stack of cash from under a reissued Polaroid camera.

"Um, what the fuck am I supposed to do with this?" TB asked, fanning three crisp hundreds. "Get coffee?"

James waved away the thought. "No. Leave it—leave it there. You'll give that to your other friend soon." He smiled before doing another bump and directed her to a travel bag next to the bed. "Alvin's is in there." Discarding the hundreds, she grabbed the bowler bag and began to bail. "Wait!" James jumped up from the desk and followed her to the door. "Partake!" he insisted, offering the bible like a plate of hors d'oeuvres. "Have you tried it? It's organic. Partake." TB checked the bag and, confirming the cash was inside, told him coke wasn't her thing and re-zipped the 20k. "Well then..." he said, touching her face like a lascivious babe-beating, gay-bashing, child-molesting drug-fuck, "How about bromance? Does that turn you on?" The Barbie told him to keep his hands to himself and smacked them away. The thin Bible hit the floor, dusting the air with organic coke, and James pinned TB to the door while giggling. As he started licking her neck, grabbing her tits, and biting her shoulders, she fought back and yelled for him to get the fuck off her. Then Score ran out of the bathroom wearing only a towel and holding a knife.

"He essentially has a flat top now." TB faces her reflection in the iron door mirror and barely drops her jaw. Smoke spills from her full lips like a lethargic, toxic waterfall. She bites off the flow and, turning back to me with the click of her teeth, details, "Bleached. Jamie said he'd put him in his next video if he cut it all off and partied with him."

I jump up, announcing that I'm extremely late for a murder, and jam for the door.

"Slow down, babe." My soft-spoken soldier continues her story. "So," she goes on, sliding her bible back into a black bookshelf lined with folders filled with pressed bugs. "Score was pointing his switchblade like some magic pink sword or something and kept spitting on the carpet and yelling all tough-guy, like, 'Motherfucker keep your hands off her.' I think he was trying to sound like Batman—he was super high but there's no way he'll admit it." TB casually crosses the room to an ornate Chinese cabinet, slides open a small drawer, and continues. "When James stopped molesting me for a second to turn toward Score, I pulled out my luger and shot him..." Steel clinks as she rummages through a collection of antique scissors shaped like cranes. "...Once in the dick, once in the balls." Making a gun with her fingers, The Barbie faces me and whispers "POP POP! Gangster." Electronic keys dangle from the thin velvet rope hung from her pantomime barrel.

Laughing, I raise my fists in celebration. "Yes! That fucking rules!" The Barbie squats with a tiny smile. As she reaches behind the red sheet of silk hanging from the front edge of the desk, the gaping sliced collar of her Sex Gang Children tee droops to reveal a small row of purple bruises on her shoulders. Sickened, I ask, "Are those his fucking teeth marks? TB, are you sure you're cool? I fuckin' swear—"

"Babe, c'mon. He didn't even break the skin. I'm fine." She adjusts her hem to cover the Drop Dead damage and slides out a piece of luggage. "But James, not so much. When I shot him he buckled over onto Score's knife." A gold monogram crumples in mocha leather as she unzips a Louis Vuitton bowler bag. "They both started screaming then Score and I got the fuck out of there. I grabbed you some souvenirs while James was bent over bleeding. He was giggling like a freak and kept yelling your name over and over. I don't know what that was all about...." The Barbie stands, gripping our spoils. "He bled a lot."

"No. Way. Did Drop Dead drop dead?"

TB shrugs, and slips a thin stack of small Polaroids into a stack of cash. I nod at the thousands. "Can I borrow that? I wanna buy Score a bat-cat as a 'thank you.' Where is he?" She shrugs again. "He was freakin' pretty bad as we were bailing. He kept saying how fucked we were and how puffy he was, then when we got to my car he said that he needed to lay low and took off running. He almost knocked over some crazy chick that was walking through the lot in kids' pajamas. I woulda thought it was Sky if I didn't know that she was busy giving you bad head in Never Everland. So..." She eyes the swollen name above my eyebrow like an unconfessed STD. "She said yes?"

"There was drama..." I pace to the door mirror and, peering through the shadows, check for tattoo damage. "Nothin' to do with her really. It's cool." I wish. I shove a hand in my jacket and squeeze the ring. "When she gets my name put on her butt I'm gonna—"

Doug bangs on the door, startling the shit out of me.

"Get it over with and get on set!" he barks as the hanging iron mirror clangs, bouncing on its hook. "We're ready on the Twilight Sleeper." The Barbie shakes her head at him, or me.

"I've gotta make-up and make-out with Kenny."

"Gross!" I cringe at my reflection. "When'd he get back?"

"He flew in with Skrillex and ZEDD on his PJ last night."

"Lammmmmme," I groan, falling back into the mattress's blackness. "I really wanted to crash in here with you tonight— it's been a pretty fucked few days." I fold my hands beneath my head and smile. "You can still let me though. We'll cuddle. Doll-dick can have the couch."

"Well, that's the real bad news, babe." The Barbie shoves the loot bag back beneath the desk then, still holding the keys and cash, paces over. "He told Doug that he'd only come back to the show if you were gone."

I sit up. "What? Like, gone gone? I'm over?" She nods, and I raise both my middle fingers in the general direction of the producer's muffled dick-voice. Fuck. I don't want to go back to The Ark. And even if I did want to, I couldn't now. Noah made that pretty clear. Maybe he's right. Maybe I am dead in this town. I hold my head, staring up at the white remains of the baby deer's head. I wonder if Drop Dead is dead. Hope so.

When the Barbie pops up at my feet and steps towards me, it feels like a comfort kitten is padding across the mattress. I really wish I could stay. Standing over me, like she did that morning two days ago, though now it seems like two months, my BF Eff gazes down at my defeat. I wrap my hands around her sockless ankles. "TB...what am I gonna do?"

She motions for me to sit up. I prop myself on my palms in a supported crunch position and The Barbie leans over, looping the velvet cord around my neck. "I told Mom that Dad's back in the country so she went to Mexico," she explains. "She won't be back at the Malibu house anytime soon."

Holding my new access charms, I ask, "Seriously?"

TB looms, blocking the extremely dim light of the bare bulbs growing from the glazed tentacles of her resin chandelier. "You should probably get out of Hollywood anyway, babe." Her butt bounces onto my lap. "Like, now." She wraps her legs tightly around me and brings her face close to mine "There aren't any idiots crying online about him yet but if that bag of dicks is still alive and groping he could still tell the cops. I really don't think Jamie's dumb enough to bring that kinda attention down on himself but ya never know, we did kinda stab him..." I try to argue, bringing up churchy fans and Christian labels, but TB interrupts. "I know." she insists, "But he could still send some sketchball for you or Score or—fuck, even me. That's what rich people do. That's what I'd do."

"He's not gonna—"

"Babe, yesterday some goateed monster was creeping around here asking for you. It felt super sketchy. I mean, I don't know why Jamie would send a guy in a sling—"

"Oh, naw, that's nothing—" I try to play it cool as I firmly discount the real threat that is Abbi. "That was just a scraper from my old crew—"

"Okay. But babe, Drop Dead still could send people. Plus, I think that Snowsimian kid's in LA and he—"

"Fuck Alexa's weak stalker, fuck the cops, and fuck Drop Dead. I'll—"

The Barbie's two-second kiss traps my rant in her parted lips then, pulling back, TB gives me a too-real look. "Listen, I don't want you hurt and I don't feel like visiting you in jail. And where else are you gonna go? Who knows, if some sketchball shows up asking about me I might be joining you...here." She presses the stack of cash to my chest. "You're taking it. If you don't, I'm taking back the keys." I try to protest, and she tugs on their cord.

"Fuck." I finally accede. "Thanks, TB. You're the best."

"Correct." She smiles, slaps my tattoo and steps off the bed. "Anything for you, babe." And, like a guardian vampire, she's gone.

I lay there with my hands over my face and my "Sky" tattoo screaming with sting, moaning for a while before I eventually stand to shuffle through the dark back to the sewing desk. I crouch and slide the loot out from under the cool silk. When I unzip the smaller version of the Louis Vuitton bag Sky was carrying this morning, I smell expensive incense, money, and Paralysis. I slip the rectangular Polaroids from the stack and flip through the small, poorly developed prints. After pocketing three delightful yet useless POV photos of what must be Jamie's dick getting sucked by an unidentifiable bleached blonde dude (with, essentially, a flat top), I return the gifted cash, close the bowler, pull out my phone, and tap my flashlight. My beam illuminates the fading initials "SM" as the director calls, "Rolling! Annnnnd...action!"

# CHAPTER 26

**Lenore's windows are cracked open.** Hot, and super bothered, I awake in the vacant lot above the WEHO flats. Birds chirp from within the vast leafy hedge, barricading me from the main road, as the sun breaks through the windshield. The scent of Drop Dead permeates my squatter snot as I sniff, wipe my clammy palms on my clammy chest and sit up in my reclined driver seat, hazily wondering why the fuck my car still smells like Paralysis. The RATT tee that I balled into a pillow now feels like I found it on the floor of the steam room. Pushing the cling-on shirt from my shoulders, I peel an animal printed Anger bag from my cheek, flick it away, and dig my shades from under my hip. I un-bend the twisted arms, slide them over my ears and stumble out from Lenore to stand in the dirt, look to the sky and stretch in the sun - gonna be a normal, summery, winter day in Hollywood. Stupid fucking heat.

My tongue feels like it's been grip-taped. I shuffle in the dust barefoot and shirtless, smacking my lips and folding my hands above my head. My tweaked joints crunch, and I gaze uphill. Sky's house is as dead as the architectural skeleton, rising from the end of this unpaved driveway. I picture myself pushing her intercom button for the millionth time once the lights turn themselves on tonight, and feel worse. Leaning back into Lenore, I crank her key. She rumbles awake just as Kevin and Bean announce Seth Rogan. "Make me laugh, man." I'm stiff, but I feel as gooey as K3NNY looks. I haven't worked out since I got kicked out of Eff House. When I bailed, not even bothering with the pathetic DJ, I slashed Doug's back tire, asked Sky's voicemail if I could stay with her, drove here, and started camping in her soon-to-be neighbor's lot. I think that was three nights ago—maybe two. Quickly crouching below the hedge, I peer through sleeping flowers at an approaching black and white sedan—just neighborhood security creeping by. Yesterday I saw two cops cruising. I'm glad it's not them again, though I think I'd rather confront the WEHO PD than the scrapers. Either way, The Barbie's right. I really need to get out of town. I just don't want to leave Sky.

To keep my position lo-pro, I twist down the radio's volume nob and lean back into Lenore to grab my phone from its new charger. Seth's gravely voice whispers about weed as I scroll through socials. Sky's not posting, but her accounts are like the 5 freeway during construction. If you Google her name right now, you'll see us kissing at Disneyland. Some 323 number tagged the photo #whores and sent it to me right before it went viral. I have no idea why. I pull an itchy shred of yellow insulation from my heel and re-open the saved shot. Stoked on it, hating it, I stand at my open driver's door and stare down at our stolen fairytale moment wondering if Sky likes it at all as another flood of messages begins. I erase the latest British slang threats from @snowsimian, Marlena's sour pleas for attention and scolding for the Tay Tay "attack," and screenfuls of poorly written scraper hatred. Then I call Alexei. His shot wasn't big money—no head to toe, our faces were obscured—but whatever little cash was made at the expense of my love life went to that motherfucker. I'm sure David is keeping Sky from me because of it. I use my nights of practice to match Alexei's '80s villain accent as I threaten his voicemail again and dig a Trader Joes bottle from under my gym bag. I'm dehydrated and kinda nauseous.

Chugging warm water, avoiding stray bolts and nails, I march up the drive and between naked beams stand at the edge of the concrete foundation below the unfinished balcony of a future multi-million dollar home. "I just tasted you on the mouth of my bottle." I type with traces of booze on my lips, pissing over Hollywood. "I'm gonna bail. Come live with me. The Bu house is bitch'n." My latest invitation to Sky pops into the endless string of my uninterrupted blue bubbles, and I toss the empty bottle into a pile of sawdust. Warm wizz spatters on my toes. This is all so fucked.

I drift back through the framework, buttoning most of my fly beneath the latent construction before I crumple into Lenore. I wait for Sky to respond, hoping she's not blacked-out somewhere for good. Kevin and Bean talk about Jamie's record. The Barbie texts me to "pick up the landline." I switch stations and tug the key at the end of my velvet necklace. With visions of that babe-thief David, a bloody Drop Dead, and the MIA, no longer shaggy-haired Score running through my brain, I lower my sun visor and flip open the mirror. The reddened Sky reflects over my eye. I tap the puffy skin around the script and wince. At least the tattoo stings less than my fucking calf.

I can feel it oozing against my jeans.

I check the rainbow around my bird bite with my heel pressed to the dash. Beyond my toes a black SUV jams uphill, cutting around the only visible curve at the bottom of Sky's street. I shut the door, throw back my seat, crank down the window, and listen. The huge hedge is completely obscuring Lenore from the road, but I still wanna be careful. Some of the threatening texts—particularly Abbi's—are starting to semi-rattle me. Seth chuckles to hedge bird song, as I slow my breath waiting for the possible scraper danger to pass.

****

"Dustin...Dustin." The gentle voice speaking my birth name kinda sounding like the Blue Fairy from Pinocchio. "Alvin, wake up," it softly demands, and I pry open my lids. Dramaramma is on the radio. I'm holding the blurred SOHO photo strip in my relaxed grip. The Unicorn and The Truebloods' sequined gowns sparkle in the twilight through the open window. Thin silvery harnesses cut lines over their broad shoulders. I dust my eyeballs blinking awake, wondering if they're wearing holsters. "We're still trying." Cam casts his faux bright blues down upon me. "She needs you. But you can't stay here. He knows now."

Behind The Unicorn, standing like a wispy, shimmery shadow against the ten-foot wall of hedge, Jaq smokes a golden cigarette watching me. Hundreds of punch colored night blooms burst beyond his black serpentine updo. He takes a drag. His gold fangs glint as he French inhales. The smoke smells like gingerbread lattes. A Santa Ana gust blows a lone petal across his cheek and over to me. It cools my bare belly. I blow it to the floor with a puff then croak, "Sup, dudes?"

An A$AP Rocky ringtone plays. Jaq shows Cam the caller's

ID. The Unicorn disapprovingly shakes his loose lavender curls at the flashing screen. Without accepting or denying the call, Jaq drops the phone into his purse and clicks shut the moth wings of a golden latch. A$AP's tone is muffled. Cam gazes toward West Hollywood then back down at me. "You have to go," he insists and, sharing an almost indiscernible expression of sadness with Jaq, they turn. Their silken wings flutter and trap stray night blooms in the wind as they disappear from my window.

It doesn't take me more than a minute before I regain enough awareness to absorb whatever the fuck just happened. Creeping Lenore up and down the hills, stalking the neighborhood trying to find out what the fuck is up with my girl, I yell their names. But The Mythicals are gone. They're just fucking gone. Sighing a "fuck" of defeat, I follow their fucking advice and head for the flats.

****

I wasn't planning to stop but when I hit 9200 Sunset, I cut into the valet beneath the tower. The Soho House reception chick totally remembers me but when I ask if Sky is upstairs, she says, "I can't give you that information."

"Well, have you seen her, like, at all?" I lean into the tall desk accidentally knocking over a small lamp. "I think she may have been murdered. Or babenapped. It's really—"

"I'm sorry but I just can't give you that information, sir."

"Sir, you!" I point a rattling lampshade at her. "Why are you being a bitch right now?"

"Sir." She glances toward valet, now looking even more bitchy than she did a second ago. "If you're not a member I'm going to have to ask you—"

"Whatever. Blood's on your hands, baby—" Safely

replacing the light, I turn and march straight into some short dude.

"Watch where you're going, buddy" he says, and tries to step around me.

I block him from the exit. "Oh, I'm your buddy now?" Grinning, I look way down and strongly suggest, "Why don't you tell me where the fuck Sky is and maybe then we can be buddies?"

David Fass furrows his little brow then turns to the sour desk babe. "You know this kid?" I throw him to the ground.

"You know exactly who the fuck I am fucker! I'm not A-list enough, huh?" I edge him across the carpet into the leather couch, lower the volume of my words and up their reality. "Fuck you, you Hollywood-yoga-fuck miniature. I can do more for her than you ever could."

"Hey—hey—kid!" He springs up in his orange shoes and backs into the elevator button. "I have no idea who you are or what you're talking about so why don't you just calm down before I get the cops over here." With his back to the wall, he dusts the leather elbows of his deconstructed blazer. Two big suited arms pin mine to my side. One of the fingers has an X tattoo.

"Chongo," whispers Martín, "You fuckin' crazy? Leave it."

I relax, and my friend walks me out. When I turn back Sky's agent is telling the desk girl she doesn't have to call the cops. "Hey, thanks David," I smile. "Keep me from my wife and I will fucking bury you in your weak sneakers. Tell Sky I love her hard." Shaking his head, Martín escorts me to Lenore. I tip him and the valet a hundred each and peel out.

As I'm speeding west toward the turn that leads to The Ark, an eastbound SUV makes a sudden sketchy left from the far right lane. Punching my horn, I swerve. The black Porsche whizzes up into Noah's neighborhood, and I gas it past wire reindeer and menorahs twinkling beneath rich people palms on sprawling green lawns. My phone buzzes. I erase a "FUCK YOU DISLOYAL SHIT!" text from some Beverly Hills number, glance into my rearview, and charge un-followed to Sunset's end.

# CHAPTER 27

## The oceanside Chevron is empty.

Easing up to the pumps, I hop out, give the register kid a hundred, and gas up. Digital dollars disappear as I lean against Lenore's grill facing the Pacific. Her metallic hood heats my thin denim and, freeing my ass before it bakes, I stand too quickly. The beach swells and deflates like I've swallowed something from The Barbie's bible. I press the cartilage of my left ear until the brain banshee chills out. My stomach makes a rodent sound. I rifle through the backseat with futile hope of finding an uneaten protein bar then the pump clicks off.

Capping my tank, I snag my keys and march back into the mini-mart. The register kid must be in the bathroom. I scan the shelves. The bad snacks look more disgusting than usual, like nightmare cartoon candy. The colors of the energy drink cans are making me sick. I grab a large bottle of Fiji from a cold case before firing behind the counter and swiping a box of smokes. I slap an extra fifty on the register, march back to Lenore, and burn up PCH.

I suck down cool briny air in heavy breaths with the radio cranked and Vega wrappers fluttering around the backseat. Def Leppard shreds through my speakers. Joe Elliot sings "Photograph. All I got is a—" as, to my left, dark waves awesomely crash against the shore. Pulling the blurry strip down from my sun-visor, I release my sharp Soho House photobooth memories into the night. The smooth highway ahead glints like a flawless glitter-rock road to salvation, like a black and white art film set in SoCal heaven, and I'm no more than two miles away from a private beach house that's all mine. Capping my bottle I shift Leonard, crank across the double yellows, and slam my breaks with tires crunching on the shoulder. I kick open the door, jump out, and barf into a beach bush in the spotlight of the high beams. The aching bite on my leg throbs like a puke-pulse with every empty wretch. I spit up burning bile. There's nothing left in me. I miss Sky. I fucking hate LA.

# MAI

IBU

# CHAPTER 28

## I haven't been listening to music.

I haven't felt like it. The Barbie's beach house has been quiet since I stopped unloading rounds into the sand from the balcony off the master bedroom. Like a gift from a gangster tooth fairy, my Deagle now just chills beneath my pillow. I've considered pulling the trigger one more time but I guess I won't. Sky may not give a fuck but The Barbie would be bummed if I Cobained, especially here in her mom's place. I burst up into the darkness awaking with one lame sob. My heart pounds like a blast beat beneath the crash of the Pacific. Mid dream, I stopped breathing, IRL—again. "Fuck." I wipe my head on the damp cotton sheets, checking and confirming my solo status in the latest borrowed bed. "Fucking good dreams. The worst."

I stand at the foot of the overthrown California King and light a Lucky. On the pastel-blue nightstand the soft pack sits crushed, like me, next to an overflowing ceramic squid ashtray. My unplugged charger cord drowns in the inches of ash and unfiltered butts. Taking a drag, I stare across the open room out the balcony doors toward the black waves wondering how long I've been in the Bu—what time is it?—and if Sky ever messaged me. I ash into the sucker of a puce tentacle and drag myself over the clean wooden floor. The swan lamp throws a seasick shadow of my grimy figure across the pale walls as a sweet and salty breeze slips from the sea to chill my thin layer of nightmare sweat. I keep the windows open. I figured the sound of the ocean would lull me to sleep. It didn't at first. For fuckin' days I was awake shooting my gun, drinking TT, and obsessing over Sky's inactive accounts. But that stopped. After using my phone as a flying target, I was forced to find better shit to do.

Shivering, I scan the hardwood floor for my grey hoodie. It's arm reaches out to me from beneath the bed but the few steps aren't worth the warmth. The sun will be up in a second. I shuffle toward the stately armoire with my cigarette dangling from my lips, wiping my palms on my thighs. Sky's ring snags on my camo boxers. I raise my hand and squint through the stinging smoke at a small drab thread wrapped around the twenty thousand dollar diamond. Snapping it from the stone's setting, I drop it and unhook my Mickey ears from the cabinet's latch. The smell of coastal morning cuts through the Lucky smoke. My eyes water as I strap on the ears.

My mouse ears make me feel a little better. I guess I've been doing better in general since I shot my phone. With my Apple's shards out there in the waves I obsess over Sky a little less. And you know what? I feel like I may have actually just slept all night for the first time—but the breathtaking nightmares still gotta go. In that last dream back there I proposed, and Sky kissed me beneath Disney fireworks. I felt her next to me in bed, whispering "yes" into my ear. I hear the brutal echo as I look back toward the empty twist of smoky cream-colored sheets.

A kinky landline extends out to the balcony from the jack behind the armoire. Treading it like a tightrope, I step through the open doors onto the slick tiled deck and around two chairs. The pastel-blue paint on their wooden rungs is chipped. The round center table has held up better but not much. A city of votives stands staggered at its weathered center. At the edge of candle-town an antique peach-colored oyster shell phone sits next to a basket of mail. Along with bottles of Chanel nail polish, a stone pufferfish holds down the curling, mist-swollen envelopes. I've been meaning to bring the mail back inside for TB's mom—when I get the strength. I eye the velvet cord worming across a to-go menu over the wicker's edge then shuffle to the southern railing. I have no recollection of dropping the keys in the mail basket. Since Hollywood, most everything has been a hopeless blur. Well, until I picked up my camera again. Lately shit's been clearing up through my lens.

I lean my forearms on cool plaster tightening the elastic strap around my chin and smoke over the rail as the first light slips across my rooftop. A string of driftwood chatters behind me. At the hollow sound of the wind chimes, my blonde arm hairs stand like their favorite singer just took the deck. I rub them flat, lurking in the useless young light. Far down shore, big colorful flags wave from my neighbor's deck like they're welcoming royalty from the west. I can almost make out their silkscreened graphics. Taking a final drag, I survey the unlit three-story house. The babe is always on dawn patrol but it's too early. She's still inside. I've got time for a drink. I snuff my Lucky into the graveyard of butts jutting from the dirt of the succulent planter then grab my camera and march down the tight winding staircase to the kitchen.

The broad island countertop looks like it's been covered in white confetti. At it's far end, amidst scraps of rolling papers next to an electric kettle, sits an enormous wooden fruit bowl. Returning from the pantry with my appropriated mason jar, I dump the remainder of my filched butt collection next to my borrowed LACMA mug and pinch one of the four green fruits stacked atop the yellow citrus in the bowl. Just yesterday, these were harder than Pantera. My fingers sink into thin waxy skin before I click on the kettle. If I ever feel better enough to be hungry, I'll make guac, I promise myself, gathering the avocados and opening the fridge. I squint in the flood of soft light then awkwardly stash the ripening fruit in a produce drawer. My empty stomach cries like a baby being dropped from a cliff as I investigate the stocked shelves. Every high-end organic thing that TB's mom left in her rapid flight from her ex-husband—every vibrant vegetable, every colorful cold-pressed juice, even the Trader Joe's chocolate syrup that I use in my tobacco tea—looks gross. "Fuck," I sigh, seeing no alternative, and grab the Midnight Moo. When I asked Star for help, before I shot my phone, she said I've gotta use "twice the sweet for the bitters" to make the love spell work. That's a lot of fucking sweet.

I shut the fridge, set the syrup on the counter next to my mug, and stretch out on the floor. Flat on my back, I watch the bubbles frantically break from the base of the silent kettle to swim up for air. When they finally catch a breath, they explode. I squirm on the tiles. Knots of lethargy and nightmares battle through my shoulders and neck against the cold slate. The knots are prevailing. I try to relax not wanting to be the bubbles. I exhale. My infected calf spasms, and I scream. Frantically gripping the stainless oven rung, I pull myself to my feet, grab my toes, and stretch. Steam whistles. My bird bite throbs. I pant from the stupid deep pain as the cramp settles then, regaining my balance, I pour the water and start the ritual.

"Sky Monroe, Sky Monroe," I whisper, picturing her face and wishing her to wish for me while crushing tobacco shreds from her butts into the mug. "Sky Monroe." Grabbing the bottle, I pop the top and choke it above the steam. Moo spatters over my boxers down to my bird bite. Whatever. I pull a teaspoon from the sink and stir in the chocolate until the water darkens. I return the little spoon with a toss and it sings its daily song clattering against the glazed pottery basin. In silent ceremony I raise my potion, sip, and shudder.

Mug in fist, covered in Moo, horrible bittersweet taste in mouth, I grimace and pad around the island counter to the breakfast nook. My laptop charges next to my Canon on the coral stained table. Posting-up on the long window seat in front of my computer, I set down the tobacco tea and flip up my monitor. My Mac whirs to life as the oyster shell begins clamoring upstairs. That thing sounds like a history lesson from a prof with a hearing problem. I glance from the digital clock on my screen to the empty beach before looking toward the primitive ringing. The Barbie must be just getting into bed. It's gotta be her who keeps calling. Though she's the only person I could even half imagine speaking to right now, and though I kinda want to, I'm too rattled to answer. I blankly stare at my background, take another taste of the wretched steaming TT, and listen. The old-timey bells chime on. If I pick up, The Barbie will tell me shit I don't want to hear. And then I'll get the wifi password and then I'll be punishing myself with

Sky's profiles instead of doing this.

My unfinished project opens with a click, hiding the desktop image of my damning Disney kiss. Somewhere, surely wasted, TB finally hangs up her phone. I table the mug and get my mind and hands on my work. In this shot I've turned yesterday's clouds magenta but they're still too dull, and not nearly killer enough, compared to the surfer underneath. As I begin enhancing them, sunlight barges into the kitchen to mute their trippy billows. I turn toward the window's annoying glare, and uttering "Yeeeees!" save the project, and stand. My unsuspecting mojito-haired model struts along Barbie Beach carrying a bigger board than she's ridden in any of my photos. She confidently strides through the dawn in her purple and black cheetah printed wetsuit toward the waves between our pads. Chugging the remainder of my bogus magic, I ditch the mug, grab my Canon, and fire out the back door to capture more of her radness.

# CHAPTER 29

**I lean against a tacky wooden post that smells like tar in the slatted deck shade.** A triple sand gnat cluster flies in my face. Gulls peck at shook crabs burrowing beneath the tide. A single wispy cloud owns the Bu sky. After an hour of bobbing in and out of cover, I've got the surf chick all over my memory card. But she's left the beach. So I think I'm safe. I scamper out from under the deck, gripping my Canon and kicking up warm sand, and make my twenty-yard dash to the stairway that crawls up the side the house. My plastic ears whistle in the wind as I bound up the splintered steps unseen.

Behind the gates of this private Bu community, locks are whatever. Rich people steal from rich people but they don't rob one another's houses. I hop on one foot through the gaping door into the kitchen grinning at my screen as I flip through my latest session. I've got some great shit to work on here. If I don't fuck it up, I may be able to put together a pretty killer show with these shots. I table my Canon in the nook, and my latent lats twinge from my stealth twist below the deck. I stretch and groan. My brain is getting better. Now it's time to get the brawn back to bitch'n. I limp over the kitchen tiles and up the hall to the half-bath. I'm going to clean the sandy syrup from my wound, sauce it with some salve, go downstairs, and get big.

****

I push open the windows, grab a coconut water from the mini fridge, and begin trotting on the gym's treadmill. All the equipment in here smells and looks new. I tap the touchscreen. It beeps like a Martin Garrix beat. The slatted belt whirs faster. This shit hurts but whatevs. I've gotta warm up. The endorphins will kick in to help.

I ignore my leg's cease and desist orders, and think about art and babes. My bare feet bounce on the rubber. I picture the surfer girl's minty hair stretched like tendrils of swirling taffy over a pink wave. I turn to my head-to-toe reflection and check myself out. I smack my flat belly. My cut abs turn pink. Despite my beard and puffy hair, I still look good after what has to be at least a week of zero training—it's crazy but thank fuck it's true. My lungs burn. I cough once. I can almost hear that sweet southern belle yelling from the window of her SF flat, demanding that I quit smoking again. When I have my gallery show I'll fly Lucky down, I decide, glancing at the healed tattoo above my eye before quickly turning away. I watch a private jet glide over the ocean through the window. For some fucked reason my stupid brain attacks me with an image of Uncle Noah on his knees with my cock in his mouth. My rod retreats into itself, and I tap the treadmill's screen beeping upward to 12 mph. I grab my cold coconut water from the cup holder. Pavéd diamonds gleam from the blue cardboard as I kill the drink and crush the box. A painfully familiar dream voice whispers "yes." Shook by the sound, I shoot the box into the bin by the fridge and tap the screen. My legs fly faster. I pant. 14 miles per hour. My brain empties into the warming air. My pulse fills the void in my healing head, drumming on my temples like Bonham. Been a long lonely lonely lonely lonely lonely time. A drop of sweat trickles from the Zep beat toward my jaw. My eyelids relax into a sober squint. I breathe. My glistening bird bite throbs silently begging me to stop. I go faster. The medicine cabinet didn't have anything helpful—just a bunch of mood meds that I swiped to someday give to The Barbie as a thank you. "TB's rad" I think, and the voice in my head glitches, repeating the phrase until it dissipates, until there is nothing. No pain, no names, no Bonham—only breath. I run from it, hard. I can't let it catch me.

# CHAPTER 30

**The sleep twitch jolts me like a California quake.** Herbal water splashes out onto the floor as I grip the tub's edges and push myself up. Bubbles tickle my mouth. Wiping away their bitterness, baffled to have slept through sunset, I stand and turn from a pervy red planet, peering at me over the French soaps that line the windowsill. It checks out my tingling, sleepy buns, and I flip on the lights. I was destroyed from the brutal muscle-up sesh that followed my warm-up—makes sense that I passed out for so long.

Relieved I didn't have a nightmare, I brace myself against the seafoam wall and grab my foot to inspect my wounded leg. The extended soak in tea tree salts didn't help the bite much. I swipe a towel from the hook on the door, pat some puss, and gently lower my foot onto the shaggy mat. The brown snail embroidered on the green cotton cinched around my waist chills over my rod as I limp to the nightstand, strap on my ears, shake out a Lucky, light up, and head out to the balcony.

The Bu sky is housing more stars than Chateau Marmont. Beneath this moon, the ocean looks like the battleground from the Pirates of the Caribbean ride. Easing into a creaking wooden chair, I prop my foot on a planter and shuffle through disintegrating junk mail. The warm breeze soothes my bitchy bite and bare skin. Relaxed, peeling a blue photocopy from a Cross Fit circular, I stick my finger in the phone and crank. The rotary dial stutters backward. I do it again—awkward but kinda fun. Hiding up here is cool. I'm pretty okay right now. I'm actually starving instead of nauseated, and I'm not even bummed on how fucking long it's taking to dial 7 fucking numbers.

"D'amore's." A dude answers, confirming my suspicion that this night is not yet a senior citizen. "Can I help you?"

"Uh..." Kinda shocked that the antique talking machine works, I unfold the damp menu and squint. "Bianca sounds hot. I'll get a large her. Forget the cheese." Twisting gravely words over my cigarette, I ask, "What kind of drinks ya got?" My voice cracks, and I realize this pizza guy is the first real human I've spoken to since I left Hollywood. I tap the tip of my Lucky into the city of wicks at the center of the table and order an Arnold Palmer. The flames of candle town struggle to survive as I lip my smoke and flip over the mailer. I rattle off the 90265 delivery address and carry the 2 lb phone base to the railing. The long coiled cord bounces against my ribs as stronger flames rise up to lick the night down shore.

The surfer chick sits cross-legged in the sand with a large yerba matte gourd in her lap watching a bonfire. Her tiny red shorts are teaching the tall flames how to be hot while a hooded figure feeds them what appear to be bible verses—at least that's what I'd guess since the cloaked figure looks like a witch wearing giant sunglasses. The black magician casually tears out pages, throwing them to their fiery death. My mojito-haired muse sucks tea through her straw as the D'amore guy tells me I've gotta wait forty five minutes for my pizza.

"Make it forty-four and there's and extra twenty in it for ya." I clap the shell phone shut, flatten myself across the warm sculpted rail, and watch the smoke.

****

There's no tomato sauce on it but this weird pizza is pretty rad. My show might be rad too, I decide, slowly nodding at my Mac then, with a sigh, take one more beach-temp bite and box the final slice. Passionately, I swipe my greasy touchpad a few more times before leaning back in the chipped wooden deck chair. I inspect the sickness on my monitor. I dip-dyed a gull to compliment the surf babe's hair and tweaked the pantones of the Pacific into zebra stripes. "Kinda killer..." I say to myself. Someone says "Fabulous", and I turn toward the small sneaky sound. The dude on the phone isn't yelling but his voice is clear enough to make out that he's a warlock and not a witch. I grab my Arnold Palmer and creep back over to the rail.

The fire down shore is dwindling. Alone now, the lanky figure paces through the smoke rapidly chattering. His giant touchscreen glows through his billowy hood. I suck down the last of my watery, lemony tea as the warlock flits his free hand like he's being attacked by night-gnats. He's pissed off—or stoked. Either way, someone's saying some gnarly shit to him. I shake small ice beads into my mouth peering over the waxy rim. The dude does a spazzy jump, gazes behind him toward the babe's house, and taps off his call. The glow of his phone dies. With cloak flowing like a skinny supervillian, he boots over the sand toward the flags.

I plop back into my chair, table my cup, and scroll through a new catalog. My mojito muse fills the monitor. She stares straight into the camera—straight into my rock'n'roll soul. I zoom. Her pseudo-detached expression is familiar, like the look the pros turn on when my flash strobes through the clubs. This surf babe is fuckin' pretty. Raising my eyes, I watch the embers rise and disintegrate into Bu nothing hoping to see her return to the dying fire.

# CHAPTER 31

**Feeling like I slept on the sun, I awake on the balcony, sweating facedown next to my computer.** I guess I passed out. I'm probably the color of Sebastian the crab, but at least I had another night without a fucking nightmare. Still missing Sky never-the-fucking-less, I peel my cheek from the table and drag myself across the dew-slicked deck tiles downstairs to concoct my daily magic. I carry the last of the butts' boiled guts to the hallway half-bath and stare at the red man in the mirror with endlessly plummeting hope. I pick a blue paint chip from my slatted temple and another from my flourishing beard, drink about a gallon of The Bu's finest sink water, then empty the linen closet.

I limp into The Barbie Beach Theater with a ball of oceanic bedding, a throbbing leg, the final mug of TT, and a stupid dying heart. After building a nest, I bail onto the floor at the foot of the 8 plush recliners that form the front row, and flick some celebrity gossip onto the big screen. This was a bad idea. But here I am.

TMZ shouts at me from the TV screen, declaring "Skamie," the new power couple. Apparently Jamie Shannon is alive, seemingly uninjured, and has changed his status to "in a relationship." I squirm on the thin carpeting, learning from Sky herself that Drop Dead Gorgeous is having his exclusive record release party at some intimate, undisclosed Hollywood club. He'll be screening the "first movement of the three part film celebrating his record." Streaming live from Jamie's Brooklyn practice pad, she tells the camera she can't wait to be there. Cut to a bigger than-life-sized image of her and Drop Dead snuggled up in a red velvet booth at the Boom Boom Room. They kiss over Manhattan. A jubilant voiceover actor announces "For Shannon, The Sky is not the limit!!!" I groan, spit back the last sip of my Tobacco Tea, carpet my mug, and switch to Netflix.

Sprawled on the floor, I torture myself with episodes of Gorgeous. Having made it through most of the first season without gaining any insight into what Sky, Lucky, or anyone sees in Jamie, I'm starting to pass out when the shell-phone begins to ring upstairs. I wonder if it's The Barbie. I need to tell her she was right. Sky never adored me. I'm not entirely sure that she even liked me. Fuck her perfect princess perma-pout.

"You cheating on me?" I open my eyes to long legs standing in fraying denim shorts. Her feet are bare. Looking down, my mojito-haired muse shows me her snaggle-toothed smile with a bag of Have A Chip cradled in her arm and a small wooden bowl in her hands.

"What? No? What?" I stutter, scrambling for the remote.

"I didn't see you out there this morning. You find a prettier girl to shoot?" She coolly accuses, dipping a chip into guacamole as I kill the embarrassing viewing. The American flag on her t-shirt is spangled with 52 multicolored mushrooms—several of them the identical color of her hair. Their neon pops in the glow of the menu screen.

Regaining my composure, I reach toward her and wiggle my fingers. "Hook me up."

"I was going to cook but all I could find that wasn't rotten was chocolate syrup and the avocados."

I grab the chip and snag some seashell-printed coverage. "Thanks!" I crunch, twisting the sheet around my waist. "So, whassup? You broke in to be my personal chef?" I stand like a flamingo, babying my peacock wound, tasting killer tang. "This guac is gnarly. I'm super—" I hop to keep my balance, and my poorly fashioned skirt falls to the ground to reveal my naked gym bod. "—horny." I grin. I was gonna say "into it" but my statement stands pretty true for the first time in forever. My muse is fuckin' hot. Making an embarrassed, peep, she turns from my casual full-frontal. I re-wrap, tell her that she's safe from the sea snake, and she faces me again.

"You sprain your ankle running from me?" She asks, staring down at my raised foot.

I bail smoothly into a recliner. "Peacock attack. Long story. So..." Crossing my legs, I strike a super dapper pose, "... You saw me out there on the beach?" and, with an unexpected hiss, extend my quad like I'm kicking the ghost of Gorgeous.

"Jeez!" The babe pulls her phone from her tiny shorts, squats, and inspects my wound. I twist my swollen calf toward her. The bite weeps in her flashlight. She shakes her head at its nasty tears. "This is pretty bad." She pummels me with pale, wintery eyes. "What have you done for it?"

"I put Midnight Moo on it. It's organic." I pull in my shin and stare at the damage.

"I've got some good stuff at my place. I'll go get it, and then we'll go for food." Smiling sweeter than Moo, she rises. "Get dressed and grab your computer. I wanna see the photos."

"Um...okay...cool." I clumsily rise to my knees. While trying to avoid another bite inspired spazz attack, I throw myself over the back of my chair and call to her back. "Hey, hey, hey—what's your name? I'm Alvin."

"I know." Her phone glows through the red shreds of her back pocket as she pads her bare feet out of The Barbie Theatre. "We've met. See ya in a minute."

# CHAPTER 32

**Her name is Cherie.** If you go to my site and search back, you'll find a bunch of shots of her and see that she's clearly one of the few babes not desperate to get covered in my flash. You know that shot of the BIPs I got inside Teddy's on that night that I met, well, you know who? Cherie was in it. She was the sour babe in the Van Halen shirt. She was blonde then which, I guess, is part of the reason I didn't remember lurking her at Bob's Donuts, standing next to her onstage as OFF! played in Echo Park, or repeatedly putting her on Al This And More. Admittedly it's still kinda crazy that I didn't recognize her cuz I was the one going after her at the parties and it's usually the other way around. Plus, Cherie looks like Ariel on legs and she's a rocker. Anyone else would have for sure remembered her but fuck, I see a lot of babes.

On the way here, Cherie insisted that we first met at Fuck Yeah Fest, showed me pictures of her cat, told me to turn up She Sells Sanctuary, and asked me to slow down before I could even get Lenore to up 80. Baffled by her lack of a need for speed, I crept into the Coogie's lot to the sound of The Cult and parked between two Teslas. We've now been same-side-sitting in this beach cafe for an entire waitstaff turnover. She said it would be easier to check out my work if she were squeezed all up on me and that, this way, all the women in the restaurant would be jealous. I'm cool with it.

In our booth beneath the starry skylight, my mojito muse points to my screen. The Beach Boys sing Christmas songs from hidden wall speakers as I rub my freshly shorn face and enlarge her chosen file. In the sicked-out photo of Cherie paddling out through pink waves, she has a fish tail made of mint leaves and sliced limes. Cherie tells me that as a little girl she'd always wanted to be a mermaid and scrolls through my catalogue. When she enlarges another photo, I accuse her of surf-vogueing.

"I can't help it." Cherie smiles her snaggled smile and, turning through the truffled air, waves back at a pilled-out Birkum classmate. "It's reflex," she defends, facing the plastic-surgery-disaster-mom in the expensive jogger. Her classmate points at me then, making a heart with her fingers, sloppily mouths "love." Cherie nods back in agreement.

After being discovered at a surf competition, my mojito muse got picked up as a model. She was fourteen then, hanging with her uncle at the US Open. On the Huntington Beach pier, Cherie played acoustic guitar and sang a song she'd written about the pros sponsored by his company. After the fashion show, an agent introduced herself. A few weeks later, Cherie signed with IMG and moved to Paris. I ask her if she's shooting anything soon, and she tells me that she rarely models anymore, that it's "unfulfilling," and that she "really wants to be a singer." I say "killer" and drag a 9th photo into a folder of her favorites.

"Al, your stuff is so unique." Cherie picks through the melted sorbet pooled in our dessert dish. She ate four scoops of strawberry on her own. It was kinda hot. "It's all so... you." Holding a drippy pineapple wedge, she pauses to consider before explaining further. "It feels like you're in every photo without actually being in them, you know? That sounds kind weird but, whatever, I really love them."

"Thanks! I've actually never been as stoked on my shit as I am on these. I guess things get radder when I put myself in them. You'll probably get radder too. Can't wait to see." Shutting down my Mac, I open my mouth and turn to her. With the fruit bedded on her tongue and her mouth half open, Cherie slowly leans and feeds me the pineapple—with no hands. As the waiter starts clearing our plates, she leans back, and I chew, stoked. I pull out the remainder of my wad and, after a legit attempt to pay, Cherie re-wraps her credit cards in a hair rubber band.

"Thank you, Al." Rising from our booth, she promises "I got the next one."

"Fuck that." I plant two fifties under our empty carafe of Winter Blast Juice, bag my laptop, and sling it over my shoulder. "Just sing whatever song you're gonna write about me at our opening."

"You've got a show coming up?" She tugs an exposed pocket of her torn super-short shorts. It rests like a white tongue, tasting her toned thigh. "Where is it?" she asks and pockets her cards.

"Nowhere. Not yet." Hoping to lure her back into The Barbie Beach house, I stand and escort her to the door. "Once I get enough good stuff, I gotta find someone who's into it. I might ask my friend who knows, like, everybody. It's weird, he doesn't really do anything..."

"I might be able to help." The yoga mom watches us with expressionless Botoxed eyes. "My uncle has a gallery. Your stuff totally fits with his deal. I think he'll love it. Let me send him some?"

"Fuck yeah! Any of them! All of them!" Lucky is the only other person to ever be truly stoked on my art.

"Cool! I can't make any promises about that song though." Moving us along, she warns, "I've gotta be inspired..."

"Pssh. I've got that..." I insist, throwing my arm over her shoulders. Cherie slides hers around my serrated ribs as we stroll past the yoga mom doing heart shaped fingers. "...but I left it back at the house." Holding open the front door, I clarify, "Up in the bedroom. With the sex."

# CHAPTER 33

**We didn't come close to making it to the bedroom.** On that first night, when we'd met for what she insists was the third time, Cherie fucked me outside of Coogie's in Lenore between two Teslas—different Teslas than those parked in the lot when we'd arrived. Back at The Barbie beach house, we showered together upstairs in the master bath walk-in before she rubbed more herbal goo on my infected leg and bailed. She said that she had to feed her cat. I lurked out to the balcony and watched her walk down the beach back to her place. We've been re-creating the moment every night since. There's something so killer about seeing her red shorts popping in the Bu twilight as she leaves—which she always does one second after dark.

I know she's going back to that warlock dude every night. I don't know what their deal is but, whatever it is, it's totally whatevs cuz I feel fucking awesome. Thanks to Cherie my leg is healed, I've been inspired to start painting over giant prints of my photos and, rather than a steady diet of TT, have been eating nothing but rad food from the farmers market. Basically my current lifestyle is this: I awake to breakfast, we surf all morning, bang all afternoon, Cherie makes me dinner then bails to feed her cat, and I stay up all night working on my art. Her uncle is stoked on the images she sent him. I think I'm gonna call my gallery show "Mer'd in Malibu".

Tonight in bed I'm finishing off the raspberry pudding that I set aside an hour ago to pull off Cherie's shorts. With my back up against the headboard of the California king, scraping the last gooey grey chia seeds from my wooden bowl, I'm watching Cherie dress like she's my favorite animated feature. She stands in front of the open balcony wearing my Mickey ears. Beyond them, the wooden chimes rattle as the sun sneaks into the ocean. I sigh and inhale mangos. My sheets no longer smell like an ashtray. Cherie washed them after convincing me to throw away my Luckys. Since then the bed smells like her tropical body lotion.

Sucking my wooden spoon clean, I set my bowl on the nightstand and grab my camera. Cherie steps into her little red shorts like one of Noah's perfectly-poised white birds. The side of her knee is chaffed from the beach bang session we had after she let me win this morning's race to shore. She grabs her little lace bra from the crossbar of a large easel. My camera flashes, capturing her in the foreground of the inky ocean sky. I'm glad she's still here. But I know she's about to bail. *Flash*. It will be dark soon, and I'll watch her shorts fade toward the deck's flags. Then I'll lay in bed wishing she'd come back before dawn. *Flash*. Cherie makes a small squeak as she stretches her shoulders. *Flash. Flash*. Her right elbow is sandburned too.

"Stopppp," she gently whines, hating on my candid shots. I drop my camera, beg her to, for once, submit to properly posing for me, and Cherie asks about my stupid ring. I look down at the diamond then shove it in my mouth, struggling to twist off the forgotten trinket.

"Thanks for reminding me." Wiping the spit on to a corner of soft pillowcase, I lob the jewel at her, "I got it for you."

Cherie's orange-sherbety bra falls as she reflexively darts in for the catch. The failed engagement bounces from her palm, plopping onto the bed inches from the glossy new skin over my bird bite. Cherie eyes the ring and carefully walks between the large, gloppy prints drying all over the floor. I watch her commanding little boobs as she bends over me and plucks the band from its sparkling crater in the cream comforter.

"For me?" she asks, playing along, and raises the stone. It glows in swan-lamp light. "But you've had it on since we met—again..."

"I knew you were coming. Felt it." I smile, and throw up my hands all shruggy-emoticon.

"You're so intuitive!" Graciously conceding to my BS, Cherie inspects the pavé. "It's an engagement ring?"

"Woah..." Scrambling to the foot of the bed, I rise to my knees and kiss her ribs. "I mean, we kinda only just met and we're both so young..."

She dodges a smooch and slips the platinum band onto her right middle finger. "We'll call it a promise ring," she declares. Cherie walks away and plucks her bra from the iron foot of the big easel. I touch my wrist, pining for my lucky lock. She resumes dressing behind a giant photo of herself slathered in drying day-glo paint. "I can't marry you anyway."

"What?" I throw out my arms all what-the-fuck-emoji. "Why the fuck not?" I definitely want to marry her now.

Cherie paces over to the grand armoire and hangs my ears on the latch. The hollow chimes clatter. Without looking at me, she raises her brows and bends to grab her shirt from the floor. "Well for one thing. We haven't even slept together."

"Um...you have a twin or something?"

Cherie calmly slips on her vintage Pyromania tee. "I mean, like, literally sleeping." She slides her snow cone hair from the back of her faded shirt's collar and gives me a pretty serious look. "Spending the night. Like people do."

"Oh! Fuck! But you always say you gotta bail by like super early for your cat or whatever!"

"You've never actually asked me to stay..."

Sensing some important yet confusing emotions emanating from her area, I bail from the bed into a thudding roll. Exiting my summersault into a one-kneed stall, I take her hand and profess, "Cherie, I know we kinda only just met...for the third time... but...will you cuddle with me all night tonight?" Gazing up, I promise, "Brunch shall follow. It will be rad."

I can tell by the way she laughs that I've chilled her out so when she pulls back her hand and says, "I can't tonight," I'm fucking baffled. Still smiling, buttoning the last brass button of her tiny red shorts, she says, "I've gotta get back."

"See!" I'm dying to scrape my tongue on her snaggle tooth. "Why?" I motion down shore. "Is it that dork in the cloak?" She looks shook.

My muse twists a limey tendril. "I've been meaning to talk to you about that..."

"Fuck him." I wrap my arms around her, locking her into

me, and insist, "You're staying. He can come get you if he wants you. Who the fuck is he anyway?"

"Well...he's in a band...and he asked me to sing on his record. And...he's a friend of yours."

"Pshh. He wishes. What band is he in?" Cherie's pale eyes grow to the size of full Bu moons, inspiring only moderate lunacy. I feel my stomach prepare to reject the name "Drop Dead Gorgeous." This isn't a totally irrational fear—her secretly hanging with James. He gets around, and Cherie is looking up at me like she's about to cliff jump into an abyss. I swear on Walt, her eyes have gone grey. "The Rolling Stones?"

"...Band Fail."

"Wait—" I release and step back onto a spent tube of acrylic. I glance over her shoulder half-expecting to see Zach scaling the balcony. "You've been fucking me everyday then going back home and fucking my brother?"

Cherie covers her mouth like she's praying to something. "What?" She asks, her folded hands muffling her rattled voice. "Oh my god, you're brothers? Like, literally brothers?" The tan has drained from her face. Her light eyebrows are cranked up to ten.

"Holy shit!" I laugh, grabbing my clothes from the corner of a spattered drop cloth. "That fucker!" Pulling on my splatter-painted jeans, I explain, "He told me he was staying on the Riv til New Year's!" I slip on my hoodie and take her hand. "C'mon!"

"What? Where?"

"C'mon!" I insist, feeling the panic in her fingers meet the excitement in mine as I drag her toward the stairs. "I fucking miss that guy!"

CHAPTER 34

**"You're disgusting."** Cherie seems more exhausted than burned when she says this. Turning her back to us both, she tosses "Al, I'll be in your bed" over her shoulder and marches down the steep wooden stairs to the beach.

Above her deck, an aquamarine flag featuring a flexing Neptune hoisting his trident flaps between two pink flags where topless mermaids whip their scaly tails. Below the trio, Score takes a sip from a skinny glass in the sunken hot tub. "Dude, you really do suck." Watching her red shorts grow fainter in the night as she returns to The Barbie beach house for the first time before morning, I shake my head at his deception. "You're such a liar."

"It's fine." Score attempts a refill then plunks an empty mini-bottle onto the planks. From its neck, torn gold foil glints behind his relaxed wrist. "She'll be fine." He rattles what's left of his ice, speaking toward her house as if its glass walls were his unimpressive accuser. "...and I didn't lie. Zach facetimed me from France. You know, your brother and I can do that because we don't shoot our phones like sociopaths." I'm pretty sure the guy calling me antisocial spent most of high school burning down old churches. "Anyway..." the pyro continues, grabbing his phone from its precarious position next to the tub. "Your big bro said it was cool for me to be in the band for the commercial." Opening his camera app, he checks his teeth then begins taking selfies. "I'm in as long as The Beats guy agrees with me—which he will," he drops his smile and widens his eyes. "It's just a better look. I'll connect with a whole different audience." Score sucks in his cheeks. When he taps his plus-sized screen I try to kick his phone into the tub. Sensing the incoming missile toe, he waves his hand away, then back, and taps the screen again. "Plus with me in it, Band Fail! will look like a real band. We should change our name though. It's dated. What do you think of Wild Baes?"

When Score heard that Cherie is into rockers, he started stalking her on Instagram. That night when I was partying with Snowmen and Marlena, Score convinced Cherie to come bang him and Stella at Eff House by telling her he was Band Fail!'s keyboardist. We have never had a keyboardist. I play drums in our band and my brother Zach, the one still in France and not the blonde editing a selfie in the bubbles below, plays guitar through gnarly effects pedals. Yet, after stabbing Jamie, and running rattled to Cherie's condo in nothing but an Alta Cienega bath towel, Score told her she has the perfect voice for the new song he's writing and producing. He suggested they work on it at her place up here—to get away from distractions.

"Dude, a fucking duet?" I scoff, and cannonball over him. Popping up in the center of the tub, I challenge his BS. "C'mon, man."

"I'm working on a duet." Score snatches my discarded sweatshirt from the deck and pats his splashed touchscreen with my hood as I post-up on the bench across from him. The sea is black against his wilting white hair.

"You can't DUE anything. Let alone a fucking et." With a jet blasting my lower back, I press my feet to the wall and stretch my Cherie-healed calf. "You don't even play. The only keyboard you've ever touched is made by Apple."

"Same keys that got me my agents—WME picked me up." His phone begins ringing in his hands. Tossing my hoodie, he accepts the call. "They're getting me a brunch with Katy Perry—" he boasts loudly enough for the caller to hear before putting the phone to his ear. "Hello, Hello!" This is the over-engaged sound of him talking to someone he wants to impress. "Oh my Moz. You have such an eye for detail, man—yeah, this and more!" I cringe and point to myself, wondering why I'm being mentioned to his agent or whomever. Looking through me, Score steps out of the tub and takes his precious convo for a walk. "No, no, not at all. He shot his phone—literally—yeah, he's a sociopath. Yeah, I know—really? Fabulous. I will—he'll be ecstatic—no, he will, he loves you. Okay. Rock 'n' roll." Score ends the call power walking towards the house.

"Who the fuck was that?" The little skulls on the back of his tiny soaked swimsuit drip onto the slats of the deck as Score peers into tall sliding glass doors. "Why were they asking about me?"

"James saw your missile toe in my post. He's giving you the exclusive on his release party but he thinks you hate him because you haven't responded to any of his texts." Score squints at his dim reflection, runs his hand through his stripped, husk-like, grown-out pretty-much-flat top, then, sets his phone atop the tall patio wet-bar. Looking down, he opens an unseen drawer. Utensils rattle. "You should do it, Al. You've been offline too long." He raises a paring knife and begins waving sharp, insane, unsolicited advice at me. "Way too long. Seriously. This'll be the perfect look for you to come back with." With an impassioned whip, his elbow knocks over a wooden bowl. Lemons thud onto the deck. Score palms a slowly rolling lime before it bails over the edge of the bar. He gingerly slices it on the stone counter. "They're not even letting people bring their phones to this thing and James is gonna have NDAs at the door."

"What in the serious fuck are you talking about?" A lemon slowly wobbles to a halt halfway between us. "No fucking way I'm covering Jamie Drop Dead's bullshit party. Dude, you may secretly be in love with that guy but I'm still in love with the thought of you having put your switchblade about seven inches deeper into his gut." Score disappears below the bar. "Speaking of that! Why the fuck is he not trying to have both of us killed anyway?" I grab the empty bottle from the deck and inspect it. "Oh! You drink now?" I sniff the mouth as it explains why my friend might be suggesting such insanity. I raise the cashed Cristal over my head. "You're drunk, puffy."

"Research for a role." Score's hidden voice rationalizes his new boozing before he reappears with a steel bucket. A family of bright orange shrimp peer out in every direction from a mound of snowy ice. He sets his victims next to the sink before surreptitiously rechecking his reflection in the glass doors. "...not puffy," he mutters then continues. "James texted me a few nights after the...accident. He said he was 'stoked on the stitches.' He said the scar would look 'tough' and—"

I hurl the empty champagne bottle. Just missing my defective friend, it quietly lands in the rectangular garbage can standing at the edge of the bar. Score glances down at the perfect toss, nods in approval, then plucks a shrimp from ice. "He said I'm a great actor and offered me a part in the second movement of the film accompanying *Meet Me at My Funeral.*" Score twists another murdered crustacean. The poor little guy's back snaps. "Jamie loves us. Says we're 'crazy'. You should bring him more of that organic coke—olive branch. You can get some, yeah?" Squeezing lime directly over the carnage, Score casually glances down at his flashing phone. His brows leap toward his dripping blonde locks. Sucking veiny white muscle into his mouth, he looks at me then back at his screen with suspicion. I ask him if it's Drop Dead. The ringing stops for a moment before starting again. Score answers, "Hello?—Um, yeah...yeah, he's right here—"

"Fuck you, James!" I bark. Score wipes his wrist across his mouth and, frantically shaking his head, covers the receiver. I raise my voice. "Like I'd even speak to a fucking piece of shit like you let alone—"

"It's Sky." he says, and passes me the phone.

# CHAPTER 35

**"Oh my god, I've been trying to reach you all day."** Sky is crying. The sound of her voice is making me faint. Or maybe it's just the heat. I step out of the churning tub. Steam enshrouds me as I stand with my back to Cherie's house, head spinning and pulsing bod dripping, to face the ocean and listen to Sky speak beneath black waves. "Cam and Jaq are gone."

"Where'd they go?"

"They went to room 32 last night. Jaq OD'd and James let him die. Cam tried to Call 911 but James smashed his phone and wouldn't let him leave. He said some shit about already having enough bad reviews." She moves her phone before she sniffles, to distance the sorrowful sound. "They watched Jaq die then James took him—"

"Oh my god." A dark breaker collapses at the loss of The Trueblood. I knuckle the sting from my eyes and palm my dripping head.

"Cam came over and told me the whole story then said he wanted to go be with his sister in Pasadena. I'd never heard him mention any family before so I thought it was weird but I—" She whimpers. "He Snap Chatted a goodbye video just before he jumped from the Colorado Bridge. He was wearing his wings."

"Oh my fucking god. Sky, I'm sorry—he's...they were... rad...holy shit." Mermaids whip above me as I trip on the death of The Mythicals, and Sky gasps a final trembling sob. Sweating in the cooling night, I look up shore. The white candles of votive city are being lit on The Barbie's beach house balcony. I watch the tiny flames multiply as I attempt to sustain the words I've been waiting to hear:

"Al, I know how awfully I treated you." Her voice reminds me of her old online videos. "And I'm so so sorry. I love you—"

"I love you too—" I blurt, losing my breath with the reflexive kick of the words. And the sand swells. I grip the wooden deck rail. The beach breathes for me until, finally, I inhale. The air must be laced with nightmare-truth drugs tonight. As I suck it in, all of Sky's bullshit floods my brain. Drop Dead took The Mythicals but he didn't take Sky. She chose him. "But —" I begin to bring up her heartlessness and my heartbreak before she cuts me off.

"I know. And I don't deserve it. I don't deserve you or your help but I miss you and I need you to be there."

I turn back toward The Barbie's house. "At the funeral?" I ask, and Cherie rises wraith-like from the chipped balcony table into soft candlelight. Everything feels wrong.

"No. No—" Suddenly sounding super composed like she hit "skip" on an "emotions" Spotify playlist, Sky explains, "You know how crazy people are going over you coming back online to cover the screening—"

"What?" Totally fucking overwhelmed, I ask, "Why the fuck do people fucking think I'm covering Drop Dead's weak fucking party—and wait, so...you guys aren't together anymore? No more Skamie?" To read Score's reaction to both questions, I whip around almost knocking over a San Pellegrino that has appeared on the rail next to me. I catch the wobbling bottle then look to the bar. With four paws on the counter, a sleek white feline bobs his face in the ice bucket. Looking up from his crustacean feast, he licks his lips and stares into my rock 'n' roll soul. That's the guy who slept with me on the bathroom floor in Eff House forever ago.

"The night we found out that his pathetic record didn't even chart top five, I caught James fucking Alice Always in his trailer on the Terror Cake set so...things were already weird before...this." Sky, reticent to say their names, pauses as I picture The Mythicals flying on fairy wings and, beyond Cherie's cat's bat-ears, the last light in her house flicks off. "...But look—please, Alvin, you have to do the event. When that fucking murderer pulls me onstage to announce my part in his next film I'm going to leave him and—I need you..."

I push down the lime wedge that my sometimes considerate, often disappearing friend shoved into the mouth of the bottle. Taking a pull of citrusy sparkling water, I stare up shore. Cherie hoists a candle into the night. Glowing, angelic, she waves me in. I pace the tub's edge toward her, gripping cold green glass. Hot water splashes over my steps. The Bu breeze hits my slick naked skin, and I shiver, drawn to tiny flames, listening as Sky summons me south. "I need you with me..."

# CHAPTER 36

**Cherie is moaning all rad.** I glance up. Swelling shadows frame the soft skin beneath her chin. Her head is thrown back. Two deck candles stand on the nightstand, flickering light and darkness across her neck. Her thighs smell like mangos, like the cool sheets clinging to my sweaty shoulders. My mojito muse tastes sweeter than Midnight Moo. Her knees close on me, muffling her shriek as she comes a second time. Trembling, she pulls me up to face her. "Fuck me," Cherie whispers. We kiss as I slip inside her. "Slow." she sighs. "Fuck me slow," and digs her fingers into my back. There will be remember-me-marks on my skin tomorrow.

Cherie asked me whose phone I was using out on her deck. I told her it was Score's. I told her everything. She didn't seem surprised or bummed. She just smiled, glanced at the "Sky" above my eye, and said, "Be careful, okay?" I invited her to come back to Hollywood with me. She said she might be going back to Paris for some high-paying shoot that she shouldn't turn down. It was the first I'd heard her mention it.

"Harder" she gasps.

I kiss her and crush her to me. This could be the last time we ever fuck. It feels even radder than usual. The last time always does. "Tell me when," I offer, knowing that I could go at any time.

"Now," she breathes. I move my hips, begin to slide out, and Cherie demands, "No! Stay." Desperately clinging, holding me in, she rapidly sighs, "Stay. Stay. Stay..."

# CHAPTER 37

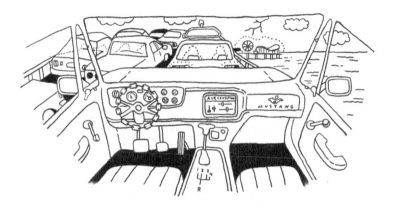

## Having finished my project in the garage, I march all the way back upstairs. With pufferfish pestle in hand, I scan the sparkling borrowed room then sprawl to check beneath the bed for forget-me-nots. Cherie snuck out in the middle of the night and took her underwear and scent with her. After my lonely dawn patrol session, I marched down to her house to find her to talk. The doors on her deck were slid wide. When I shot in, a cluster of ladies jumped like startled kitchen chickens. Hugging bags and boxes filled with fresh produce and Windex bottles and looking at me as if I were a lesser Disney Villain, they told me Cherie was gone. I asked about Score. Judging from their bristly vibes, I knew that he was also gone and they'd have liked me to be the same. I said, "Gracias mamas," and came back here to follow their cleaning lead. I've gotta go but I can't leave TB's mom's place all fucked. And it isn't. There's nothing here under the bed except my drop cloths. The rest of the house is spotless.

The keys around my neck rattle as I rise to glance over the made bed, still palming the pufferfish. I toss and catch the heavy paperweight, inhaling the sweet-pea cleaner that I found next to the washer/dryer stack and used to scrub speckles from the floor. "I'll miss you sire," I accede, addressing the California king. "You ruled...through cold sweats and hot ones." I pick a green hair from a white pillowcase, pocket the strand and, wondering where I'll end up sleeping tonight, saunter toward my last standing photo.

Bright, heavy brush strokes are still drying over Cherie's wetsuit. I squint at her jagged smile. She made this whole place better. I hope my gallery show helps her song go viral. Score thinks that after I cover Drop Dead's bullshit party, anything I touch will burst into fame. I gaze over the collection of hyper-colored photos stashed safely about the room. I didn't come here with anything but a headful of nightmares, a bellyful of earthquakes, and some bullets. Except for what's left in my clip, all of that shit is pretty much gone. And yet, I am leaving a lot behind. I can't fit my prints into Lenore without fucking them up so they're all staying.

I walk out to the balcony, tapping the chimes as I pass. Their skeletal rattle sings for me one last time as I table the paperweight and peer through the afternoon gloom. Down shore, the flags have collapsed like quitter socks. I watch the beach for Cherie, wiping blue dust onto my splattered jeans, imagining her walking up the sand and paddling out into the hazy breaks. The ghost-surfer stands to catch a two-footer. She cuts towards me, and I salute. "I'm out," I say to her and the private Barbie beach. "Thanks, babes."

Shoving my hands in my jacket pockets, I grip the baggie of decimated pills I'd planned on saving for TB, turn from the motionless mermaid on the dead flag, salute the powdered pufferfish paperweight and, shuffle back inside. TB's house keys bounce from my abs on their velvet cord as I lug my shit back down to the garage and reunite with Lenore.

****

The afternoon gloom stayed long enough to defeat the sun. It melts into the ocean as I flip on my low beams and cruise from the driveway past quiet houses that look like art museums. When I stop at the community gates, the guard asks me about the green-haired girl. I tell him that it's not easy leaving green unless you're on your way to see a hot brunette. Matching my lie, his thick stash reveals a big white smile. "I'll be back soon," I promise, hoping that Cherie will let me shoot her again, and pull forward. He tells me to stay gangster.

From the post of the "Coast HWY" sign, a seagull watches me turn onto PCH. The clock in my dash tells me to hit the gas. I do. Lenore rumbles, and the massive white bird chills as I speed away. The road feels rad. 69 mph. It kicks ass to be moving again. The pufferfish pestle made quick work of crushing the Diazepam though the search for the cashed custom dime bag (eventually scrounged from the musty RATT shirt stuffed beneath my driver seat) really slowed me down. But it will be worth it. Tonight will be a lot easier if that piece-of-shit James thinks that I like him. The animal print baggie will give the faux Anger authenticity. 82 mph. I cut into the right lane and pass a vintage Fastback. I lag just enough to give the ancient driver a thumbs-up before shrinking his Arizona plates in my rearview. 103 mph.

I turn on KROQ. The Chili Peppers sing something about California. As I begin wondering if I can make it back in time to hit the Apple store before it closes, the Santa Monica Pier appears below the crack in my windshield. The Ferris wheel blinks far beyond an expanse of static brake lights.

# ENC

# RES

# C H A P T E R 38

**The Roxy is historic.** The New York Dolls played here. The Ramones played here. The fucking Crüe played here. Tonight the small club has been reserved by a poser fuck who demanded scented roses be strung all over the room. They dangle from the low ceiling on fake spider webs, polluting the air. Inhaling Paralysis and vape clouds, I march down from the side stage clusterfuck and through the misty crowd toward the VIP. A white bloom smacks my forehead. Sending the soft, stinky petals swinging, I hit back and carry the slap into a high-five-one-arm-hug combo.

"Dude!" I pat the muscular back of my man guarding the stairs. "What the fuck are you doing here?" Stepping back, I get a good look at Martín. He's gotten buffer since he pulled me off of David Fass. "You quit the Ark?"

"Naw. He fired me cuz I didn't eat some açaí shit that he sent to the booth." He unhooks the velvet rope. "It's cool.

That guy's a bad kinda crazy." Martín squeezes my shoulder. "Man, I thought I'd never see you again, Chongo. You good? You still going up there?"

"Naw. I fired him! Fuck that POS forever!" We fist bump, and I step up a status level to slip into Franco's crew.

James Franco is far from the only fame here. Though his album essentially flopped, Jamie Shannon's self-indulgent movie screening has drawn tons of superfame and received more than its fair share of forced applause. Now that the credits have rolled, he's continuing to punish us all by performing his new record—front to back. My memory card is packed with embarrassing shots of him singing the first half of *Meet me at My Funeral*. I don't have any photos of his band. Before the show, Jamie informed me that tonight is about "this" and framed his face with his hands.

As Drop Dead announces track 11 (he's been calling out each by number,) Franco asks me how I feel about the Skamie power couple, when I will announce Alice Always as Ms. Pac Man on my site, if Score is really signed on to produce the second DDG film, and what "was that blue shit in the baggie?" I yell over Jamie's wailing, telling Stella's boy-toy that the powder was crushed Sweet Tarts—and that I'm fresh out.

Franco was backstage talking with Sky in the flyer papered hallway when Jamie booted over to tell me that AlThisAndMore "should feature Jamie Shannon for a week." I diverted him from the nightmare suggestion with narcotic distraction. "The bluer the purer," I free-styled, and palmed Drop Dead the baggie of Anger. "This shall prepare me for the real encore," he said, called me "rock 'n' roll" then took Sky and skipped away. Like literally skipped, back to his private room. I've barely seen Sky tonight. She rode here with Drop Dead. So that he won't sense her impending break up, they've been hanging hard: her plan. I was bummed that she'd already left when I showed up to her house but whatevs. I know that I'm gonna end up back in her blue room tonight.

Stella, standing next to Franco in the Eff booth and overhearing my candy claim, pauses her conversation with Alexa Chung to squeal, "I want a Sweet Tart!" I tell her, "fresh out," and the drunken Eff asks Alexa if she remembers me. Tugging the thin hem of Score's shrunken Ramones shirt, the Brit it-girl looks over my shoulder towards the other booths. "Of course I remember Al," she stutters, seeming kinda rattled, and bails before I can take her picture. Alexa disappears into the sea of fame offspring on the main floor, and the music drops. Through the quiet synth-scape Jamie whispers into the microphone "Raise your rose!" He spreads his arms, and a Haunted Mansion's worth of fog spills into the room. "We're all gorgeous. Raise your rose."

Like submissive students of bullshit, every fool around me follows Drop Dead's command. Hundreds of party invitations wave like a white sea of flowery suck. I hoist my poor Canon above the waves of weakness—*Flash*. I check my shot, and something soft smacks the back of my neck. Kinda on edge about everything and pretty much ready to wreck anyone, I calmly turn toward a table stuffed full of big—and I mean supersized—Drop Dead Gorgeous fans. Each of these dorks paid 5k for a limited edition ninja mask that admitted them to this poser parade. My assailant, wielding the spider rose, flips up the DDG logo to unblock her big mouth and, in some generic American accent, tells me to shoot them. I tell them to shoot themselves. Sensing my violent mood, Franco pulls me away and introduces some dude I recognize from photos of yachts on the French Riviera. The Beats exec sends my brother's love, tells me that Cherie speaks highly of me, and then asks if The Barbie would be into having her own headphones.

"She hates music" I say, pocketing his card, and step higher into the VIP fog desperate to find shelter.

Near the center aisle of the third tier, Marlena Lopez, Taylor Swift, Ellie Goulding, Tegan, Sara, and Sia are bunched in a circular booth. At the edge of their table, a kid lurks over the pop-superfame. The fur lapels of his long coat glow white in the club's dim light. As I squeeze by them, the six babes look at me all at once. The lurker kid turns to see what's so rad. "Hey mate," he says, quickly tugging his nose as if removing a trace of coke that suddenly talked trash to his nostrils. I give the superpop squad a nod and, fucking finally, make my way up and back to the only halfway sane person in the room. In black on black with her hood up, knees raised and fingers locked over her Balenciaga buckle boots, The Barbie is perched on the arm of the last booth on the fourth tier.

"What a fucking shit show," I lean against the wall between her and the exit. "I'm so fucking glad you're still here. I know y'got major alcohol tolerance but I figured this thing might have already had you back puking in your dark throne..." I shout, decrying the event with a smile, before following her bummed gaze. "You okay, TB?"

Too many steps off the stage-right wall, Score is dancing as if he's been hired. Clustered behind him stands Katy Perry, Alexa Chung, Floyd Mayweather, Justin Bieber, Chris Brown, Joaquin Phoenix, Leo Di, 7 Wilhelmina models, Kobe Bryant, Drop Dead's Redhead and Belarusian accessories, Skrillex, ZEDD, and K3NNYDOLL. The bleached blonde Asian with her heavily tattooed arm over The DOLL's shoulder has about three inches on him.

"Yeah...I'm good." Turning to me, TB waves the fog from

her welling eyes. "Jesus, this shit is killing me. They could at least mix it with hemp oil." Reaching into her "Narc by Narc" UNIF tote, she pulls out her giant shades and slides them on.

I notice the pop babes watching us as I nod toward the stage. "I meant, y'know, K3NNYDOLL and Kat Von Double Ds."

"They literally look like a sideshow." TB stares at the trashy couple. "It's just fucking insulting that he'd think I'd believe he married her to keep her in the country for ZEDD." We peer at the newlyweds. Kenny's wife pokes him until they're both singing along to DDG. "Better hope your import stripper's English is good enough to learn my songs," TB utters, frowning at the tattooed blonde that, I'm pretty sure, I saw at SOHO House with Drop Dead's Belarusian accessory. "...Not that anyone's gonna give a fuck about Pink Corvette without me." The Barbie turns back to me with her slight smile. "Of course the producers are dying over the whole thing. KV Double Ds works at the Vegas Spearmint Rhino. They want us to go to the club to shoot and have Ken and me get back together while she's on the pole."

"Fuck that." I throw my arm over her shoulder. I can feel her secret sadness as I squeeze her tight. "Want me to break his fingers? Fucker won't be dropping the bass then."

"Yeah, maybe..." The Barbie pretends to consider the great plan. "What about you? How you doing with that thing?" Her fingers give a dismissive flick through the fog at a transfixed Sky swaying between two kids in western wear. From stage left, in front of Alice Always and the young cast of Terror Cake, she watches Jamie like he's Elvis Jagger. The Barbie looks back up at me with concern. "She doesn't look like she's leaving with you tonight, babe."

"She's over that fuckface. Just wait 'til the encore. Skamie has mere minutes left to live."

Jamie struts to the mic and insights the crowd to clap. Projecting over the cracking rhythm of morons, our waitress offers drinks: "In celebration of the final song! Compliments of the band!" We each take a shot from her tray as one of the wispy western dudes onstage tips his white Stetson and whispers to Sky.

"Maybe I'm wrong. Maybe she's riding the range." She tosses back the glowing green booze and, hissing through the alcohol's burn, asks, "What's up with her freaky cowboy friends and why the fuck is she hanging with Alice?" I don't really have answers to these questions. Passing her my shot, I'm about to admit this when I'm interrupted. The sucker punch hits me hard—hard enough to knock the words from my mouth, the drink from my hand, and me to the ground.

I taste salt oozing from the fresh molar marks in my cheek while a very solid brothel creeper-toe kicks in my ribs. I hear "Get up you fucking bender—" over my own grunts, the big closing hits of the DDG drums, and the high-pitched sound of a one-note head solo. @Snowsimian doesn't have to ask twice.

I spring up. "Hey man..." With raised open palms, I step towards him, catching my breath and grinning. "...I don't wanna fight." The ringing in my head starts shredding like Slash and, as if from a different dimension, The Barbie's stern voice calmly advises the kid to leave. Holding his stance and puffed up in front of the fast approaching security, @Snowsimian continues talking British shit.

"Well maybe you and your poofter, second-rate-Shannon mate should have thought of that before getting so familiar with my girl—"

I spit crimson saliva onto the murdered-bunny fur of his lapels. @Snowsimian's shocked expression is pretty rad. I swing. The kid falls. The crowd erupts. Jamie bows and leaves the stage. I gleefully shake the sting from my fist and begin roughly undressing Alexa's stalker. As I slip on his bloody overcoat, Martín seizes his limp, wheezing body, and shoves @Snowsimian outside. Beyond the back exit a Cayenne idles in the alley. As Martín drags the scrappy stalker past the churning black SUV, I grab my camera bag and throw my fellow Ark exile a double peace. Martín nods and, after cluster of rabid DDG fans slip through, a second security guard slams the double doors.

I turn through the influx of squealing fans to give The Barbie a painful, salty smile. The crowd chants "Drop Dead, Drop Dead, Drop Dead," and, granting my performance silent applause, TB lightly claps her hands before I bail into the booth below her perch. I feel my adrenaline drain as I watch the show. The hired studio musicians have stopped playing to join the side-stage onlookers who erupt with the crowd for Jamies' grand re-entry. Striding down from his dressing rooms and now wearing a tuxedo jacket over his Muumuu, Drop Dead boots past the cloistered celebrities. Blue powder dusts his peak lapel. His coat tails flop against his 'DDG' emblazoned tights as, like the Prince of Poseuria, he waves from behind the mic stand.

"You are my family." Silencing the chant, he addresses the room while giving outrageous heart-felt glances toward the side-stage superfame. "It is very meaningful that you've joined me tonight. More meaningful than you know, for I have news for my family...but, before I share..." He glances toward Sky then scans the packed floor. "Where'ze?" he slurs, "Whir'you go?"

I look up at The Barbie with wide eyes and ask, "What the fuck is this?" Shaking her head, TB giggles and Jamie repeats the question. "I think he's super wasted," she laughs, and Drop Dead spots me. He points toward the VIP.

"This history MUST be documented," he decrees. "Al, please grace us with your presence here on stage." Folding his hands, Jamie wobbles then bows.

"Here we fuckin' go!" Pushing myself up from the bench, I round the booth. "He's gonna announce Sky's role. She's gonna shut him and his 'second movement' the fuck down, and then her last name's gonna be Thisandmore." Grabbing The Barbie's waist, I lift her and set her on the floor. "You're coming."

"I still don't really get it but..." Tugging her billowy hood to further obscure her face, she peers toward Drop Dead. "But whatever it is I'd like to see it from up close."

I raise my red knuckles above the club full of craning necks. "On my way dude!" I yell, and barge toward him. As their roses wave me in, I can feel the excitement of the guests. Jamie could say anything and most of these idiots would love it. Dragging The Barbie out of the VIP, I lean into her ear, and ask, "Did you hear that shit back there? Some ninja psycho started freaking when I got up—he was all, 'you loved me first,'—like he was burned that Jamie didn't pick him to come onstage. These people are all fucked."

# CHAPTER 39

**The wispy cowboys are gone.** I've taken their place. Standing between The Barbie and Sky, a few feet to the left of Jamie, I raise my camera. I'm locked on the actor acting like a rock star. I focus. Score's slicked hair stands out in the background, reminding me of The Unicorn's plastic-fascist-soldier days—though, rather than exuding Cam's stoicism, Score looks like he's going to explode with glee. James motions to his techs. His face looks floppy. Sky scratches her shoulder.

"Don't be nervous," I whisper, as two dudes in baggy jeans push a keyboard to center stage. "You're gonna kill it."

Sky stares intensely at Jamie. The lights go dim. Jamie taps the Yamaha keys. I switch my Canon to video and press record. An ethereal synth piece begins. I'm pretty sure this piece is tracked. The stage turns blue. A fog machine hisses. The synth line—tracked as fuck—continues as Drop Dead leaves the keyboard, wavers through the fog back to the mic-stand, and addresses the room.

"You. You. YOU! You are all my family. And I'm elated to tell you, now, here, tonight, that our family is growing. My Sky... Sky?" Beckoning her, Jamie reaches towards us. I hold my lens on him as Sky walks into frame. A spotlight hits Skamie. Smiling, acting, Sky takes Drop Dead's hands, and he turns to the crowd. "Now, here, tonight, now, I announce our new partnership." He mumbles something inaudible to himself like a schizo. "Our new trinity! We are pregnant."

The room gasps then cheers. The Barbie and I say, "What the fuck?" and Drop Dead drops to one knee. Keeping the mic, he releases her hand and raises a zillion dollar ring. Sky is looking away from the gargantuan diamond over her shoulder at me when the first gunshot cracks.

# CHAPTER 40

**Screaming, fleeing, full-on raging-fucking-chaos is behind us.** A second bullet splintered a gutted Marshall cab a few feet away from me after the first went far over Jamie's head. Having slipped behind smoking holes in the DDG banner and bailed out of the stage's secret loading doors, we're some of the first outside.

I sprint up Sunset holding Sky's hand. Alice Always and the Terror Cake supporting cast run ahead of us past One Oak. A panicked mob pushes out from under the Roxy's marquee at our backs. People are tripping over each other and scrubbing onto the ground. Alexa, gripping the laces of a waving, studded Louboutin low top, whizzes by in her striped socks, thanking me for knocking-out her stalker. "NP!" I yell, and block The Barbie from the scrapers filming the terrorized fame scene from the steps of the bank across the street. Clustered in front of us at the corner of Rainbow Bar, some of my old crew videos the bedlam. Their spotlights disappear as the black Cayenne screeches out of the alley, clipping the gear from the hands of the pimply fuck in the Lion King beanie. His crew retreats across Sunset through traffic, toward their parked ride and, ID'ing me, the less fearful scraper in the beanie stares. With his smashed camera at his Adidas and his phone at his ear, he says my name—to Abbi, I've gotta presume—before taking off toward the bank.

I drag Sky around the corner into the alley where my ride awaits, throw open Lenore's doors, and stuff in the girls. Sky jumps into the back and her soon-to-be fucking-baby-daddy throws back his seat. Drop Dead flops down next to me. He slams the door. I crank the engine, command "Buckle the fuck up!" and burn west on Sunset. Cutting into oncoming traffic, I pass the Cayenne, pump the brakes, and flip a bitch. Cars honk as the scrapers cut away from the bank's curb to begin the stupid chase.

"Fuck!!" I yell, checking my rearview, jamming east. Cameras are raised in the windshield of the Caddy catching up to us. As the scrapers' Escalade cuts directly behind me, the black Porsche swerves behind it. The fucker at the Cayenne's wheel is driving like a drunk 8-year-old-in a bumper car. "He turned around. He's following us," I announce, glancing to and from my mirror at the same SUV that was idling in the Roxy's alley right before the show got shot-up. Vying for the scrapers' place up my ass, the Cayenne sideswipes a Land Rover. "I knew those fucking bullets were for me."

The girls are silent. Jamie is laughing. "He's after me, dude." With his elbows on my dash, his fingers link over his topknot. "Psycho pervert thinks he owns us. He's so fucking crazy."

"What?" I ask, looking at him before turning away to pass a Volvo on the left. "Why the fuck would Abbi want to kill you? Your posing pays his Porsche bills. Psycho's after me." Dodging a head-on with a Star Tours van, I cut back into the left lane, and Jamie flops onto me. As I shove him from my lap, he laughs.

"Jonnnnn," He sings the name like a Lil' Wayne hook, like a syrup-fueled nursery rhyme. "Jonjon J-jonjonjon. It was Jon. I saw him. In the back. His DDG mask wasn't even limited!" Jamie guffaws. His eyes look like they might roll out onto his tights. "That crazy, jealous, faggot fuck. Thinks he owns us. Right, Sky?" Jamie fucks with his seatbelt, still trying to latch it. With his motor skills melted like my Boneville's engine and his lips and fingers flopping like coke-dicks, he asks again, "Right, SKY?" as if blaming her. The blue shit that I crushed up with the pufferfish kicks his brain as Jamie attempts to swivel in his seat. Giving up the fight with his besieged nervous system, he lolls his head back, chuckles at the woman carrying his unborn famespring, and says, "No wonder you're so fucked up."

Shoulder to shoulder with their knees on the seat and their heads pressed against the sloping glass, Sky and The Barbie stare out of the back window toward the tinted Porsche. Its driver honks at my Escalade tail. "Oh my god." Sky looks back to James. "I think that's one of his cars."

"Who the fuck is Jon?" I yell, and cut the double yellow again, almost slamming into a Prius to pass a Smart Car.

"Al." The Barbie calmly squeezes the back of my seat. "He's catching up."

The Escalade is on me like Jamie on a go-go dancing groupie. A scraper in the backseat shoves his cam in and out of his window as we zigzag through traffic. I catch glimpses of Lion King beanie dude, sitting shotgun, yelling into his phone.

Cutting it hard, I screech right down San Vicente and both tails stay tight until the driver of the wagging Porsche starts shooting—then the scrapers bow the fuck out. Their Caddy slams to a stop at a red curb as wild bullets slice the WEHO air.

"Oh my fucking god!" Sky cries, and my girls drop to the floor.

"Stay down! Hold on!" I demand, downshifting Leonard, and hitting the gas.

"Alvin! Alvin!" Laughing, covering his head as if the long row of DDG crested buttons of his tux sleeves might stop a bullet, Jamie yells, "Al - VIN!" Then sings, "JonJon, Jon-j-jon-jon-jon..."

The light at Santa Monica is red. I charge through then stomp my breaks. They scream as we stop centimeters short of another SUV. The Jon Song dies with Lenore's engine and the snowy crunch of Jamie's head against the windshield. I see Abbi through the cracks. Trapped behind the wheel of his Land Rover, the beastly scraper meets me with his green monster eyes just before the apocalyptic sound of metal embracing metal explodes like my worst Sky nightmare.

The Porsche, having just swerved around our near T-bone, cut through the crosswalk, jumped the curb, and crashed into a blue light-post in front of Millions of Milkshakes. Bare wires spark over the Cayenne's crumpled hood onto the sidewalk. Watching their cascade, I think of fireworks and fairies, and a bullet shatters the storefront window, tearing through a poster for "Le Petit Morte." In the immortal ad Drop Dead sips a black shake while, IRL he sits slumped in his seat next to me, wondering aloud about the chasm in his forehead. Another shot takes out Abbi's windshield. Like a giant wiry-haired rodent in a sling, the scraper scurries out from his passenger side to join the other fleeing drivers.

Jamie slumps closer to me, looking like a last minute Halloween costume with his face dripping red. "See…" Bopping and quietly reprising the Jon song, he curiously dips his finger into his gushing forehead and laughs, "This doesn't even hurt!" James wipes a line of his blood over the script above my eye as I watch Uncle Noah tumble out of the Porsche.

"Fucker drives like he shoots." I softly curse and smack away Jamie's incoming finger-paint. His sticky warm fluids cake on my tattoo while my prodigal uncle limps towards us. Screaming obscenities, bitching about betrayal, Noah reaches into his silk sling-bag, pulls out a clip, reloads, and points his HK at Lenore. "Girls, stay the fuck down!" When I turn for my Deagle, I find my passenger door wide open. Drop Dead's heels clop out of site as I pop my glove box and grab my gun.

Weaving through abandoned vehicles like a bee on benzos, wavering like an A-list marionette, laughing like a total fucking nut job, I hear Drop Dead blurt, "Fuck you Jon!" Noah squeals, "You loved me first!" and fills the surrounding shops with holes. A rainbow flag clipped from heaven drifts to the street and, suddenly, my passenger seat pins me to the dash. I grunt and the girls fly out of Lenore.

"No!" I beg as they dart from my ride, making themselves easier targets for the scorned psycho. Totally fucking bummed and grossed-out to discover that I have way too much crossover with Drop Dead, I crawl out of Lenore. In the sour smell of burnt rubber, I crouch taking cover behind my driver door, and aim. Noah halts his shuffle. Teetering in his drugged-out struggle to focus, he points his gun at Jamie and, from the other side of my ride Sky screams,

"Daddy, no!"

Shots ring. Jamie falls and, with the sling-bag bouncing at his side, Noah hops in the street. Laughing, celebrating, cursing his wounded ex-boyfriend/client, he throws cash. Three—for sure, hundred dollar bills—flutter down through the sulfuric air, nowhere near Jamie's body. They paper-up Noah's Prada slippers as he reaches back into his silk sack.

"Oh my fucking god!" Sky, exposed, hugging herself like she was the one who got shot, commands, "Shoot him, Al! Fucking shoot that piece of shit!"

Unfortunately Sky doesn't want me to finish off that piece of shit Jamie. She wants me to shoot that piece of shit Uncle Noah—her fucking father, the animal-loving creep who has always treated me with the same bizarre reverence that he affords his other broken pets. I might not even be ruling Hollywood if it weren't for him. I look from Sky to Noah to Jamie. Sky's "daddy" baby-talks his deaf Kinkajou as the bleeding superfame reaches up for the side mirror of an evacuated Aston Martin. Barely managing a grip, Drop Dead struggles to pull himself up and Noah, expressly pissed off by the stubbornness of Jamie's pulse, lowers Kinky and raises his HK. I take aim.

The Barbie appears over my shoulder like an Amerasian fallen angel. "Al, don't."

"Fucking shoot him—" Sky screams.

Noah fires once. I pull the trigger twice and both fuckers fall.

"Oh shit..." The Barbie gazes at the bodies then faces me. "Nice shootin', babe." She squeezes my traps. "Right. Let's get the fuck out of here."

TB runs around my trunk to take shotgun, and I move toward Sky. She's draped over Drop Dead, weeping beneath Noah's screechy animal-like wailing. Two exhumed kinky corpses lay strewn with him on the asphalt. The lone living night monkey crawls across its satchel and curiously sniffs the blood spilling from Noah's knee while he makes noises like a peacock from hell. This shit feels like a video game I'm about to win.

"Al…" The Barbie calls from behind me. "Al, come on!" I keep walking. "Fuck— Al!" Sirens begin to wail from the north before I hear her say "…fucking cunt."

If Disney had a Silent Theater Silverlake Land, its Princess would look like The Barbie does as she strides into my line of sight, down San Vicente, and disappears into an alley graceful as fuck.

I jog toward my dream girl. "Sky! We gotta fuckin' go!" She briefly raises her head before cowering and hiding her face. Below the static streetlights, I stop, turn from her tears, and fire. The Lion King scraper's cam explodes in his hand as it juts from the Escalade. The driver squeals away before he even realizes that I've switched my aim from his passenger to him. The Caddy weaves through the abandoned rides, and I turn back to face mayhem: Sky is petting Drop Dead's gushing head. "Sky, fuckin' c'mon!" I yell until she stands and paces toward me—way to slow.

I run through the searing scent and sounds of justice and revenge to grab her bloody hands. Coaxing Sky back to Lenore, I shut her in, fire behind the wheel, and crank the engine. Jamie's voice sings through the speakers as his blood drips from my dash to her knees. I hit the gas. I kill the radio and disappear into the alleys to the sound of distant sirens and Sky's sobs.

# CHAPTER 41

**This desert has a raging, vital silence.** The night feels charged and alive, as if the looming black hills might begin howling were I to get too close. I'm far enough from them now to avoid feedback and further from LA but still feel Hollywood's side effects in the air as, at the concrete base of the stairway, I end my peripheral wander through the dust. I carefully climb the solid steps to the landing. From the second floor, the scattered red rocks look like they were placed about the hotel's property by set-design. They remind me of Thunder Mountain Railroad. Wishing I were in the Happiest Place on Earth, I lean over the iron railing and stare down at the pool. A wind ripples the water. The lamps hidden beneath the cacti branching from the bordering succulent gardens slice lines through the steam rising from the hot tub. People would be partying out there if it weren't so close to Christmas.

I turn to the window behind me and blow my battle-bruised, highway-frozen hands. I'm gonna need new gloves now that I'm riding again. For an early Birthday present, Sky found my bike. Yeah, the very racer that I rode in on. My Boneville was waiting for me in her garage when we finally rolled up to that dark space age house, both shook and silent until she asked Reggie to make Lenore disappear for me. For us. Caring less than I'd have ever imagined, I said goodbye to my bloody Mustang while Sky dried her swollen eyes and stuffed a travel bag. Then we bailed. I hugged Highway Ten and Sky gripped me like a ghost, saying nothing until we hit Palm Springs. At the city's welcome sign, yelling over the wind, she told me to stop, that she needed to smoke, that she was too cold, too tired. I was too—still am.

I know everyone here at the ACE Hotel. When The Barbie had her summer day-party DJ residency, I put the night manager all over my site. He got super laid and has hooked me up every time I've come to stay since. Tonight, after checking me in under a fake name, he put our incidentals on his card. I was too burnt to argue the last favor but he's getting paid back for anything that Sky drinks.

With my car-crashed, gunshot ears soloing on a shrill note, I pick someone's blood from my thumb's cuticle and peer into the comped suite. Through the crack in the curtains, I count what's left of the white tablets scattered over the LA Times article that Sky pinned to the unfinished wooden table with a bottle of cherry Absolute. As we fought, she chased pills with long shots of vodka between swearing that she's not pregnant, that she'd lied about it to Jamie, that she didn't know he was going to propose. With both hands on my screaming head, I yelled, "If you don't love him then why the fuck are you crying?" She looked at me like I'd said some crazy shit, and I came out here to deal with my brain. I threw the door harder than I'd thought. The slam would've bummed out the neighbors if we had any—all of the surrounding rooms are as empty as our suite appears to be.

Sky's Louis Vuitton carrier sits zipped and bulging on the couch where I left her. The bag is from the same set that Jamie used to deliver The Barbie my blackmail money. Daddy-Uncle Noah must have a hook-up on LV and gold monograms. I suppose he gave a set to both James and Sky. I stare into the thick darkness beyond the open bedroom door. Sky must be in there, passed out, dreaming of Drop Dead or The Mythicals or Jon, I guess. The pane steams with my breathing, and I turn from the vacant scene back to the mountain-shaped holes swallowing the night. I told those voids about the Ark and my trigger finger's half second of hesitation, but never told Sky that I knew her father. No reason to, really. I'm not sure that she'd even care about my deal with him. I'm not sure that she cares about anything. She's probably not dreaming at all, I decide, before escaping the looming hills' atonement.

I shuffle to the opposite end of the landing, grip the cold rail, and ease down the stairs to continue my brain-sliming stroll beneath the festive star lanterns strung from palms. The gate at the pool swings open smoothly, clanking shut as I pace past the shallow end, my whole bod aching with every breath, with every step. Alexa's soccer player stalker sure knows how to kick. He must be a forward. At least he doesn't aim for the vitals like Sky does. I shove my hands into the pockets of his warm coat and drag myself to the front of the hotel.

I enter the bar holding my side. Last call was a few minutes ago. Whoever was drinking in this hunter's lodge for the murderously hip is now probably wandering the hills, looking for the perfect #wanderlust selfie. Standing with his black apron latched at his lower back and a joint burning in the ashtray behind him, the bartender tells a story to the murdered creature rearing from the mirrored shelves. The taxidermy brown bear stares at me from below bare bulbs. Lurking in the doorway, I nod toward his snarling nuzzle then, thinking of The Barbie and hoping she's okay, drag myself past him through the lobby and into the remixed roadside diner.

I think this place was a Denny's once. It's less fucked now. Leaning over the old-timey cigarette case, a young pig-tailed hostess plays Candy Crush as I shuffle toward her. I stare at her for a second then say hey. She stands, drops her phone in her cardigan, pushes up her glasses by the bridge of their thick tortoise shell frames, and asks if anyone will be joining me. I tell her I don't need a table. "We close at two." She smiles genuinely. "But no rush."

"I won't camp," I promise, pass back a menu, and drift to the counter tapping every felt stocking hung along the way. The empty red socks swing from the craggy lava rock wall, and I bail onto the center stool. I unbutton the long commemorative coat and, rubbing my head, stare toward the kitchen just kinda breathing. A few deliberate breaths pass before a waitress announces her coming. The redhead bounces out of the swinging doors and bubbles across the brown tiles to ask me what I'd like. Only looking for a place to recover, I order coffee and she grabs the pitcher behind her. Headlights cut over my shoulders. Her faint freckles pop then disappear when, looking away from my battered face, she dips her head below the beam of light and fills my mug. A hypnotic car engine dies. The redhead spins, and returns the sloshing dark roast to its warming plate. I sip my coffee gingerly, watching her thigh tattoos as she skips back to the kitchen. A car door slams. I turn from her two tombstone outlines toward the sound.

In the front lot just off the highway, two identical SUVs are parked next to each other. A steady puff of exhaust churns from one of the tail pipes. I can feel unseen eyes peering through the black windshield of the idling G550 when, in my periphery, I catch a glimpse of a steaming red basket coming my way.

"Oh! You're rad." I thank the waitress for the unordered app as my mug warms my palm. To be polite, I snag a fry and pop it in my mouth.

"Oh, no hun, they're not yours." The redhead glances beyond me. "But I can get you some." Her kind smile is almost sympathetic. I must look as demoed as I feel.

"U'shit. Shorry." I fan my searing tongue and garble through greasy pain, "Naw. Ahm'goo. Jes d'check."

The nurturing babe pours me a water then bubbles away again. I drink too quickly, hissing when the cold glass presses against my swollen lips. As the burn chills out, I eye the basket sitting next to me which I suppose some local revenant ordered. From the kitchen, over the sound of sizzling and scraping, the redhead's gravely voice announces in Spanglish that she's about to clock out. Suddenly starving, I set down my glass, take another fry, and dig in my pocket. With the potato between my teeth, I mouth-breath hot air and grab my cash to close my tab so my waitress can cut out sooner. Sky's engagement ring falls from the wad. It pings from the handle of a butter knife before thwapping onto a newspaper laying atop the stool to my right. Cherie must have hidden the diamond in my jeans before she bailed. I hope she's not too burned. She's killer. I kinda miss her.

I grab the ring, bummed to have it returned but also relieved. I need to polish this up and give it back to its rightful owner. From a too familiar LA Times article, Drop Dead and

Uncle Noah watch me scarf the fry, suck my finger, and force the platinum band over my greasy, raw, puffy knuckle. My pinky throbs as, sliding a piece of mojito hair from my tongue, I grimace down at those haunting fuckers' faces. I pocket the lime-colored strand and a tight pair of heavy jeans replaces the paper.

My new neighbor folds the Drop Dead article into a tight rectangle with dainty hands, slips the wedge into the inner pocket of his fleeced jacket, sits, and tips his black Stetson. Wood clicks against steel as he props his boot heels on the footrest and assesses me from behind cop shades. I try to squint through them, and the wispy cowboy turns away. Sliding a golden comb from his back pocket, he hoists the napkin dispenser like a crystal ball and, reading his reflection, grooms his dark beard before replacing the chrome box on the counter. I wonder if he saw our future.

The cowboy pockets his comb, settles into his seat, and delicately removes the longest fry from the red basket between us. He nips the tip. Steam rises from the starchy bite like potato vape as, chewing slowly, he turns to me, and says, "Well, you're all over-ish." His fey voice is as startling as his question. "Why so upset?"

The waitress had me suspecting that I might be giving off slightly rattled vibes but I didn't expect this guy to immediately pick up on it like some sort of wizard. Maybe it's because I'm so emotionally demo'd, or maybe it's because he seems so gentle and weirdly familiar, but I don't even hesitate to answer. "Fuck, man," I help myself to a cluster of his fries and, as if confiding in my brother, admit, "I'm in love."

He and the small brass skull on his brim smile together. "Cowboys always are." Peeking out from below the midnight bristles of his mustache, a gold tooth winks at me before he turns into the headlights blasting through the roadside windows again. High beams explode like suicidal stars in his mirrored lenses. I slide on my own shades and follow his gaze into the lot. One of the G550s is gone. At the open driver door of the remaining Benz, another wispy cowboy stands waiting in white. His aviators are mirrored too, but the rims look silver. A sudden gust flutters his duster, sending sand over his boots as he stares. A fucking tumbleweed the size of Score's murdered bean bag rolls up the road behind him, and I've gotta look away to see if the hostess, or someone, is directing this shit from the cigarette case. No one else is in the diner.

My gentle buckaroo in black rises from the bar. "Don't let'm slow you down killer. These parts need your kind." He touches his brim. "See ya soon." Leaving his long nibbled fry next to a newly materialized pair of brown tablets on an unused napkin, the cowboy clops toward the lobby combing his beard.

"Later dude." I salute him tentatively. The previously unheard spurs of his snakeskin boots jangle as the waitress bounces back to see if I need anything else. I retrieve my wad from between my legs and sort through small bills.

"You're taken' care of, sweetie." She smiles and skips away.

"Oh, okay...killer." I finally make out the "love" engraved on one of her thigh headstones. The doors swing to a stop behind her before I can read her other tattoo.

I stand, and my knees crackle. Bracing myself on the back of my stool, I break off a fifty, leave it next to the mystery pills, and snag another grip of the cowboy's fries to fuel my journey back to the suite.

CHAPTER
42

**I listen outside our suite.** I can hear the landline through the door. I slide in my keycard. Thinking of clamoring shell phones, Cherie, The Barbie, Bianca pizza and the Bu calm, I step in and the ringing stops.

The front lounge smells like cigarettes. The only things left on the table are the fashion and culture magazines. Avoiding the upsetting striped skin splayed across the floor, I amble between the table's edge and the murdered Zebra remains into the dim bedroom. Sky turned on a single reading lamp, cranked the heat, and left her small impression in the tucked comforter. She, her drugs, and her monogrammed overnighter are gone. I'm not surprised. With a weak sigh of relief, I drop my commemorative overcoat, pull off my Mousketeers shirt, and loom in front of the wall mirror tapping the British bruises on my ribs. Exploring the pain, I bathe it in her absence. The darkest blotch hurts less than the others.

With sweat tingling through my scalp, I shuffle away from the sorry site of myself, turn off the thermostat, and throw open the doors to ease my suffocation.

The chilled desert night blooms through the dead, manufactured heat, hooking up my lungs like soft CPR from Princess Elsa. An unlikely, badass roadrunner springs from the corner of a raging fire pit. Landing with a bounce, he turns his beak toward me and blinks. I salute him and, with the pain of slow stab wounds that came without knives, I gasp, quickly dropping my arm. The bird darts off the ledge. I calf-raise and peer over the flames into the darkness crawling up from the red rocks below. Fuck, I hope that fast guy can fly.

I lower my stance and limp to the desk, babying my brothel-creeper-tweaked knee. My camera bag hangs over the back of the chair. Its windshield-worn latches resist as I fuck with them, my fingers stinging as I force the bent metal to unclip. With a click it finally gives, and I flip the pouch wide. The sad, smashed mouse ears peek up at me. I ignore a vague temptation to upload the fucked memories I've yet to erase, push my camera aside, and hook my finger on the elastic band. The Roxy video is not going online anytime soon. My name didn't make the news—aside from Jamie's and Noah's, none of ours did—but if I don't keep quiet for a second I'm fucked.

I strap on the damaged ears, slide my Deagle from my waistband, and amble to the bed to stash my gun under a floppy pillow and lay down. Everything hurts. I roll off my purple hip. Taking a deep breath of Sky's chocolate perfume, I stare at the art on the wall. The fire she left behind crackles. I should put it out and get out. I should be moving—not that I know where the fuck I should go—but I'm resting first, just for a second.

A photo of a cow skull hangs clothespinned to the white wooden slating above the desk phone. I sit up to the unsettling sound of ringing and scrutinize the sepia-toned shot. I imagine it sicked-out with Cherie, nude, holding the skinless bovine face over hers. I should go back to The Bu and make that happen. The Barbie would be into a shot like that—she'd probably like this one right here. Whenever it's safe for me to hit Hollywood, I'm dragging her to Disneyland, I decide, forcing myself up and across the room to unclip the print. I carefully slide the present into my bag, hang up the unnerving call, click off the reading light, then bail back onto the bed and pass out. When the ringing wakes me from an unsettling dream about roadrunners, I leap into darkness. Barely conscious with my fallen ears scraping my scaps, I rush to end the noise. I snatch the phone. "Wrong room." Then I hear my name. I'm only shook for a nanosecond before I recognize her soft voice.

Shrugging the receiver to my tender ear, I pace, twisting my ring, assuring her that I'm fine, that I think we're safe now, that I'm so stoked to hear from her. I step out to the balcony and, moving toward the ledge, ask her where she ran off to. The awkward spiral chord springs taught, halting me before I can check on the roadrunner. The archaic phone clacks onto the hardwood, and she tells me that she's okay. I knew that she would be but, still, I ask if she's positive. In the dim, my faint reflection appears as crushed as my mouse ears in the bedside mirror. Averting my eyes from the stygian script above my brow, I watch split lips tell her I'm sorry for all the shit that went down, that I have something for her, and that she's getting it in Fantasy Land whether she likes it or not. My platinum band taps against the plastic receiver, and she says that she already misses me. My knees give out.

"I miss you too," I confess, caught by the mattress' edge. With my exploding head in my bejeweled hand, even more relieved than when I'd first heard her quiet voice through the sizzling silence seconds ago, I tell her "I fuckin' love you hard," and the statement reopens the wounds inside my cheek. I shove my tongue into the salty, fleshy holes as she cries, and I make promises: to return too soon, to work on my shit, our shit. She tells me to slow down, that "we should do this in Hollywood," that she should go. Keeping her on the line, keeping her with me, I speak faster. Each word hurts more than the last, I taste blood with every vow, but there's no way I'm letting her go now. No fucking way.

# About the Author

The lead singer of AFI, Blaqk Audio, XTRMST and Dreamcar, Davey Havok has released over sixteen records, acted on screen and performed on Broadway. He also contributes to the dark and beautiful design behind Eat Your Own Tail. His debut novel, Pop Kids, was published in 2013. Born in New York, raised east of the San Francisco Bay by vegan non-believers, Havok currently resides amidst watchful livestock and diaphanous garments in a Southern Californian institution of higher learning. This is his second novel.

CPSIA information can be obtained
at www.ICGtesting.com
Printed in the USA
BVOW09s1426290118
506560BV00013B/175/P